SNOWFALL

Book Two

Katie J. Douglas

Snowfall

Printed in the United States of America

* * * * *

This book is a work of fiction. Places, events, and situations in this book are purely fictional and any resemblance to actual persons, living or dead, is coincidental

* * * * *

Edited by Dr. Megan Hennessey-Croy

Cover design by Rachel Christmas

Photography by Ashley Elicio Photography

Formatted by Debora Lewis / deboraklewis@yahoo.com

ISBN-13: 9781694267962

To my mama, who taught me to love
without restraint and to my dad,
who taught me to fight.

I

"This tale is true, and mine. It tells
How the sea took me, swept me back
And forth in sorrow and fear and pain,
Showed me suffering in a hundred ships,
In a thousand ports, and in me."

~ *The Seafarer*, author unknown
Translated by Burton Raffel

Wyatt walked with the setting desert sun beating down on his back, sweating beneath his helmet and Kevlar. Like most things in his life, war was not what he expected it to be. Actually, he didn't know what it was he expected when he joined the Marine Corps. Lately it felt like he wasn't in control of anything in his life, like it was all pre-planned and mapped out for him even though he knew it was him who walked into that recruiter's office and signed his name on the enlistment contract. "Wyatt William Sterling," he'd written neatly in his impeccable cursive. It was him and no one else who forced him to do it. It never ceased to amaze him how that one turn, one decision changed it all.

June in Iraq wasn't so different from June in Arizona, so Wyatt, unlike the rest of his platoon, adjusted easily to the scorching, dry heat. The days were long and the heat unrelenting, hardly a cloud in the sky. His fellow Marines from the American south were the hardest hit, missing the humid air of their homes, cursing their dry bloody noses and skin chapped by the sun. Patrolling in full gear was miserable for everyone, though, Wyatt included. Complaining was always kept at a minimum since whoever cried uncle first was hopelessly ridiculed for being a puss. But the sun was finally setting that June evening and they'd be headed back to camp soon. He was in no hurry, though; he'd realized soon after setting foot in country that down time meant something different for him than it meant for the other guys. It meant time to think, and that wasn't something he was interested in. Patrol, or whatever mission of the day, however dangerous, was a distraction. Just like boot camp had been. He'd gone almost a year with playing that game with himself. How hard could he work, how far could he push himself, how much danger could he find, if only not to stop and think? His limits, or lack thereof, amazed him. She'd been right about that, he was stronger than he thought.

Just keep moving. He'd told himself over and over again. *Don't stop and it won't hurt*. So that's what he did. From the moment he arrived at boot camp, he kept moving. He ran faster, pushed harder, and studied longer than the guy next to him, sometimes by double, and it was never enough for him. It didn't keep him from feeling the pain and emptiness that consumed him anytime he had a moment to think. He had no satellite phone calls to make, no letters to write, and none to read except the occasional note Garrett would slip in a small package of Mexican candy and chewing tobacco.

"No rain this spring- we're fucked for fire season. Stay safe." – Garrett.

As close as he'd grown to the old man, sometimes he wished he didn't have any contact with anyone at all. All it did was remind him of that place, of that summer, and of her. It had been easier than he'd thought to write off his parents, a mother who seemingly had no interest in him anymore and a father who was too stubborn to take back the things he'd said in anger. But Garrett had saved him, there could be no denying that. So there was no way to write him off, even if he wanted to forget it all.

Wyatt's eyes surveyed the ground to each side of the dirt road around him for the telltale signs of IEDs. He turned and looked behind him at the small unit of men trailing him, doing the same. He liked being point man and being the first to walk over an area, knowing that it was him and no one else who was responsible for the men behind him. He thrived on the pressure, the urgency he felt to protect them. He adjusted the M16 in his sweaty hands and grinned back at his best friend behind him.

"Almost back," Wyatt said loudly over his shoulder to Patrick's exhausted face.

Patrick shook his head. "Bout damn time. Don't know why you had to take that long ass way around camp. Son of a bitch. Gonna miss chow time."

Wyatt laughed. "Naw, man. They won't start without us. You know how important we are."

"Shiiiit," Patrick said, drawing out the word. He wiped his forearm across his face, moving his weapon nonchalantly as he did. "I got a date, cowboy. I got a book to finish tonight." Patrick grinned at him, his straight perfect teeth shining in contrast to his ebony skin.

"You and those books," Wyatt said, still searching the ground around him. "There anything you won't read, man?"

Patrick shook his head proudly. "No, sir. Specially out here. What the hell else is there to do? Told you, I'll even read that cowboy shit of yours. Speaking of, don't you think I'd make a great cowboy? I mean, in your life, how many black cowboys have you seen? You know how much girls would like that?"

Wyatt smiled and shook his head. "Haven't seen many."

"Exactly. And you've seen how we clean up when we go out together. Something about this ebony and ivory thing just makes them go crazy!" Patrick turned his head, spitting over the top of his gun. "Yep," he mused. "Gonna get me a cowboy hat and everything when we get back. Texas girls won't be able to handle it," he said, winking at an amused Wyatt.

It never ceased to amaze Wyatt that every conversation with Patrick always found its way back to women. No matter what they were talking about, Patrick could work women in, a habit that increased even more once their unit deployed and there were hardly any around. Patrick loved the ladies and, in turn, they loved him right back. He could charm the pants off of any girl he met, a technique that also benefited Wyatt by association. He was right, girls hadn't been able to resist a pair of 6 foot something young men in full Marine regalia. Flies to shit, is how Patrick put it, as poetic as ever.

Wyatt looked at the road in front of him and camp in the distance. Barbed wire curled around the top of the chain-linked fence in front of huge berms of sand stretching high above it. The place wasn't exactly a state of the art camp, but Wyatt had quickly realized that the wheels of the military turned slow and unlike the immaculate recruiting office that he first walked into, wartime was a mess. The U.S. had just passed the year mark of invasion but it looked like they could have landed the previous day for all that needed to be done.

Wyatt checked his unit one last time, all safe from the afternoon patrol, and he counted himself lucky after what he'd seen. If for no other reason, he was happy to be back at camp that day, back home once again. He was exhausted from another long day of patrol. He knew that at any minute, more action would find them. The days it didn't, he was always surprised by his disappointment, his yearning for more and more danger. But no matter how tired he was, he silently steeled himself against what he knew was coming. The silence of the barracks and nothing else to distract him. He was powerless to stop what he knew would happen when his head hit the pillow. But still, he steadily walked his men home.

The Museum Club in Flagstaff was a town staple. Built in the 1930s, the wood building looked more like a cabin than an actual bar. But once someone crossed the threshold and hit the unmistakable smell of whiskey and stale beer, there could be no doubt. It was still early that Friday afternoon so most of the patrons were the die-hards, the contractors and construction workers who finished work early, headed directly to the bar, not leaving until closing time, their dusty boots and tattered clothes irrelevant. Flagstaff was a lot of things, but pretentious wasn't one of them.

Charlotte vigorously wiped down the bar, taking orders from customers as she did. Her long blonde hair piled high on her head and a dishrag hanging out of the back pocket of her snug jeans, she looked every bit the formidable bartender. She liked working there for a lot of reasons: the money, the flexibility with her class schedule, but most of all because she could dress casually. When she moved to Flagstaff officially that spring, she'd applied at several bars in town, many of them right next to campus. She quickly realized that she wouldn't be well suited for something that required her to wear a short skirt and platform boots each night. She knew the kind of trouble that could invite and gave herself a week until she punched some handsy college kid. So the second she walked into the Museum Club and saw the waitresses hanging off the bar in jeans and tank tops, she knew she'd found her place.

The bar manager hired her on the spot, putting her on the floor as a waitress that very night, and Charlotte soon saw why. The customers loved her. Mostly older men, cowboys, and blue collar workers, the rough crowd not only enjoyed the way the new girl looked, they fell in love with her intolerance of nonsense, as well. She was the only waitress of them all who was in college. The rest were older, working-class women hardened by years of working in the service industry. There is no one on earth more jaded than a woman who has been waiting tables 20 years. Charlotte knew that already since her own mother worked in the industry on and off for years, so she didn't take it personally when the girls wouldn't acknowledge her. She knew she had to prove herself before they would treat her with the least bit of respect. Truth be told, she wasn't in the market for friends anyway, so even if they never did, she wouldn't mind.

Charlotte took to waitressing like most anything else; she realized that as long as she kept moving, kept doing something, she couldn't really mess up. It was all about timing and the faster the time, the bigger the money. So she kept moving, did everything the senior bartenders asked her to do and quickly. She only had to be told once how to do something and then she had it down. Her efficiency annoyed the girls, though, because the only thing worse than a new girl was one who was going to show them up. So they barked orders at her without saying thank you and rolled their eyes at each other when Charlotte's back was turned.

The shift manager, Willow, was the worst of them all. In her mid-20s, she, too, had started there as a college girl, fresh as a daisy. She stayed in class for two semesters before getting kicked out due to her grades. She didn't care. By that time she discovered cowboys and cocaine were way more fun than class anyway, so she started at the bar fulltime and never looked back. Until a girl like Charlotte was thrown in her face and she was reminded of who she once was.

"New girl, ice!" she shouted at her, throwing the bucket across the crowded bar.

"Ok, where–" Charlotte started.

"Fucking figure it out," Willow snapped, opening up the beers wedged expertly between her fingers.

Charlotte walked the only way she could think of to find more ice, toward the walk-in fridge and luckily, she found it quickly, filled it to the brim, and moved behind the bar to fill up the trough. The men sitting at the bar all watched her closely as she leaned in to pour out the ice. Charlotte noticed the same group of men had been perched at the end of the bar all night, clearly marking their territory. The bartenders called them by name, giving them a hard time, laughing and joking with them. "Johnny" was seemingly the ringleader. Sitting with his arms crossed over the bar possessively, he looked Charlotte over, his rotund frame spilling over his barstool.

"How much," Johnny said that first night.

"How much what?" Charlotte said over the noise of the music and people.

"Your tits. How much did you pay for 'em?" he said, eyeing her and licking his lips.

Charlotte took a deep breath. She tried to ground herself and harness her temper. She could feel her hands start to tremble and the familiar feeling of being out of control of herself. She looked at the mug of beer in front of Johnny. Thought about how it would feel to hit him across the face with it. *No.* She thought to herself. *No, you can't do that. Stay calm.* But he only grinned back at her angry face, beads of sweat already forming near her hairline.

"What?" he laughed, the men around him going quiet and shaking their heads, ashamed by association. "You got them on layaway or something." He chuckled, looking around for reinforcement.

Just that quickly, she knew she'd lost herself, and soon her job, on her very first night. She knew her Aunt Rose wouldn't care but she still took a beat and stared back at him across the bar, giving him a chance to take it back. But he only grinned at her, grossly exposing the tobacco stuck in his bottom teeth. Charlotte took a deep breath and walked the length of the bar, lifting the opening hatch and walking around toward Johnny.

"Ah, now, don't go. I'm only fuckin' with you," he said, shifting in his chair as she approached him. Without another word she grabbed the bottom legs of the stool and pulled with all her might, sending

Johnny tumbling to the floor, his hairy stomach flopping out of his shirt for all to see.

"Go fuck yourself," she said consciously before heading to the office to retrieve her purse, leaving the regulars roaring with laughter, pointing at Johnny's shocked face. She was still trying to get ahold of herself when Willow walked in after her.

"Whatcha doin?" she said, hopping up on the tattered desk scattered with papers.

"I'll go," Charlotte said, pulling her purse off a hook on the wall. "I won't make any more trouble."

Willow laughed, and lighting a cigarette. "You can't go yet. You're closing with me," she said matter of factly, crossing her long legs in front of her. Willow, unlike most of the girls, chose to wear cut off jean shorts and cowboy boots to work which Charlotte was sure didn't hurt her tips for the night. She was stunning fire red hair and fierce green eyes, but there was something terrifying about her. Something hard.

"I just pulled a regular off of his barstool," Charlotte said.

"I know," she said, exhaling a long stream of smoke. "Fucking hilarious. What's the problem?"

Charlotte sighed, exasperated. "Pretty sure that's not allowed."

"I'm the shift manager, you know. The only one on duty right now. And I say you stay. So go grab a keg of Coors Light, we just had one blow. There's a dolly in the back you can throw it on."

Charlotte stayed quiet and looked at her. She shifted the purse on her shoulder, hesitating.

"Ok, but I can't wait on him," she said, not trusting herself.

"I had the bouncers put him in a cab. Tomorrow he'll be all, 'I'm sorry, I'm sorry,'" she said, rolling her eyes. "Then he'll tip a benjamin and it'll all be forgotten, K?"

Charlotte nodded, hung up her purse and set back to work. And Willow was right, her very next shift he apologized, tipped her generously, and pretended like it never happened. Meanwhile, the rest of the regulars were at her feet, retelling the story over and over again whenever there was a new pair of ears around to hear it. And that was all it took for the other girls to respect her. She had proven herself and on that very first day. Record time for anyone, especially a pretty blonde college student.

And so the Museum Club had become her second home in Flagstaff other than the tiny apartment. Even though she missed working with Rose everyday, missed the magic of Spirit's Soul, she was nothing if not adaptable. She had created a new place for herself, once again.

Charlotte finished taking orders and wiping down the bar, making sure her regulars had all they needed. She cleaned the sticky liquor bottles, putting them back with the labels out and aligned, fixing up Willow's mess as usual. She grabbed the ice bucket and headed toward the back.

"I'll stock ice before it gets crazy in here," she said to Willow who was bent at the waist and talking seductively across the bar to one of the bouncers.

"Kay, thanks," Willow said without looking at her.

Charlotte hustled toward the back, and dropped the bar bucket in front of the ice machine as she kept moving. She pushed open the back door and took a deep breath as soon as she hit the cool mountain air. She could still smell the pines since she hadn't been there a year yet. One year, that's what the locals said it took until you stopped smelling them. One year until it would just be normal to her. She walked out into the dirt parking lot and looked out into the horizon.

The sun was sinking behind the mountain peaks in the distance, jagged with pine trees at the top. Rose had adamantly prescribed this to Charlotte. Nature, daily and often, grounding required.

"You're still recovering, babe," she'd said over and over again to her. "Let the earth help heal you."

And of course, Charlotte listened. She knew that her aunt was right. She still didn't feel like she did the summer before, but she also didn't think it was possible that she ever could again. Not with everything that had happened. Not with him being gone.

Charlotte took a deep breath and grounded herself like she did every day, planting her feet into the earth. *I am loved.* She reminded herself over and over again. She closed her eyes then, savoring her last bit of fresh air before she'd be held prisoner to the bar until the wee morning hours. She thought of him then, like she always did. She squeezed her eyes tighter and prayed like she did whenever she thought of him.

Please God. Please keep him safe.

Wyatt always found it funny how happy his fellow Marines were to be back in the barracks. There was nothing inviting about them. Thrown haphazardly up months ago with wood siding and sandbags piled high outside, they consisted of rows and rows of bunk beds covered in drab green sleeping bags. Some men hung pictures of their families, wives, girlfriends, parents, on the wall next to them, some hung American flags, but not Wyatt. His bed was always impeccably made and his ruck perfectly organized underneath him. Only the occasional book, usually Louis L'Amour, would sit on top of his pillow. He had no pictures hung and nothing else personal around.

"Cowboy's a hard dude, man," a Marine named Seth said that evening when Wyatt was out of the room. "Not one picture of his family or nothin'. Doesn't ever talk about no one. Shit—nobody knows a damn thing about him."

Seth looked at Patrick, raising his eyebrows for an answer. Patrick lay on his back with a book open in front of him, not bothering to stop reading.

"Well, McMurtry?" Seth said, slapping Patrick's bunk with his large hand. Seth Casey was a big southern boy and wasn't used to people being unaffected and unafraid of his imposing presence until he joined the Marines. A fact which annoyed him to no end.

"He talks plenty," Patrick said shortly, still reading.

Seth shook his head. "Naw, man. He don't say shit. All he does is try to be the golden boy and outdo everyone else."

"The fuck you tellin' me this for, man? Tell him," Patrick said coolly.

"I'll tell him. I don't give a fuck. I ain't scared," Seth said defensively.

"Ahh," Patrick said, setting his book on his chest and grinning up at him. "There it is. You ARE scared. That's what they call a Freudian slip. No wait, I'm sorry. If that were Freudian, you'd have to talk about his dick. You talkin' bout his dick?" Patrick said to the laughter of the Marines strewn across beds around them.

"Ah fuck, nevermind. You're always talkin' out your ass," Seth said, waving him off and leaving the room.

Wyatt passed him on the way, a towel wrapped around his waist exposing his lean stomach.

"Ah come on!" Patrick said after Seth. "Look at him, no one can blame you for talkin' bout his dick," he shouted.

Wyatt looked at him, confused as he pulled his ruck out from under his bunk. "What's that about?" he asked casually. "Nothin. Casey might be in love with you," Patrick answered, sitting up on the edge of his bunk.

Wyatt shook his head, smiling. "You're no good at making friends, Pat."

"What the fuck I need more friends for? These guys have to love me and plus, I got you," he said, batting his eyes at him sarcastically.

Wyatt nodded briefly before dropping his towel and slipping on his Marine issued silkies, or as Patrick called them, freedom panties. He zipped up his ruck neatly and lay down on his bed with his hands behind his head.

"Long ass day, cowboy. You hear we gonna push out soon?" Patrick said, looking at Wyatt.

"I'll believe that when I see it," Wyatt said, stretching his lean body out over the hard mattress, his feet almost hanging over the edge. He hadn't been in the Marine Corps long but he'd been in long enough to know how plans changed, and how long it often took for things to happen.

"I heard the Captain talking bout it today. Says it's about to go off. Bunch of hajis just killed some contractors over in Fallujah. Fucking White House is pissed."

Wyatt could always count on Patrick to know the happenings of the moment. Since he was so well read, he always seemed to know the geography of the country and the political implications like no one else did. Most every other Marine he knew just waited to be told who to shoot and when without bothering with details. Patrick, Wyatt had realized since meeting him, was an astute observer of everything around him. He adapted to every situation and had survival skills that simply couldn't be taught to someone. His, he was born with. He was so much like her that sometimes it hurt Wyatt to be around him. But Patrick was his best friend, had been since advanced infantry school where the two competed for top spots in everything physical and academic. No one could beat them and they went back and forth beating each other so much that they should have been enemies, but it just wasn't possible. Their skills complemented each other too much for them to be. So a team was what they became. Patrick was just as Rose told him he would be. And Wyatt was thankful.

"Well, we'll be ready then. I could go for some more action, actually. Patrol gets boring."

Patrick shook his head. "Man, you crazier than I am. I wanna live, goddamnit. Marine Corps wanna pay me to just sit here on this base and look pretty, I'm fine with that." Patrick gestured his hands toward his bare chest, rippled with muscles. "Look at me," he said. "Look at how goddamn pretty this is. I don't need any holes in it, you hear me?"

Wyatt laughed. "You love it just as much as I do, don't lie. I saw you smiling in that firefight the other day. You sure didn't look like you wanted to sit and be pretty then."

"Adrenaline, man. Adrenaline. It does fucked up things to you." Patrick plopped down on his bunk, the sound of the barracks winding down behind him.

"Alright man, whatever. You and Casey gonna be ok or is this gonna be another fight you're getting me into?"

"No fightin', don't worry. He'll get over it. Told you. He's in love with you. Or he just wants to be you. You gotta know that. You almost as pretty as me," Patrick said as he fluffed his pillow behind his head and turned on his side to go to sleep.

"Almost," Wyatt said quietly, closing his eyes and listening to the sounds around him.

The barracks were a lot like the bunkhouse, only there were more men and most of them spoke in English. There were a couple men in his unit, though, who spoke to each other in Spanish on occasion and those times were even more difficult for Wyatt, bringing him back to his home, so far away. Bringing him back to that place. A lot of times he remembered the good parts. He remembered the feel of her under his hands. How alive he felt when he touched her. But mostly, he couldn't stop reliving the ending.

He thought about that day she left for good. How hopeless it felt. He went to Garrett a blubbering mess and Garrett never once made him sorry that he did. He treated him like a man, but also like a son who needed help. He sat up all night with him, talking to him when he wanted to talk and letting him doze off when he could, all the while sitting vigil next to him. He'd silently retrieved Wyatt's things from the bunkhouse and moved him into the big house a door down from his. For the whole two weeks before Wyatt left, Garrett helped him, mostly by listening. He'd tried to help him find Charlotte, asked around after where she and Rose had gone, but it was no use. They'd vanished like they were never there to begin with. And plus, Wyatt reminded himself, she broke up with him before leaving. She wasn't required to do anything more than that.

When Wyatt refused to eat for days, Garrett coaxed him out of it by making him hearty meals of chili and beans. He told the vaqueros Wyatt was sick and wouldn't be out on the range anymore. He simply took care of everything for him up until the day Wyatt left, getting on a plane to basic training, still with shaking breath and an aching heart. And boot camp, although he wouldn't know it until later, would save him. He had no time to grieve. No time to think. The punishments of basic training were a blessing to him. He owed the Marine Corps a lot and he owed Garrett even more. He had changed so much in the last year, but still, his heart wouldn't allow him to lose the old man, his only tie to home. Now there was only him. Him and his fellow Marines, brothers all of them, even the ones he couldn't stand.

Wyatt placed his hand over the Archangel Michael medallion resting behind his dog tags, holding it tight against him. As angry as he continued to be with her, he couldn't take it off. Something about it made him feel safe, even though he knew that was nonsense. He closed his eyes tightly, trying to get the images of her out of his head, but no matter what, there she'd be, sitting by the lake waiting for him. There she'd be, blonde hair strewn across his pillow with her hand against his cheek. There she'd be, deep in the corners of his heart where he could not move her.

Downtown Flagstaff was eclectic, just like Charlotte saw on her very first trip there the summer before. The people were a mixture of the type that frequented her bar juxtaposed with outdoorsy hippies and folks that Aunt Rose liked to call "new age weirdos," a fact that amused Charlotte to no end. She didn't think her aunt realized that most people probably categorized her in the same way. But they'd be wrong, of course; Rose was far too original to be pinned down in any category.

Charlotte walked through the dark streets of Flagstaff toward her small apartment. She and Rose had found it when she moved there for the spring semester, and at first, Rose refused to allow Charlotte to take it.

"It's the size of a closet, Charlotte!" she'd said, putting her arms up in exasperation. "I'll pay for something nicer. No need to live in squalor. And it's right above all of these shops! It'll be so loud!"

But Charlotte had insisted. Not only did she not want her aunt spending more money on her, she actually liked the little place. It felt like home to her and for once, she wanted to be near other people. Leaving Rose would be difficult enough and for the first time in her life, she was terrified of being lonely. So she rented it. And for $400 a month, the small studio was hers. Charlotte's twin bed doubled as a couch and the tiny kitchen and bathroom were no more than three strides away from her at all times.

She opened the door that evening and was relieved to be home, as always. The work at the Museum Club was hard and the hours on her feet left them throbbing at the end of each ten hour shift. But she could not complain. She never walked out of a shift without at least $100 in her pocket, allowing her to pay her rent and bills early each month with money left to spare, or in Charlotte's case, to save. Rose had offered to pay all of it for her. Offered for her to just focus on school after all she'd been through, all the while knowing the girl wouldn't take the money. As much as she wanted to help her, she knew Charlotte could do it all on her own.

Charlotte walked straight to the shower and stripped off her clothes, turning the water as hot as she could make it. She wouldn't think of sitting on her bed coming straight from the bar with its thick cigarette smoke and beer and liquor splashed all over her. She put her head under the stream of hot water and felt it burn over her body, all the while cleaning her energy and all of the people she'd encountered, washing all of it down the drain. Rose had warned her about working at the bar because it was thick with other people's energy, some that could be toxic to her and Charlotte knew that the very next morning in their daily call, Rose would ask her if she had done it. She also knew Rose would check to see if she was lying, so Charlotte did as she was told.

When she finished showering, she slipped on her favorite pajama pants and tank top, sitting down on her bed. Rose, true to form, wanted to buy her all new furniture when she moved, but Charlotte wouldn't let her, only allowing Rose to buy a new mattress and bedding for her while she found the rest at yard sales. She loved finding treasures that were all her own, often stopping at the hardware store to buy paint or stain to refinish her pieces. The result was a funky little apartment with splashes of color everywhere. She kept a picture of mother Mary decoupaged onto a wooden board hanging on her wall, constantly looking at it for strength and guidance.

Next to her bed she had a framed picture of her and Rose at the Grand Canyon, both bundled tight in winter jackets, Rose smiling with her arm holding tight to Charlotte's waist. She loved the way Rose looked in the picture. Just like she always did, happy with cascading love and light bursting from her eyes.

It was for that reason she kept the picture and no other. She tried not to look at herself in it since all she saw when she looked at it was that time in her life. That dark spot. Her smile looked like it could crack at any moment and Charlotte knew that was because it truly could have. She was still, at the time of the picture, trying like hell to pull herself out of the hole she found herself in. She felt like she would never be able to do it, but there she was, in her own clean apartment, a college student and a real adult who paid bills. She was holding it together, she reminded herself. Things could be worse.

Charlotte sat on her bed in the quiet apartment pulling her book out and reading slowly. This was her way, decompressing after a long day of summer school followed by the bar, only to wake up mere hours from then and do it all over the next day. Most of the girls got off work and went directly to whatever after party there would inevitably be that evening. They'd asked her to go, countless times, so had the bouncers, but as afraid as she was of being lonely, it was the last thing she wanted after a night of working a bar shift. The comfort of her home and the pure energy that came from that solitude was too big a draw to pass up.

She read only long enough to make herself sleepy before shutting off the lone lamp on her refinished nightstand and laying down. The night was quiet except for the occasional train roaring through town. The bars were all closed, no stores open, only the empty streets with a few stragglers headed home. Charlotte hated that time of night, when the town was no longer alive with the sounds of people and the movement of her little city.

She closed her eyes and once again said her prayers, holding the people she loved in her heart and asking for their protection. Per Rose's instruction, she always prayed for herself, too. And it seemed that her prayers were always answered, that she knew of anyway. She didn't know about the ones she said for him, of course.

When she thought of him, she tried to think of their good times together. Tried to think of the love they felt for each other, but no matter what, her thoughts inevitably went to what she'd done to him. How she'd broken his heart in her very hands and then left there for good. Maybe he didn't look for her after that, she'd tried to tell herself, but she knew that wasn't true. She knew him, sometimes it felt, better than she knew herself. She knew his very soul and that he wouldn't have left like that. He was, after all, much more pure of heart than she was. Another reason she hated herself most of the time. She knew she'd done the right thing. That he didn't deserve to be with a woman like Lily Holt's daughter. That he didn't deserve the tragic end that would no doubt meet him had they stayed together.

She tossed to the side, fluffing her pillow underneath her, willing sleep to take her. Pleading with herself to stop thinking of him once again, but it was no use. No matter the energy cleaning, the disconnecting she tried to practice, he remained.

It would be an early morning for them, but Wyatt preferred it that way. Ever since working the ranch he'd become accustomed to waking up just as the sun rose, accomplishing a whole day's work before lunchtime. Anything less now just seemed lazy to him. Some of his platoon members, though, did not agree with him. But that morning they grabbed a quick MRE breakfast and a strong cup of coffee on their way out, resigned with the duties of the day and the fact it wouldn't be fun or dangerous enough for most of them.

"Alright listen, assholes," Sergeant Stevens had said early that morning, men huddled around him outside the barracks. "We've been told to play fucking nice. You might have noticed that we're not exactly a *welcomed* presence here. So I know I've told you it's not your job to make them like you, but now I'm telling you different. This one's coming from the top in Washington. They want us working with these civilians, playing nice with the kids, all that shit. It's the only way to get information from them about insurgents, or so the Washington boys think," he sighed, exasperated.

Stevens was in his late twenties but behaved like he was a middle-aged man, years of responsibility and wartime morphing him into a Marine, head to toe. He treated everything casually in wartime, exemplified by his scruffy graying beard and hair still disheveled from sleep. Wyatt stood next to Patrick with his arms across his chest, listening intently to his sergeant. He could feel Patrick shifting from foot to foot next to him and shot him a glance over his shoulder, pleading with his eyes for Patrick to keep his mouth shut.

"So we're gonna have alpha team start on the east end of the main drag and work their way up. Bravo team, I want you to start up north and work your way up and down the side streets. Sterling, you got that?"

"Yes, sergeant," Wyatt replied steadily.

"Excuse me, Sergeant Stevens?" Patrick piped in.

"Yes McMurtry?" Stevens replied, rolling his eyes toward Partick in anticipation.

"How the fuck- I mean, how would Washington like for us to know the difference between insurgents and civilians? There some name tag I don't know about? Cause they all fuckin' hate us."

"You think I don't know that?" Stevens barked at him. "Fuck, I don't know McMurtry. Use your best judgment. That's what we're told to do, which scares the shit outta me based on the judgment I've seen from you guys."

"10-4, Sergeant," Patrick said, biting into a granola bar and grinning over at Wyatt.

"Grab your shit and hop in the humvees. Radio base if you need backup," Stevens said before walking off back to headquarters.

"You just can't resist, can you?" Wyatt said, picking his pack up off the ground and putting it on his back.

Patrick grinned. "You know you love me, cowboy. You'd be bored as fuck without me here, admit it."

Wyatt smiled at him, starting toward the humvees with the rest of the unit. Patrick had made him laugh at some of the lowest moments in his life and in some of the most dangerous he'd ever encountered.

"Got the candy for the kids?" Patrick asked, walking at his side.

"Mmmhmm," Wyatt said sarcastically. "Sure it'll fix all of our problems."

The men loaded into four humvees and began their short trip to town. Wyatt sat next to Patrick, staring out the window as they drove. It was hardly daylight and the temperature was already climbing higher and higher. Wyatt wiped the sweat that formed just under his helmet, looking out into the distance, not participating in the men's conversation. He watched the dirt that surrounded them continue on for miles, the horizon feeling so far away. It made him feel isolated each time he did it but he couldn't stop himself, his Arizona upbringing making him search the skyline for mountains to let him know where he was. But there were none for miles and miles and even those, he knew, were tainted. They weren't like the ones in Tucson, stretching high above him, protecting his city. These were riddled with danger. With insurgents and a violence that he'd only seen part of. That part irrevocably differed from who he once was.

"Wyatt," Gus was saying from the driver's seat. "Sergeant said to enter up north?"

"Yep, wants us on the side streets. Park up by that fenced-in house," Wyatt said, leaning up and pointing it out for him.

Gus looked from side to side, actively searching his surroundings just like any good humvee driver would and Wyatt could sense his fear. Gus Barrett was a good Marine, a solid guy in general but at less than a year younger than Wyatt, there was something so childlike about him. He had large blue eyes and cheeks that, despite the rigorous training of basic and advanced infantry, still had baby fat on them. He was short, too; at only 5'5 he took a lot of shit from the other guys, until he had wrestled a few of them and they realized that Gus was, as Patrick dubbed him, all-day tough.

Wyatt slapped Gus on the shoulder in silent reassurance as he parked with the other humvee of men pulling up beside them. They had a solid squad, and had a reputation for completing any task they'd been given and always returning together. Wyatt, Patrick, Gus, and the always silent Tate Harvey rode in one humvee while Seth, Gabriel, Griff, and Hunter rode in the other. Seth butted heads with almost everyone except Griff, who tolerated him more than the other men ever could. But despite being difficult, his skills as a Marine made him an asset to the team which no one could deny.

The men assembled in front of the humvees, putting on their packs and getting their bearings. The town was small, much smaller than some of the cities they'd been in but not quite as rural as some of the villages they'd been through. Dilapidated brick buildings lined the dirt streets littered with run down cars. The town was just coming awake with vendors setting up their shops, putting merchandise out on the makeshift sidewalks for any passersby to see.

“Alright,” Wyatt said, informally. “Searg wants us to patrol up and down this north side,” he said pointing down the street. “Let’s split the street four and four.” He opened his pack and took out the bags of lollipops he’d been given, passing them to each man without explanation.

“We have a goal in mind here?” Seth said, already sounding irritated.

“Man,” Patrick said, annoyed. “You were at the same damn briefing as we were! Why you always asking shit no one has an answer to just so you can get pissed about it?”

“Fuck off, Pat,” Seth replied, stretching his arms over his head in boredom.

The men set off down the road, M16s in their hands in contrast to the message they were supposed to be conveying. Nothing says, “we’re here to help you” like an automatic weapon, an irony which Wyatt had thought several times since finding himself in the middle of that strange desert.

The Marines split the street and walked down each side, waving to the townspeople as they looked around and up into the higher buildings. It was common to see people peeking out at them from behind curtains, pulling away when they were spotted, a fact that unsettled the men to no end. They knew the terrible things that could happen. The worst-case scenarios constantly plagued their minds. It was rare to get a wave back unless it was from a child who didn’t know better. The later it got in the morning, more and more of them would scamper out in front of them, speaking quick Arabic and putting their hands out.

Wyatt stopped, squatting down and laying his rifle across his knees to give a group of children some candy, trying like hell to make a good impression on them.

"Marhaba," he repeated over and over again. *Hello* was all he could say to them, even though he tried to make it sound like so much more. "Marhaba," he repeated gently. *I won't hurt you, I want to help you.* He wanted them to know, but they always ran off giggling with their candy, no doubt making fun of the American who couldn't say hello correctly.

Wyatt stood up and continued walking with his unit. The morning was getting later and they hadn't seen any suspicious activity as of yet, but they all knew it was there, lurking under the surface or in plain sight- a frightening reality.

"Wyatt?" Gus called from behind him. "I gotta piss, bad," Gus said, dancing the slightest bit. "Sorry, trying to stay hydrated."

Wyatt nodded, holding his hand up to stop the rest of the unit. He wasn't used to anyone calling him by his name anymore. Most everyone called him by his last name or his nickname, Cowboy, given to him by Patrick, of course. Gus was the only one who called him by his name and he actually liked it. It reminded him of who he used to be instead of who he'd become.

"Barrett's gotta piss," Wyatt said over his shoulder, knowing that the men would all stop where they were, holding their positions.

Gus darted down a small alley, trying to get out of eye-shot. The Marines had been briefed on a lot of things since coming to Iraq, some of them things that they could never have imagined coming out of senior officers' mouths—where to piss being one of them.

Wyatt's eyes searched the buildings in front of him, sweeping the landscape for danger. He never knew how beneficial his hunting skills would be until he got there and used them to look for insurgents, looking for anything out of the ordinary. It was just like trying to spot a deer in the distance, only the stakes were higher.

A group of children ran out in front of him, playing and yelling back and forth to each other, all holding one of the lollipops they'd given. One boy, Wyatt figured about 8 years old, ran to the opposite side to the street to his mother, clad in a long black dress and hijab covering her head and neck. He held up the lollipop, talking excitedly to her and pointing to the Marines. She looked up, her brow furrowed in concern, and Wyatt caught her eye, smiling softly and putting a hand up to wave to her.

The woman smiled only slightly and raised her hand up in a reluctant wave. Almost immediately a man who Wyatt assumed was her husband walked out of the shop behind her and aggressively pulled her arm, spinning her around to face him. He yelled loudly, speaking so fast that Wyatt couldn't even tell which language came from his mouth. Wyatt felt himself get hot immediately, tightening his grip on his rifle and taking a step toward them. The man continued yelling, ignoring the child clinging tightly to the back of his mother's dress. Without warning he wrenched his arm back and brought his open hand hard across her face.

"Hey!" Wyatt shouted, stomping toward him.

Gus emerged from the ally at that moment and Wyatt continued walking.

"Sterling!" Patrick yelled from being him. "Leave it alone, man!"

Wyatt could hear his men scrambling up behind him and he knew he should listen. That they should just continue on. This was one of those things they'd been trained about. You can't fix it all- only do what you can, or else you might just lose your mind. But he couldn't keep walking. Simply couldn't pass it by.

"What the fuck are you doing?" he barked at the man, still striding toward him, the woman shrinking down behind him, hand on her already red cheek.

The man yelled back, an unintelligible stream of what had to be insults. The language barrier was thick there, but anger was universal, he realized. So, too, was fighting. As soon as he was within reach, Wyatt reared back and punched the man hard across the jaw. The man, much smaller than Wyatt, dropped hard to the ground and before he could kick him blissfully in the teeth as he wanted to, he felt Patrick grab him from behind, pulling him back.

"We're leaving now," he said authoritatively. "Right fucking now, you hear me?"

It took Patrick's serious voice to pull him from where he'd been. He looked at the woman, pulling her son off the road back to the man on the ground, bleeding profusely from his mouth. He woke up then, snapped back from his anger and realized how he'd put his men in danger. Local men were coming off the sidewalks then, yelling at the Marines and pointing at the man on the ground. Just that quickly, the whole squad came together all facing out and assessing the situation for danger.

"Let's move out, boys," Seth said steadily, jaw set and eyes swiveling the crowd.

Gus silently patted Wyatt's arm and the men turned quickly back to the humvees, all the while townspeople still shouting at them angrily. For as much as they tried to pretend the Marines were invisible, they sure noticed when they did something wrong, Wyatt thought grimly.

"Sanchez," Seth barked, taking charge. "Radio camp and tell them we're headed back early. Tell alpha team to pack it in."

"10-4." Gabriel murmured, pulling his radio out and executing as Seth told him, still walking briskly back.

The men double timed it back to the convoy, loading quickly into the vehicles and turning back to camp. Gus looked nervously around while Harvey sat stoically in the passenger seat, looking in the rearview mirror to be sure they didn't have any stragglers. Wyatt took off his helmet and ripped at the velcro on his bulletproof vest, tearing it off roughly, working hard to catch his breath. The humvee was quiet except for the hum of the engine and his panting. Patrick said nothing, knowing his friend well enough to know when to stay quiet.

"Fuck," Wyatt said, running his hand over his cropped black hair. "I'm sorry, you guys."

Patrick shrugged. "Don't sweat it man. Can't be perfect all the time. You ain't me." He grinned over at Wyatt, winking at him in reassurance.

"What happened anyway? All I saw was that haji bleeding like a mother fucker," Harvey laughed.

"Lady waved to me, then he hit her. Hard," Wyatt said. The men were quiet. They, all sons to mothers somewhere back home, knew this was no joking matter.

"Shit, man," Harvey said.

Wyatt tried to gather himself, tried to calm his breathing and slow his heart down. But he couldn't. He'd seen some awful things since he'd set foot in Iraq, most things he had absolutely no control over. He felt like so much of it he'd become numb to. He never imagined that he'd be able to be rattled by anything, but he'd been wrong about himself once again. There, a world away, he'd looked into that woman's eyes and seen her. Seen Charlotte just as she was at the fair. Afraid. And that was all it took. She was right there, just like she always was. And with that, he'd lost himself.

Sedona was quiet that morning, nothing but the creek streaming over the rocks and the distant sounds of birds calling. Charlotte sat cross-legged on the red rocks, wearing her favorite cutoff shorts and a tank top bearing her college's name. NAU was sprawled out in gold letters, offsetting the blue shirt. Rose bought it for her and she'd worn it proudly, hardly believing that she was actually a student there, even after a whole semester of classes and well into summer school. Her palms facing upward, she kept her eyes gently closed, grounding herself into the nature that surrounded her.

Angel's Retreat was a compound of sorts, but Charlotte hated that word, associating it with cult-like, scary things rather than what it actually was. Which was, per its name, as close to heaven as one could get on earth. The only place ranking above it, in Charlotte's mind, was the oasis of Patagonia Lake. Angel's Retreat sat on Oak Creek on the outskirts of Sedona, quiet compared to the bustling tourist town only a few miles away. Charlotte loved the place despite her memories there the fall before that.

It was there that Rose had brought her early that fall. Charlotte packed her bags and told her aunt she had to leave, that she couldn't stay anymore except she had no idea where she would go. She just knew she had to go, far away from where she could hurt him. So Rose told her she would take her, that she would leave with her. And in desperation, she'd taken her to Angel's Retreat, a spiritual rehabilitation of sorts, usually reserved for the extraordinarily wealthy. But Rose, somewhat of a legend among Arizona clairvoyants, knew the right people, and so Charlotte was taken on as one of the patients. She could hardly remember those first few weeks there when she refused to leave the small cabin on the creek that she shared with Rose. She'd laid in her bed all day and all night, most of the time unable to sleep except for a few uneasy moments here and there. Her dreams were the worst they'd ever been, ripping her from rest anytime she'd closed her eyes. She was losing the fight within herself, allowing the darkness to take her, and all Rose and the others could do was watch, because, as they all knew, it was only Charlotte who could climb her way out.

The people who worked at Angel's Retreat were just that, angels. Charlotte didn't even know if they were of the earth for all of their love and patience with her, so much like Rose. So for months she'd recovered there, and even though she'd refused to do anything they'd suggested at first, she woke one day ready to leave her cabin. And slowly, eventually, she started to listen. She meditated, she hiked, she put her feet into the ice cold waters of the creek, trying, as they taught her, to reconnect herself with the earth. She began eating more regularly, undergoing spiritual counseling which often ended in her screaming at the stoic counselor before storming out into the wilderness to be alone.

It was, she recalled, a darkness that overcame her, that pushed her to the edges of herself. And Rose was right, she still wasn't the same. She still felt the hole in her spirit like a physical wound she had to protect from infection. That's what brought her back to that place. Once a month, she'd take a Saturday off from the Museum Club to be back there, to check in with herself and her teachers. Spiritual practice for her was no longer something she did because she found it fascinating. She did it because it saved her, because she didn't know if she would have survived without it.

And so she sat, feeling the Arizona sun beat down on her shoulders and the warm rocks heating beneath her.

I am loved. She repeated in her mind, trying like hell to believe it. Trying to believe that she deserved it. She listened to the creek, emptying her mind of anything except the stillness within herself, retreating to the safe place inside her mind. It was still early that morning and the place was quiet around her. She heard nothing but the sounds of nature around her, but she knew Rose was there. She felt her long before her aunt walked up and sat down quietly next to her.

Rose said nothing as she sat with her, reaching over for her hand. A smile spread across Charlotte's face but she didn't open her eyes, continuing her mantra in her mind, feeling the love pulsing through Rose's hand and into her body. They sat like that for a long time before Rose sighed, squeezing her niece's hand.

"Ahhh," she said happily. "Good shit."

Charlotte opened her eyes and laughed, hugging her aunt close to her.

"Great shit," she said back. "How'd you get here so fast? I wasn't expecting you until lunchtime."

Rose shrugged. "I woke up early as hell like a little kid on Christmas. It's my favorite day of the month, after all!"

They'd done this since Charlotte moved up to Flagstaff that spring, met at Angel's Retreat which was closer than Flagstaff for Rose to visit. It was unspoken that Charlotte couldn't come to Patagonia for a visit. Her heart couldn't take being back there and Rose, knowing her better than anyone, made it easy for her by suggesting that they meet there instead. Charlotte, Rose knew, needed her more than the girl would ever admit, but she realized how much she needed the girl right back, her house and shop so empty without her there that she had to remind herself daily that the change had been in Charlotte's best interest.

"I'm glad," Charlotte said smiling softly. "What do you want to do today? You wanna shop in town? There's this place I want to take you for lunch."

"Whatever you want," Rose said looking at her adoringly. "You look good, babe. You've been outside a lot?" she said, brushing the color on her cheek.

Charlotte nodded, looking out over the creek. "Been hiking a lot after class and before work. There are so many places up there."

Rose nodded, still watching her close. "And how's the bar? Those old bitches still a little hard to handle?"

"Naw," Charlotte said. "I've seen worse."

"Pfft, well yeah, that's not saying much." she balked. "Once you go through the dark night, not much can faze you."

Charlotte hated talking about it, cringing each time she heard the phrase. Those two words encompassed more than she could ever put into words.

"And how about school? What summer classes are you taking again?"

"Right now it's Shakespeare and grammar."

Rose cringed, making a face. "Grammar sounds like water torture. But Shakespeare," she said wagging her finger in the air. "That guy knew his shit. Changed the way we all thought, really."

Charlotte nodded. "That's what my professor says, too. He's brilliant. Just kinda... I don't know..."

"Too smart for his own good?" Rose completed for her.

"Exactly," Charlotte said, laughing.

"I've been called a lot of things but that's one I've never been accused of." Rose grinned.

Quiet fell between them, mostly because Rose didn't want it to seem like she was grilling Charlotte or worse, lecturing her, even though that's exactly what she wanted to do. She saw the girl so clearly, and it killed her to have her so far away when Rose knew she wasn't ok yet. She'd prayed for a solution, but she was still waiting for an answer. The spirit world, it seemed to her, sure took its sweet time answering prayers sometimes.

"Baby?" Rose ventured. "Are you ok? I don't want to nag you, but you're just so tough I know you won't tell me if there's anything wrong. If you're still feeling bad. I just worry, honey."

She tried not to cry, but she teared up looking at her. So young, so beautiful with her wild blonde hair falling around her face. Her green eyes showed the wisdom and experience that shouldn't have been there at her age. Rose wanted nothing more than to hold her, to make all of her decisions for her, to shield her from the world, but she knew she couldn't. This, she'd thought over and over, this is what it is to be a mother. To love something so fiercely, but to be unable to take upon the hurt of the world for them. It was more tortuous than any dark night Rose had ever encountered.

But Charlotte, true to her nature, gave Rose a brave smile, reaching out to grab her hand firmly.

"Look at me, Aunt Rose. Don't I look ok?" she stared steadily into Rose's eyes, holding her gaze. "You're the magical one." Charlotte said lightheartedly. "Check my aura and you tell me if I'm ok." She grinned.

Rose smiled sadly and looked squarely at her niece. It was true that she could see the light sparking from her as she always could. The child was more special, more divine than she could ever imagine. She practically carried her heart on the outside of her body for all to see. She looked at her with the morning sun shining through her hair, but all she could see was the empty place that she'd lost, the hole that not even Rose could fill.

"You're perfect," she whispered, putting her arm around her shoulders and holding her tight to her side.

The hum of the engine had lulled most of the men to sleep, but not Wyatt. The darkness out the window mesmerized him into a trancelike state. The men were filed in the back of a large truck like cargo, heading toward Fallujah. Patrick had been right, it was about to go off, as he put it, and not in a way the Marine Corps wanted it to. The city was packed with buildings, tall and intricate, creating many places for insurgents to hide. Simply put, the Marines knew it was like a death trap around every corner. And they all wanted to go.

This, they knew from the history that had been drilled into their heads in basic, was so much like the pitfalls of Vietnam and would not be their preference for battle. But Washington, it seemed to them, didn't care about logistics like that, they only wanted the job done. The news of the contractors, all ex special forces members, being murdered, bodies mutilated on the streets of Fallujah, was splashed across every TV in the states, showing the grim reality of the fight. Yes, America would prevail, but not without pushback. Not without carnage.

Wyatt, like the rest of them, knew the dangers of what awaited them in that city. They'd been hearing about it for months, only waiting on the call to go. Waiting for the signal to pack and be ready once again to fight, but it was different this time. It was not the fighting that popped up across dirt fields with shots fired far away into a treeline, the men mostly unsure of whether they'd ever hit a target. This, they knew, would be much more personal. And Wyatt, sometimes not even recognizing himself or who he was before, wanted to go with every fiber of his being. He needed desperately to be there to protect the men to either side of him. To do what he knew had to be done.

But sleep evaded him once again and he was left to listen to the sounds of the men around him. He shifted his head against the hard siding of the cargo truck, closing his eyes and willing sleep to take him. He could feel the tires bouncing along the dirt road, rattling him slightly. He crossed one large bicep over the other, settling himself in, trying like hell to turn his mind off. His mind, though, was constantly betraying him. For if he was not thinking of war, there was only one other place he could go.

Wyatt was lulled into a dreamlike state and immediately there he was, back at the lake. It had rained that day, hard. He'd left work in a panic because he knew she'd be at the lake waiting for him. The storm had seemingly come out of nowhere, like storms late in the summer often did. Giving no warning with ominous clouds that teased rain all morning, these were the things flash floods were made of. Sudden violent rains that blew in from Mexico, took hold, then left just as quickly as they arrived. And she'd been there waiting for him, stuck in the rain and in danger.

He'd blown down the highway, racing to her as fast as he could through the pouring rain. When he hit the turnoff to the lake he slammed on his brakes. He had no idea why, but he reversed quickly and turned his truck to the front parking lot at the lake, not their normal meeting place. He could hardly see through the buckets of water falling from the sky, the sound of thunder cracking closer and closer. He rolled through the empty parking lot slowly, looking around for her. And there she was, sitting on a picnic table, rain falling indiscriminately sideways under the canopy above her. She got up, smiling, and jogged through the rain and to the truck.

She was wearing her swimsuit as always, cutoff shorts and tank top covering her. Her hair was drenched through, her clothes soaking.

"Are you ok?" he said, throwing the door open for her.

"Yeah!" she said laughing. "That storm came outta nowhere!"

Wyatt looked her over, his brow furrowed. Her body was covered in goosebumps and he could see her shaking.

"I'm so sorry," he said, putting the truck in park and turning on the heater. "I should have left work earlier to get you."

"I'm fine," she said, shaking out her hair. "That'll let you know you're alive," she said grinning over at him.

And she did look alive. Her tanned skin was slick with rain and her black eyelashes were clumped together. He stared at her a moment, looking at her perfect strong body before remembering he needed to take care of her.

"Here," he said, taking off his button up work shirt. "Take that off. You need to be dry."

Charlotte widened her eyes at him, smiling naughtily. "Is this just a ploy to get me naked?"

Wyatt laughed, trying his hardest not to blush. "It's not, but it is an added bonus."

Charlotte stripped her shirt off over her head and unbuttoned her shorts, shimmying them down her wet body, leaving her only in her swimsuit. Wyatt watched her, holding out his shirt and trying to keep his thoughts pure. He could see that the goosebumps spread the length of her body, covering her flat stomach and hardening her nipples beneath her suit. Charlotte smiled at him as she pulled his dirty shirt around her shoulders.

"Thank you," she said, pulling it tightly together.

Wyatt looked out at the storm which still showed no signs of stopping. The sky was dark, no sign of the storm breaking on the horizon.

"We might have to wait it out at bit. The washes were starting to run on my way here. Don't know if we can cross safely yet," he said, still looking out to scrutinize the storm. "Are you sure you're ok? I feel bad it took me so long to get here."

He looked back at her and she was still smiling, looking out at the storm.

"I'm fine. Just a little cold. I kinda liked it," she laughed. "It was exciting."

Wyatt looked at her, wet hair dripping over his shirt. She was perfect like that, scrubbed clean by the storm and alive with adventure.

"Come here," he said quietly. "Let me warm you up."

Charlotte scooted toward the middle of the truck where she usually sat and he brought his arm around her shoulders, pulling her tight to him. She was cold to the touch as he moved his hand up and down her arm to warm her. She looked up and smiled into his face.

"Hi," she whispered, brushing her lips to his.

"Hi," he said back, kissing her longer that time.

"How did you know I was up here, Mr. Earp? Did you go to the back of the lake first?"

He hadn't thought about it until she brought it right out for him to see. Why had he come there? Stopped his truck in motion and backed up to the exact spot she'd be?

"I-I don't really know," he said, looking down into her green eyes. "I came here first."

Charlotte smiled at him, holding her mouth closed. She nodded and he continued.

"I knew you'd be up here," he whispered. "I don't know why."

Charlotte put her cold hand up to his cheek, bringing his face closer to her.

"You knew because I told you, in my head," she said, widening her eyes in humor.

Wyatt laughed. "You mean like magic? LIke, *Rose* kinda magic."

Charlotte laughed, stroking his cheek. "Something like that."

"Mmhmmm," he said, putting his other hand on her thigh and moving it up and down. "And how do you know that's why?"

"Because stuff like that happens to me all of the time," she said, matter of factly.

"Like when?" he asked, still on the verge of teasing.

"Every time you come and meet me here. Or at the library. I always know when you're about to be there."

She was staring into his eyes, holding his gaze so intensely he almost had to look away, only he didn't, looking right back and feeling the pang hit his gut deliciously.

“What do you mean?” he asked, whispering into her lips now.

“I can feel you before I ever see you,” she said back, not breaking her gaze.

Wyatt felt his mouth go dry and his heart ache. He was a month from leaving and he didn’t know it at the time, but their days together were numbered in a way he couldn’t imagine. But looking back on it, he thought, maybe he did know what would happen. Why else would he have felt his heart breaking as she sat there in his truck, monsoon pummeling the earth around them?

“Me, too,” he whispered. “I can feel you, too,” he said, bringing her face to his and kissing her slowly as the rain persisted outside their window.

The campus at NAU was much emptier than it was during the school year, so many of the students returning to their homes in Phoenix and Tucson, and other cities scattered across Arizona. Charlotte couldn’t understand why they wanted to go. The weather was perfect in Flagstaff during the summer with chilly mornings and afternoons that hardly got above 80. She didn’t understand why anyone would want to leave that to go back to the bustling cities farther south, baking in the relentless heat of summer. But she was thankful they did since that meant campus was as good as empty, only the overachievers or slackers left willing to be locked in the old buildings for summer classes.

That spring Charlotte had excelled so much that she and Flower knew she could handle a heavy load that summer. But no matter what she did, she always felt behind her classmates who all belonged there more than she felt she ever would. So she had to work harder than them, she knew that was her only way, the only edge she'd ever have over anyone else there. That spring she'd sat in Flower's office looking over her progress report for the semester, a 4.0 scrawled across the bottom of the page. Flower looked from the paper to Charlotte sitting opposite her in her office, shaking her head.

"How did you do this, Charlotte?" she asked disbelievingly. "I just can't- I mean, this is incredible."

She stood from her chair and embraced Charlotte, hugging the girl warmly against her. Flower, it seemed to Charlotte, was cut from the same cloth as Rose. An angel walking among people. She knew this for many reasons, but most of all because of how Flower had helped her. She'd enrolled her in correspondence community college classes that previous fall semester, set it up for her entirely so that Charlotte could apply to NAU for the spring as planned. She'd hand delivered assignments to Angel's Retreat, called Rose weekly to check in, and would never accept compensation from Rose for all of her work. She quite simply wanted to help Charlotte, and help she did.

And so with proud tears in her eyes she enrolled Charlotte in five summer school classes, stacked start to finish for the entire summer. She knew the girl could handle it and Charlotte didn't mind. She loved school, every class teaching her things that she'd only been able to read about in books in the corner of libraries across the US wherever she and her mother called home that week. No, she was far away from that now, looking out the window of historic brick buildings to the pine trees growing out of a manicured lawn. She silently thanked the universe for this gift every time she set foot on campus.

Charlotte tore her eyes from the window and looked back at her professor. Dr. Croy, who was the smartest man she'd ever encountered, spoke in such a way that made it clear he didn't care who was listening. His words were so practiced, yet so indifferent to the reception of anyone hearing him. He wore sweaters like Mr. Rogers, always on top of long sleeve shirts no matter the time of year, his gray hair trimmed impeccably close to his head. Most people said he was the most boring professor in the department, but there was something Charlotte liked about him. Perhaps it was his indifference, the way he didn't care what anyone else thought. Mostly though, Charlotte enjoyed being in the presence of someone with so much knowledge to give. And so she listened to his every word, droning voice notwithstanding.

"It must not be overlooked," Croy said, looking above the heads of his students, "That *Henry V* exemplifies the very bravado that we still see associated with the military today. These are the very bones of Shakespeare. Why he's still relevant today. Love, sexuality, war!" Croy said, getting passionate. "These things do not change, nor does human nature, in a large part."

Charlotte stopped jotting notes and looked up at her professor, alive with his lecture, holding his hands out and gesturing wildly, still not looking at the students in front of him.

"Listen to the words," he all but shouted, articulating each word. "Listen!" He closed his eyes, standing just before the first row of desks.

> "O War! Thou son of hell,
> Whom angry heavens do make their minister,
> Throw in the frozen bosoms of our part
> Hot coals of vengeance! Let no soldier fly.
> He that is truly dedicate to war
> Hath no self-love, nor he that loves himself,
> Hath not essentially but by circumstance
> The name of valor."

He quoted the passage without opening his eyes, furrowing his brow together as the students sat silently watching him. For a moment he said nothing, keeping his eyes closed tightly before opening them wide and looking directly at them for the first time that day.

"The name of Valor," he reiterated. "This is the stuff war was made of, and still is for that matter. Remember that. That a man who is truly dedicated to war cannot be selfish. Valor and selfishness cannot live in the same place."

Charlotte swallowed hard, feeling her heart pound in her chest. She avoided watching the news of the war, unable to stomach the images of that desert so far away, the explosions and gunfire haunting her dreams whether she watched the news or not. Valor only had once face in her mind and it was his. His perfect crystal eyes iced over into someone else. She felt him as if he were right next to her there in the classroom.

Croy continued talking, assigning an essay on valor before dismissing the class for the day. Charlotte walked slowly out of the English building onto the brick path that led through campus. A slow drizzle started while she was in class, making other students scurry quickly to their cars or other buildings, but Charlotte walked slowly, letting the rain fall on her, thinking only of him, war, and the valor that she knew he'd pay for with his soul.

If Wyatt's platoon thought that their first camp in Iraq was primitive, it was nothing compared to what awaited them just outside of Fallujah. Camp Fallujah was a mess, overcrowded and crudely thrown together in such a way that Wyatt knew would drive his Captain crazy. But there'd be no choice. This would be home for the remainder of their deployment and this, as they'd been told over and over again, was where the action was. A hotbed of insurgent activity that had to be stopped. The Marines were there to ensure it would.

Wyatt and Patrick walked side by side, cooling off after their morning jog around the perimeter. Both shirtless, sweat dripped down their chests and they fought to catch their breath in the early morning heat.

"Man," Patrick said, still panting. "This place is a shithole."

Wyatt looked around, nodding. "Yeah, not the best camp, I guess."

"Naw, I mean this whole country. Place is a goddamn shithole. Never thought I'd be so thankful to grow up in shitty ol' Detroit until now." He shook his head. "This place makes the inner city look good."

Patrick talked about his hometown frequently and Wyatt knew, even when he bashed it, that he missed it just as badly as Wyatt missed his. Wyatt hardly talked about Arizona to Patrick or anyone, but it was in his heart and he thought of it everyday. He thought of the desert, how it smelled after the rain, the clean smell of the rain hitting the creosote like nothing else. He knew that right then at that very moment the monsoons would be starting up, people watching the horizon religiously, waiting for the first drops to fall. Was it only a year ago he'd been there with her? Only a year since he'd held her watching the first rain hit his windshield, her snug against his side? Sometimes it felt like a lifetime ago and sometimes it felt like yesterday, time and space suspending for him since he joined the Marines.

"So whaddya think, man? You think we gonna get to go today? Finally?" Patrick said, bringing him back to the present moment.

Wyatt shrugged, putting his hands on his hips, sighing heavily. "Don't know. Everyone wants to go. Sounds like it's time for the big push Captain was talking about," he said spitting out in front of him, surveying the sky above them.

Patrick nodded. "Think I'll call my mom, then. She'll be pissed if I don't."

Wyatt smiled. He'd yet to meet Patrick's mother, but felt like he knew her already. Patrick was one of the toughest guys he'd ever met, not intimidated by anyone except for one person: his mom. Wyatt knew she must be special if she made even Patrick follow directions.

Wyatt nodded at him. "You should. She sounds like she'll whoop your ass if you don't."

Patrick widened his eyes at him. "No for real. She will. My mom is scary, man. Scarier than some of these insurgents. She's who we need over here. Have this shit all settled in a day. Guarantee you."

Wyatt laughed, steering them back to the barracks. "What about you, man? Think you ought to call your family?" Patrick said carefully.

Wyatt stiffened and didn't make eye contact. "Naw. Not gonna do that."

Patrick nodded slowly, not wanting to push his friend. He knew more about him than anyone else, but still felt like he didn't know Wyatt at all sometimes. It had only been that one drunken night after graduation from infantry school that Wyatt told him all of it. Drunkenly crying, he told him about his parents' divorce, his mom leaving, and his dad essentially disowning him, shrugging off Wyatt's potential death in war like it was nothing. And he'd told Patrick about her. How much he'd loved her and how quickly and violently it had ended. Patrick, true to his nature, listened to Wyatt, feeling his pain for him. He'd put his arm around Wyatt's shoulder and allowed him to talk, not saying a word but just being there. The next day, they both acted like it never happened, ignoring the fact that Wyatt, a Marine at the top of his class, and one of the toughest Patrick had ever encountered, had cried like a child. He never brought up or mentioned his family again, until that moment.

"Alright, man. I'm just thinking, you know. It's gonna be dangerous. Everyone's always told us to call home before something big, you know?"

Wyatt nodded, not looking at his friend. "I'll call Garrett," he said shortly.

"What about her?" Patrick said quietly.

Wyatt stopped in his tracks turning to put his face near Patrick's.

"Don't, Pat," he said in as calm a voice as he could manage.

"I know, man. I just think–"

"Fuck, Pat. Just stop. If we die, we die. You get that, right? Nothin' we do, no one we call is gonna change that."

Patrick looked at the ground and Wyatt felt immediately felt awful. How could he say that to his friend? To the person who had sat steadily by his side for almost a year, sometimes the only thing that kept him going? But Patrick was resilient and knew his friend too well to be mad at him. He looked back into Wyatt's face shooting him his signature smile.

"You do your thing, man, but I'm gonna call my mama," he said and turned to go into the barracks.

Wyatt stood outside for another moment listening to the sounds of the camp mobilizing. He knew today would be the day. He didn't tell Patrick that, but he knew that day would be the day they entered Fallujah, because some things he just knew to be true in his heart. Wyatt took a deep breath and tried to gather himself. She'd told him so many times that she could feel him without seeing him, that she could hear people when they talked to her, no matter where they were. Maybe that was still true. And maybe Patrick was right. Maybe he should contact her. He closed his eyes, lightly placing his hand over his St. Michael medallion, thinking of her face.

Goodbye, Charlotte. He said in his head, then walked into the barracks to dress for war.

II

"What's done cannot be undone."
~ William Shakespeare

The bar was packed that Saturday, the dance floor full of men in cowboy hats swinging the local women across the floor. It was rodeo week in town and the girls in the bar had excitedly hyped it up for Charlotte. The band would play all weekend, the tips would be more than double normal, and cowboys, they'd reiterated over and over again, there would be cowboys. And not just any kind of cowboy, but rodeo cowboys, a whole different breed according to WIllow, who appeared to be quite the connoisseur of the breed in general.

"For christ's sake, Char. Couldn't you have at least worn shorts or a skirt tonight? It's always gotta be those old jeans?" Willow said, rolling her eyes as she scooped ice to make a drink.

Charlotte shrugged, popping open several beers in her hand. "I always wear this. What's wrong with it?"

Willow sighed, passing a drink across the bar to a patron. "It's rodeo weekend. It's like hunting season, but for dudes. I mean, you're gorgeous, don't get me wrong, just thinking you could have dressed it up a little."

Willow wore a short jean skirt, cowboy boots, and a halter top that exposed her perky breasts, pushed together, on full display. Despite the heat in the crowded bar, she kept her red hair down and wavy around her face, flipping it off her neck seductively every time the opportunity presented itself. Charlotte found her annoying, lazy, and wildly promiscuous, but she couldn't bring herself to dislike her for some reason. Maybe because of her affinity for men, or her lack of self control. She had a little of her mother and Rose in her, so Charlotte couldn't help but like her.

"Well?" Willow persisted.

Charlotte hefted a box of beer off the ground and began loading the cooler in front of her while Willow watched her, hands on her hips.

"You can have all the cowboys, Willow. All yours," she said, wiping sweat off her forehead.

"So it's true, then?" she said, raising her eyebrows with a smirk. "You don't swing that way, huh?"

"What are you talking about?" Charlotte said annoyed, breaking down the box and discarding it to the side of the bar.

"I mean, it's true you're a dyke?" Charlotte frowned at her. "Jesus, ok, a 'lesbian,' I mean," she said, holding air quotes up around the word.

"No," Charlotte said, briefly. "Why would you ask me that?"

Willow shrugged. "The bouncers all have a bet that you are. They said Paul asked you out and you said no, so we all just figured you were."

Charlotte laughed, turning to fix more drinks. "Nice logic," she said, not committing further.

"Well!" Willow said, finally getting another round of drinks for the waitress. "They've got a point. Who wouldn't want to fuck Paul unless they're a lezbo? I can tell you firsthand that there are worse ways to spend an evening," she said, grinning wickedly.

Paul was handsome, even Charlotte had noticed. A football player at NAU, he'd lost his scholarship after an injury, promptly dropped out, and started working at the bar. He had a formidable presence at well over 6 feet tall, with dark brooding eyes and wide set shoulders that made it clear he'd played the sport for years. And he was nice, too, always helping the girls haul kegs and boxes of beer, technically not in his job description. But Charlotte didn't hesitate when she'd told him no. Not an ounce of her wanted to say yes.

"Well fine then, you take him," Charlotte said indifferently.

Willow shook her head. "Clearly you didn't hear me. I already had him. Why would I want him again? Look out there," she said sweeping her hand out to the dance floor, cowboy hats popping up through the crowd. "See the little ones?" she said pointing to a group of stocky Cowboys. "Those are roughstock guys. Bull riders and such. Crazy little sex monkeys but never have a dime to their name. Those tall ones are ropers, and the big ones, steer wrestlers. They fake being a gentleman well enough and they always buy you shit." Willow looked back at Charlotte. "All of those cowboys and so little time."

Charlotte went back to taking orders from patrons, trying to ignore Willow and every cowboy hat she saw. More than once that night, she'd seen the back of a few tall cowboys, their muscular forearms flexing out of the bottom of their pearl snap shirts and she'd had to remind herself that it wasn't him. Over and over again she had to convince herself that he was probably a world away by then, not there in her bar. He was far away in an unreachable place and the young cowboys in front of her only served to emphasize the heartbreaking truth of that.

There was a lull in the rush and Willow took that opportunity to sit up on the beer cooler and light a cigarette while Charlotte cleaned up around her. Willow eyed her, taking a long drag.

"You know," she said, exhaling, "I wouldn't be upset if you did swing that way. Been awhile since I've dipped my foot in that pond, but for you I might reconsider."

Charlotte rolled her eyes, wiping down the bar. "Whatever, Willow, you're the straightest person I know."

Willow shrugged. "Not necessarily," she said stretching her arms up above her. "Just saying you shouldn't rule it out. But what is it really? You have a boyfriend or what?"

Charlotte cringed to think of it. How could she tell Willow, or anyone for that matter, that she didn't have a boyfriend, not at all, but that she belonged to someone more than she could even explain? There was no way to say it.

"No, I'm just- I'm not really interested in dating. School and work are enough."

Willow narrowed her cold blue eyes, assessing her. "Hmm, ok. I'll tell the other girls that Paul's up for grabs then."

"I'm gonna take out the trash really quick," Charlotte said, ignoring her.

"Kay," Willow said, indifferently, examining her nails.

Charlotte pushed down the back hallway, crowded with people waiting for the restroom. She put the trash over her shoulder, politely refusing help from several of the rodeo cowboys drunk and occasionally catcalling her to the laughter of their friends. When she made it out the back door she inhaled a fresh gulp of air and quickly tossed the trash into the dumpster. The night was cool, a stark contrast to the thick air of the busy bar.

Charlotte stood in the parking lot looking up at the stars. They were just as he'd told her they were in the mountains, clear and closer than ever to her. She planted her feet and tried to clean her energy per Rose's recommendation. She knew the busy days at the bar could be harmful to her and she'd tried to overcompensate by hiking each day before she came there, and most days it worked. Most days she was able to feel her connection to the earth, coming in refreshed and prepared with her imaginary shield up firmly around her. But not that day. That day, she felt riddled with fear and anxiety. She'd woken with a pit in her stomach and couldn't shake the feeling all day. It didn't help that she saw him wherever she looked, feeling him so strongly that she'd prayed over and over again for his safety.

It wasn't enough, no matter what she did she couldn't stop herself from worrying. But worrying was all it was, she tried to tell herself. It was not because he was in trouble, despite what she felt in her heart, despite her dreams which told her just the opposite. Somewhere deep inside of her she knew that he needed her more than ever. No, she told herself again and again, he will be ok, he will return, she thought in the quiet parking lot, willing it to happen with everything she had.

Wyatt had been right. They entered Fallujah that very day but it wasn't as they had hoped it would be. There would be no charging forward and taking the city as they wanted to, as their leaders had continually asked permission to do. The bureaucracy of Washington constantly got in the way of the fact that all the Marines wanted to do was fight; they simply hadn't been given the chance to yet. Fallujah was a bustling city compared to everything else they'd seen in Iraq. It was crowded with tall buildings and interspersed with trees, offsetting the drab brick coloring. Roofs had high edges around them, creating rooftop balconies, making the perfect place for insurgents to hide high above the roads.

Word traveled quickly around camp that this had been the way of it: endless random fire-fights with hajis who would shoot and scoot their way through the city, hiding away in civilians' homes, only to pop up again and mortar attack Marines on patrol or sitting on rooftops. Almost a dozen Marines had lost their lives there. Wyatt knew because their helmets sat at the front of the camp, draped over the fallen man's weapon, sometimes with his bloody boots sitting beside it. Wyatt, like all of his platoon, had stopped to pay his respects to each man, although he didn't know them. But they were Marines, and all his brothers, so he stopped just the same. He tried not to look at it again after that though, each time finding himself consumed with an anger that scared him. He felt it pumping through his veins and knew it couldn't be contained.

When they entered the city that day, their fellow Marines quickly squashed any dreams of channeling that anger into retaliation. *Hold up, hold up, do not push forward... not yet... not yet... ok now... nevermind... pullback.* Those were the orders from Washington, the constant back and forth stopping them from doing what they knew needed to be done. The city needed to be emptied of the insurgents who were stuck there like a disease, infiltrating every corner, making them indistinguishable from the regular citizens. Negotiations with the town elders continued and it was always the same story, they made demands and the military listened, rejecting the demands and giving them money for other supplies, vehicles, anything they could to persuade them that they wanted to help and not harm the people of the city.

But it was never any use. The donations were often destroyed; even a soccer field the Army spent weeks building was rooted up under the cover of darkness, scrapped of the fresh sod and goal posts, leaving a vacant dirt lot instead. After all, what more could send the message that the American presence was not wanted there than people looting actual dirt? But the messages from Washington remained the same. Negotiations could still be made, collaborations with the Iraqi Army, there was still another way other than the Marines ripping through the city and exterminating all insurgents they found.

And so they sat on a rooftop that first evening, awaiting orders, waiting for the call that said they could finally do something to make an impact rather than just volley with small firefights back and forth. The sun was just setting that evening and Wyatt sat with Patrick to one side of him and Gus to the other. Their orders were simple: engage only if engaged first and when complete darkness falls, move to the next building up, closing the gap between the Marines' front and the enemy. Hurry up and wait, again, but this time the stakes were higher, and Wyatt could feel the tension in the air. He could feel the impending battle looming and he could hardly contain his need for it.

"Goddamn, stays hot here even when the sun's down," Patrick said, shifting his weapon across his body.

They sat with their backs against the side of the wall built up around the top of the building, making cover for Wyatt and his platoon. The men were scattered around the rooftop while Griff kept his head poked over the edge, looking through the scope of his sniper rifle.

"You're gonna hate this, McMurtry," Griff said without taking his eyes off the scope. "Bet we don't shower for three weeks."

"Yeah, pretty boy. No cologne either," Seth chimed in, grinning over at Patrick.

"Man, fuck you guys," Patrick said, shaking his head. "I'm a pretty boy because I like to be clean? The fuck? You stinky bastards just don't understand hygiene."

Wyatt smiled at his friend, but stayed quiet in the exchange. He'd long since learned of Patrick's affinity for personal hygiene. Patrick was capable of almost anything and in training, Wyatt had seen him rough out unspeakable circumstances without complaining, dirt and all. But after that it had become clear: Patrick hated to be dirty and took his appearance very, very seriously. His hair was always cut perfectly and clothes always impeccable ironed, even his civvies. The first time they went out together Patrick had stopped Wyatt at the door only to make him turn around, take off his shirt and allow him to iron it for him, refusing to be seen with him unless the problem was remedied.

"You really think it's gonna be that long?" Gus asked, looking to Wyatt for an answer.

Wyatt patted his shoulder briefly, "Naw, man. I bet this is over faster than everyone thinks."

Even as he said it, Wyatt knew that was a lie. He'd overlooked the city that afternoon, long enough to calculate the number of buildings and how much work, how much carnage he knew it would involve to clear each one. But he grinned at Gus's nervous face reassuringly.

"I don't even like to go that long without a shower," he said to Gus.

"That's because you're clean!" Patrick said, getting back to his point. "Some of us raised to wash under our nuts. You hear that, Casey?"

Seth rolled his eyes, looking away from Patrick. "Just because I don't spend all day in front of a mirror don't mean I don't wash my nuts, Pat."

Patrick cocked his head. "That right?" he said sarcastically. "What about that time you ended up in the infirmary for a whole week because of that boil on your ass?"

All of the men laughed then, even Griff who always sided with Seth. Gus began giggling uncontrollably, a habit that increased the more he was around Patrick.

"Shhh," Wyatt said, laughing himself.

"That was an ingrown hair. Fuck you, Pat. Shut up, Gus," Seth whispered fiercely.

"No really. You know what a dirty bastard you gotta be to have a boil on your ass? Hiking for three weeks in the sticks and didn't wash it. Ended up dick down in the infirmary for a whole week. Nasty," Patrick said, shuttering.

"Why you always gotta be such a dick, Pat?" Seth fumed.

Patrick shrugged, feigning indifference. "I'm just calling it like I see it."

Seth's face grew red like it did every time Pat picked on him and Wyatt knew they were bordering on dangerous territory. Wrestling in the barracks was one thing, but a whole other on a rooftop in Fallujah.

"Alright, alright," Wyatt said, placing an arm on Patrick's shoulder to stop him. "I'll take first watch before we move out in a few hours. Who wants to sleep now?"

Seth raised his hand and promptly closed his eyes, as pouty as a child. Harvey and Gabriel raised theirs and Wyatt nodded.

"I'll stay up with you and Gus, man. You honkeys are my favorite anyway. Don't smell or nothing."

Gus started giggling again but checked himself quickly when Seth opened an eye and stared at him. The rooftop grew quiet again, the men listening for sounds of action in the distance. Wyatt looked up at the sky at the changing colors with the setting sun. The sunsets in Iraq were surprisingly beautiful, casting an orange glow over the desert and the city buildings. Still, it was nothing like his desert home, sun sinking low over the mountains in the distance making the whole place feel warm. This sunset had an eerie glow to it, the contrast of nature and silhouettes of helicopters flying in front of it giving Wyatt an unsettled feeling. He adjusted his back against the hard brick behind him, looking over at Gus whose eyes never stopped moving, but remained on a constant swivel. He felt it, too, then, Wyatt thought. Gus knew, just like Wyatt knew, that there was a very good chance he was not getting out of Fallujah. Wyatt wondered why it was, then, that he didn't feel upset or scared about it, but only eager. The boy he was, forever changed into the man sitting there, kevlar heavy on his chest and his jaw set for the battle that awaited him.

Charlotte's days fell into a routine the way she liked. She'd always been a creature of habit, her mother's unorganized and wayward ways giving her an aversion to anything that didn't offer the kind of structure she liked. Each day she woke early to meditate, reveling in the silence of her little apartment. Next, she'd dress and go to class, stopping under a tree after to eat her packed lunch and do her homework for the day. If she had time after that, she hiked anywhere she could. Mount Elden was her favorite since that's where most locals went, not the tourists who overran most of the other spots in town. The trail wound up the mountain and had such treacherous drops that there was a sign-in sheet at the trailhead where Charlotte always signed her alias. "Charlotte Bronte," she'd write, smiling to herself before embarking on the trail alone in the quiet of nature.

Finally, she'd return to her apartment to dress for her long shift at work, trying to give her personal appearance some attention since she'd surely be chastised if she didn't. She stayed in a constant state of motion, always focusing on only the job in front of her. "Buddha says to do one thing at a time. If you're eating, only eat. If you're drinking, only drink. If you're..." Rose had said, winking over at her, "Only do that."

The way to be fully in your body, according to Buddha (and Rose), was to just do one thing at a time, and to do it with all of your heart. And so that's what Charlotte tried to do. What happened because of it was just what Rose said would happen: magic. She excelled in school, everything coming to her much easier than she ever anticipated. At work she became one of the most sought after waitresses and bartenders, mostly because the other girls knew if Charlotte worked with them they'd make more tips together AND Charlotte would do the majority of the work. A win-win for all of them. Simply put, Charlotte was succeeding at everything she tried and the harder she worked, the more she noticed her success.

Something else started to happen as well. She started knowing things before they happened. Sometimes little things. She'd turn a corner and knew she'd see a person before they came into view, she'd know minutes before a fight would break out at the bar, pegging the troublemakers before they so much as raised their voices. She'd walk up to the bouncers and tell them, pointing out the patrons and at first they'd shrug, not seeing anything worth kicking someone out over. She was right so much of the time that the bouncers had made a nightly joke, asking her to peg who would be kicked out at the beginning of the night. Sometimes it was obvious, a loud mouth who clearly was looking for trouble, but others, it would be someone less descript. She was always right.

Part of her hated how much her skills were developing. How much she knew in her heart to be true. After all, what did that mean for him? What did it mean that each day she woke thinking only of him? She'd open her eyes to the morning sun only to close them tightly in prayer for Wyatt, calling in St. Michael and invoking the protection she knew he would provide. And she knew he needed it. She felt it in her very soul.

But that Friday Charlotte came to work happy, knowing it would be her final shift that week. Rose would be in Sedona the very next day, meeting her for a weekend trip up to the Grand Canyon. She needed the woman more than she liked to admit to herself, always leaving their visits recharged and full of light, so much so that she often wondered if Rose performed some kind of magic on her. But when she asked, all Rose would do was smile.

"Must be that Sedona Vortex they always talk about," she'd said, grinning. But Charlotte knew better, no vortex could ever beat Rose.

Charlotte set to work cleaning the bar vigorously, doing all of the side work the girls had skipped the night before that. She didn't mind, though. She never liked to just sit anyway. Willow walked in with the register drawer and set to work, not looking at Charlotte.

"Char, I need you to work tomorrow." Charlotte looked up at Willow and frowned. She never turned down a shift, but her time with Rose was non-negotiable. Willow knew that.

"I know, I know," Willow said rolling her eyes. "It's Aunt Rose weekend. But listen, Barb can't work and we're gonna be slammed."

"Why can't she work?" Charlotte asked, annoyed. Barb worked when she had the flu the previous winter, refusing to give up her shift since she had rent due. She all but fist-fought less senior bartenders over shifts if any were ever cut. She simply refused to give up shifts to anyone if she could help it.

Willow shrugged. "Guess her dad croaked or something."

Charlotte inhaled sharply, immediately feeling Barb's pain, the emptiness of her loss.

"Oh, god," Charlotte said. "That's awful."

Willow shrugged again. "I mean, I'm sure he was old, right? Barb's old, it happens," she said, counting money expertly and putting it into the register.

Charlotte stared at her a moment, shocked and annoyed by her response. Willow, true to her nature, didn't really care about Barb or her dad, only that she had a shift to cover since she would be directly affected by it. Her indifferent selfishness was becoming increasingly obvious and Charlotte thought regularly about slapping the shit out of her for it.

"Ok," Charlotte began, "I'll cover it. I just need to call my aunt to tell her to come here instead. Give me a minute."

Willow didn't respond, not taking her eyes off the money in the register. She knew that Charlotte would take the shift even though it was her only Saturday off a month. Charlotte was a sure thing in that way.

Charlotte walked to the back office to use the phone and at that very moment, she saw Barb walk through the back door. Barb was middle-aged but dressed like she was 21, her clothes ill fitting and her bleached hair always showing her black and gray roots below it. Years of smoking and work at the bar made deep set wrinkles appear early on her face, a strange contrast to her compact body and young tight clothing. She'd been nice to Charlotte, but not overly warm, since her years at the bar and her life experience told her that Charlotte was a short-timer, just passing through before she moved on to bigger and better things. A stinging reminder that Barb long since missed her chance to escape the same way. The bar was her life, and always would be.

She raised her head and Charlotte noticed that it was the first time she'd seen Barb without makeup on. Her eyes were rimmed from crying and her hair was piled on top of her head haphazardly. She'd even ditched her signature tight tank top and tight jeans for sweats. Charlotte was immediately hit with a cloud of grief when she saw her, a wave of sadness that nearly knocked her over.

Barb gave Charlotte a tired smile, "Hey, Char," she said quietly, heading to the office.

Charlotte opened her mouth to speak but nothing came out at first. How could she tell her what she wanted to say, what she knew Barb needed to hear?

"Barb-I," she stuttered, "I'm so sorry about your dad."

Barb sighed and turned into the office with Charlotte following her.

“Thanks, honey. I just wasn’t ready for it. Kind of sudden.” She inhaled a shaky breath that indicated how much she’d been crying, all too familiar to Charlotte.

“I’m gonna take your shift tomorrow,” Charlotte said dumbly, trying to offer any kind of support she could.

“Thanks,” Barb said. “I came to get my check- are they in yet?”

“Yeah, in the drawer,” Charlotte said pointing to the desk.

Barb crossed the room and pulled out the folder containing the checks, looking through for hers, all the while praying that it would be enough to get her to New Mexico. Charlotte remained quiet, watching her closely. She felt the tingly sensation hit her head, the lightness of the messages, popping softly into her subconscious. She began chewing on her bottom lip, fidgeting from foot to foot. Barb pulled her check out of the stack, opening her tattered purse to put it inside.

“Thanks, Char. I’ll see you next week,” she said, heading for the door.

“Wait–” Charlotte started. “I just- I want to tell you something.” Charlotte said quietly.

Charlotte hardly spoke to people at the bar unless it related directly to work, so Barb squared her shoulders to her to listen, raising her brows in question. Charlotte cleared her throat, wringing her hands together nervously.

“Your dad. Was he in the Navy when he was young?”

Barb looked at Charlotte, staring blankly for a moment before she responded. Then she widened her eyes at her, dropping her jaw open a bit.

"How did you know that? I've never told anyone about him," she said quietly, taking a step closer to Charlotte.

"He's ok, Barb. He made it over just fine. And he loves you. He loves you so much. He says you're his sweetheart."

Barb's eyes welled with tears. "That's what he called me! He called me his sweetheart!"

Charlotte stepped toward Barb, taking her hands in hers. She focused hard, pumping as much love and peace into Barb as she could, infusing her with the light that she knew the poor woman needed.

"He's at peace and he wants you to be at peace, too. And he said he always wanted to die in his sleep, so don't feel bad for him."

Barb's tears flowed freely down her cheeks and she let them, not moving her hands out of Charlotte's to wipe them away.

"He did. He always said that," she said, squeezing her hands tighter. "Char, how? How do you know this?"

Charlotte shrugged. "Anyone can hear angels if they know how to listen," she said quietly. "It's gonna be ok, Barb. It's fine to be sad but you need to know it's going to be ok and that he's ok. He's so happy. He's free now," Charlotte said, smiling at Barb with her eyes.

Barb shook her head in disbelief. "I don't even know what to say. I–" she said, dissolving into tears.

"Thank you. Thank you so much." She hugged Charlotte to her tightly and Charlotte patted her back, finally pulling away.

Charlotte walked to her purse and opened her wallet, removing a hundred dollar bill. She walked back to Barb and put the money in her hand.

"This is to help get you there. He left you enough to get back home, too." Charlotte said quietly, hugging Barb again as she sobbed into her shoulder.

It was time. Finally, the signal had been given from Washington. They'd been pushed to make the decision to invade the city when all other negotiations failed. This decision was compounded by the fact that the Iraqi Army had no interest working side by side with the Marines, unwilling to risk the lives of their families by associating themselves with the Americans so blatantly. And so the Marines would have their way, finally able to infiltrate the city which had been dangled in front of them like a steak in front of ravenous dogs chained to a pole. They'd finally been unchained and the excitement was palpable. Wyatt's whole platoon reconvened inside the house they'd held down for days. Sergeant Stevens arrived with orders and was cleanly shaven and dressed for battle head to toe.

"Why Stevens look like he dressed for prom?" Patrick said quietly to Gus and Wyatt. "Sick bastard looks happier than I've ever seen him."

Wyatt and Gus laughed under their breath, thankful as always for Patrick who inevitably took the edge off of any tense situation, the biggest battle of their lives, no exception.

"Now," Stevens said, his eyes dancing with excitement, "We're gonna head north up this first block." He gestured toward the road, tactical gloves strapped tight on his wrists. "One house at a time, that's the plan. We'll have a platoon behind us for backup and two more to the other side of the street. Our orders are to extract if possible, destroy if necessary. They're not gonna go easy now, though, so don't hesitate," Stevens said, looking at his Marines.

Wyatt assessed the men around him. His jaw remained set, his mind already on the road outside, troubleshooting all that could go wrong. Seth Casey bounced from foot to foot, anxious as a kid on Christmas Eve. Harvey, always one ready for battle, remained cool, having just woken from a nap, his favorite form of preparation. Patrick, too, looked steady as can be, but Wyatt noticed he'd continuously prayed that morning, growing quiet and discreetly crossing himself after, kissing the tips of his gloved fingers. Gus for all of his nerves, faked it as well as he was able, trying like hell to tell himself he could do it, remembering why he had to, the men on either side of him always reminding him. He repeated inside of his head: *God and country. God and Country.* And he worked hard to believe it. To believe he was worthy of fighting next to these, the bravest men he'd ever known.

Wyatt, always in tune with his friend, looked over at Gus and smiled, widening his eyes humorously at Seth, all but dancing with excitement inside the crowded house. Gus smiled back, inhaling a long breath and looking back to Stevens. Wyatt could feel the excitement in the air but also the nerves. Even the men who appeared excited, he knew, felt nervous on some level. He looked around at his fellow Marines, saying a silent prayer to himself that he could protect them. That they'd all get out of Fallujah.

When Stevens finished his briefing, the men collected their weapons and headed out the front door and onto the north side of the street. Pat and Wyatt, being battle buddies, stuck close to each other's side, both with M-16s ready in their hands. Wyatt glanced behind him as they approached the first house, feeling his heart pounding in his chest. He remained outwardly calm as he nodded to Gus, eyes wide behind his tactical glasses, the sturdy Harvey to his right, a wad of chewing tobacco hanging heavy in his bottom lip.

Before kicking down that first door, Wyatt felt overcome. An image of the Archangel Michael came into his mind and he felt his medallion sitting flush against his skin. He remembered then what Rose told him: to call on Michael whenever he needed him. And so he did; in that split second before placing his boot on the door, he asked for help.

If you're really real, I need you now. My brothers need you.

And with that, the battle had begun. He kicked down the first door through which all the men entered, ready to fight, separating out and flashing lights against the walls, weapons pointing high and low wherever they searched. Seth burst through a bedroom door that wrapped back to a living room, scaring the shit out of the rest of the men when they realized it wasn't an insurgent. Especially since they'd come close to firing. They went through two more houses that same way, clearing through each room only to find a deserted home, no insurgents or civilians to be found. Just as they came out of the third house, action found them. They heard the patter of bullets firing in the distance, then closer.

"Get the fuck inside!" Stevens yelled to his platoon, the men scrambling inside the next house with a dozen other Marines hot behind them.

The machine gun fire came fast and hard, hammering down on the street and the house they entered, windows breaking all around them. Wyatt set to clearing the house with Patrick, both intent on securing their position since they knew what was coming.

"Board it up, Goddamn it." Stevens ordered as the men gathered couches and other pieces of furniture to put up over the windows.

The fire was coming heavier then, the whole building pounding with bullets and explosions.

"House is clear, Sergeant." Wyatt said.

"Where you want us?" Pat said.

"Up on that roof, fuckers are firing from next door on the rooftop. Intel says they have RPGs a few houses down. Harvey, pop a few out this window, they're out in front, too."

Harvey nodded, finding a small hole that his sniper rifle fit through, sticking it out in the street.

Almost immediately he fired, pulling his rifle back in and looking at the front of his scope.

"Fucker was close," he said, wiping the blood off the front of the scope with the elbow of his uniform.

There was chaos in the house, Marines, yelling to each other, heading up the stairs two at a time. Wyatt nodded to Gus before he left him standing next to Harvey, still shooting out the window. Gus, not being the marksman Harvey was, set to work supplying him with ammunition and stacking furniture over every opening to the front of the house. Seth and Griff were two of the first ones up, firing wildly as they hit the top of the roof, laying down protection for those coming after them. Wyatt and Pat entered the rooftop in much the same way, firing their weapons toward the building next door even though they couldn't see what they were hitting.

They sat down hard next to Seth and Griff, bullets whizzing over their heads and hitting the cement just above them. There were twenty-plus Marines on the rooftop. Wyatt glanced to the other side of the roof and saw several Marines stomping out a fire from a Molotov cocktail.

"There's one, there's one!" Seth yelled. No sooner did he finish his sentence before all of the men fired and two insurgents on the opposite roof dropped.

"Grenades," Wyatt yelled above the noise of the firefight.

Wyatt and Seth pulled grenades from their pack while Pat and Griff laid down fire so they could stand and throw them. They listened for the explosion, reloading to continue fighting. They heard the screams of the insurgents after the explosion and continued mechanically on, firing back to the rooftop. The fight lasted much longer than anyone anticipated. It seemed like they'd been out there for hours even though Wyatt knew it was more like 30 minutes at that point. They'd seen several Marines who had to be carried downstairs, injured by the gunfire and RPGs hitting around them, sending cement splattering over everything near it.

Gus and Harvey joined the rooftop battle sometime later after more men were injured and had to leave the fight to get bandaged, only to hobble back up the stairs and continue peppering the insurgents with machine gun fire and grenades.

"Down lower, Gus!" Wyatt yelled as Gus shrugged down, clinging his weapon to his chest.

Harvey spit out in front of him, removing a grenade from his vest.

"Lay down some for me, Gus," he said, turning to face the enemy. And Gus didn't hesitate, raising his weapon over the side of the wall and firing back and forth so Harvey could throw his grenade.

"We keep fucking killing 'em but then more come!" Seth yelled to the newcomers. "Motherfuckers are like rabbits."

Gus chewed on his bottom lip, looking around at his fellow Marines, following their lead.

"We have any new orders?" Patrick yelled to Harvey.

Harvey nodded once. "Kill 'em."

Pat grinned back at him, hot with anger from the long firefight. "Copy."

"Grenade!" A Marine from the other side of the rooftop yelled.

The men all turned to the wall, shielding their faces from the shrapnel that came flying toward them.

"We've got one down over here!" Someone yelled from father away.

"Get him downstairs!" Wyatt yelled back, turning back. "Go, now! Now!"

Pat stood up next to Wyatt, as did Seth and Gus, all firing so they could get the wounded down the stairs. When they sat back down, Wyatt turned and looked at Harvey.

"Harvey!" he said, crawling toward him. "You're hit, man." Harvey grimaced, just barely, looking down at his bloody arm.

"Ain't bad." He spit. "Dress it here, Sterling."

The wound could have been shrapnel or a bullet, Wyatt couldn't tell since it was bleeding so profusely. He kept his face even and nodded to Harvey, pulling a bandage out of his pack and wrapping it tight around the wound. His gloves were covered in blood when he pulled away.

"Good?" he said above the gunfire.

Harvey nodded and pointed his weapon back to the insurgents.

"Fucking taxis are dropping more off!" Griff said disbelievingly.

Wyatt peeked his head over and saw, sure enough, men pouring out of taxis to join the fight. Harvey stood to get a better angle and fired his weapon down the street below, taking out two insurgents who wouldn't make it to join the fight.

"Sit the fuck down!" Pat yelled at him.

Harvey grinned, sweat and blood dripping from his brow. "Fuck it."

The fire finally started to die down late in the afternoon when Stevens came out on the roof, looking frazzled but still with those same excited, alive eyes.

"Medevac is finally coming. We need help getting some of the wounded out."

"Yes, Seargent. Still some RPG fire coming from that house a few blocks away," Wyatt said, pointing with his chin.

"Delta guys are gonna shoot their thermos," Stevens said. "That'll take care of the rest."

All the men turned to watch the new explosive toys that the Delta Force guys had, much to their envy. When the thermos made impact with the building, a whole corner of the building all but crumbled before their very eyes.

"Army guys always get the cool shit," Pat said, gathering his things and heading for the door.

Wyatt waited until all the men stood.

"Move. I'll lay some down," he said stoically, firing as his friend ran back into the building.

When he hit the stairs, he could hardly believe what he saw. Blood covered the floor to the point that men were slipping on it down the stairs. The room was crowded with wounded Marines and the rest were figuring a way to get the men out.

"We need a stretcher!" one man yelled loudly.

"You're gonna have to make do! We don't have one!" Stevens walked over to the wounded man. "That's a scratch, for fuck's sake. You're fine."

Wyatt looked down at the man who was almost yellow with pain, his leg seemed to be hanging by a thread, but his stomach wound was even more troubling, a green substance oozing from the exit wound when the medic turned him over. The medic looked up at the able-bodied Wyatt.

"Help carry him. I don't have a stretcher," he said, looking around like one might appear.

Wyatt looked around the room, spotting a bedroom door. He signaled Pat to help him remove it roughly from the hinges and laid it down by the bleeding man. The medic nodded approvingly.

"Help me move him," he instructed.

Wyatt sat down on his knees with Pat next to him, doing the same. He read the last name on the wounded man's uniform.

"Come on, Alverez. Gonna get you outta here," he said, ignoring the man's listless appearance.

Alverez moaned as they moved him. "Tell my mom..." he mumbled, morphine induced.

"I don't need to tell her shit. You're gonna tell her. Hang tight," the medic said, patting Alverez's shoulder hard.

Wyatt felt his throat catch, but quickly checked himself, lifting his side of the door and hustling out onto the street, still active with gunfire. He ducked down as low as he could, keeping hold of his side of the door with Patrick on the other side and two other Marines behind him. They reached the armored ambulance and deposited the man inside before running back to join the men. They waited just inside the threshold of the door for orders to move out, and Patrick looked over to Wyatt, his dark heavy eyes in contrast to the smile he cracked for his friend

"Made it," he said quietly, looking him in the eye.

"Made it," Wyatt said. But he couldn't muster a smile, not even for Pat, the image of his fellow Marine clinging to life haunting him. "Made it."

The Monte Vista Hotel in downtown Flagstaff was allegedly haunted, but Rose didn't care. She stayed there anytime she came up to see Charlotte since there was no room for her at her tiny apartment. Plus, she'd told Charlotte over and over, the Monte Vista *did* in fact have ghosts, but ghosts needed help, so why wouldn't Rose stay there just to offer her services?

"Ghost is a ridiculous term," she'd told her. "They're only poor souls who haven't gone to the light so they stay here and fuck around."

And so that's where Rose insisted on staying, always talking to them in her head, sometimes out loud. Some she helped and some didn't want to listen, but either way, she wrote the hotel bill off on her taxes. Plus, the breakfast was the best in town, the dark smoky bar offering spicy bloody Mary's and a hearty breakfast with fresh ingredients she approved of. She was sitting at the bar waiting for her drink when Charlotte walked in.

"What's wrong?" Rose all but gasped when she saw her.

Charlotte gave her a tired smile. "Nothing," she said pulling out the chair next to Rose and sitting down. "Long night at the bar."

Rose looked at her. She had bags under her eyes and Rose could tell she'd been crying. She took a beat, considered playing along, then promptly decided against it.

"Bullshit," Rose said, turning in her chair to face her. "Please, babe. Don't make me invade your privacy and check the magical way because I will."

Charlotte smiled sadly and took a shaky breath. "Can't get it by you this time, huh?"

Rose shook her head slowly, reaching out to brush her hair off of her niece's shoulder. "Not this time. Tell me so I can fix it."

Charlotte shifted in her chair, looking out the window to the sunny street outside, just coming alive with people. She shook her head.

"I don't think it can be fixed, Aunt Rose. I just- I haven't been sleeping." Charlotte grew quiet as the bartender placed a Bloody Mary in front of Rose and a cup of coffee in front of her.

Rose took a sip, thinking about her response. "Are you gonna let me break our rule and ask about him?"

"There's no rule," Charlotte said almost defensively.

"Babe," Rose began, "not all rules have to be spoken, you know. I know you don't want to talk about him. But it's him, isn't it? It's Wyatt."

Charlotte flinched at the sound of his name and looked away from her aunt again, her eyes on the bar in front of her. She felt her throat tighten and her eyes well up but she willed herself to stop, to get ahold of her emotions like she'd been so good at doing for the last year. Finally she nodded and Rose said nothing, waiting for Charlotte to talk.

"He's not ok. I- I dream about him every night. I'm just- I'm so worried." A tear creeped its way out the side of one eye, but she wiped it quickly. "I can just feel him, Aunt Rose. And no matter what I do, no matter how I try to disconnect, I can't. I can't wash him off."

Rose frowned, feeling Charlotte's pain for her as clearly as if it were her own. She shifted in her chair, uncharacteristically at a loss for words. Charlotte looked straight at her aunt, her deep green eyes serious.

"What should I do, Aunt Rose? I've prayed. I've meditated. I've cleaned my energy," she said, ticking off Rose's normal recommendations. "I just- I hurt for him," she said, her voice barely above a whisper.

Rose rubbed Charlotte's back gently. "Write him. Why won't you write him?" she asked quietly.

Charlotte shook her head. "You know why. That regression. I know what I saw." Charlotte felt her stomach churn just thinking of it.

"But Char, that doesn't mean that–" she stopped short of finishing. "That was another life, babe. This is a new one."

Charlotte leveled her eyes at her aunt. "I can't be with him. I won't do that to him."

Rose sighed, taking another long drink. She knew the girl wouldn't budge, but she couldn't help but try.

"Ok. If there's nothing I can do to change your mind. Just keep praying. And talk to him in your head. Just because you aren't in his life, it doesn't mean you're not in his heart," Rose said gently. "And ask your guides to bring him home safely. Ask them to give you a sign that he will come home."

Charlotte nodded, willing to try anything to help.

"Ok," she said, taking another shaky breath." Ok, I will."

Rose didn't say anything for a moment, but stared out the window instead, listening to the sounds of the city. She turned back to Charlotte and spoke softly to her.

"Never forget, Charlotte. Never forget- God grants miracles."

The days that followed that first major engagement in Fallujah were more of the same, only with shorter, smaller skirmishes which the men now felt better seasoned and more prepared for. Even the greenest of them had been broken in like they never could have imagined. Baptism by fire was the term utilized and it worked in more ways than one. The men fought with more ferocity and sureness than they had when they arrived in country. They were, as Pat put it, always sitting on ready.

That first battle had left many injured men, but only one was wounded bad enough to be extracted and there still wasn't any word on him. Wyatt thought of his face every day, though, often waking from sleep struck by the image of his yellow, bloodied skin, and his low moans, his mother's name on his lips. He knew he shouldn't, but he counted the Marine's grave injuries as his own mistake. If only he could have been closer, helped him somehow. But he wasn't, he reminded himself. And he couldn't help them all- a more heartbreaking realization than he ever anticipated.

It was nightfall in Fallujah and the men were hunkered down for the night, holding their front which they'd fought hard for and wouldn't give up. There would be no returning to the crude camp just outside of the city, not that night. Wyatt never imagined such an awful camp would look so appealing in comparison to the deserted house they sat in, the foreign objects of the home's occupants unsettling for him to look at.

He should have been sleeping that night since another platoon had first watch, with snipers on the roof and tired eyes looking out the front window, ready for anything. Wyatt sat with his back up against the wall with Gus to his right, curled up like a child on the floor, head resting on his pack, his breathing deep with restful sleep. Patrick was to his left, sitting against the wall with his eyes closed. His full lips pressed together in a serious line. Wyatt looked at them and the other men lying scattered across the room, counting all of them safe. Seth, Griff, Harvey, and the others. All accounted for.

Thank you. Wyatt said in his head to no one in particular.

The night was quiet, almost unsettlingly so. Wyatt knew at any moment, at any given place in the city, there'd be another engagement. It was anyone's guess where it would be. Maybe right there. Which is why he should rest, he told himself. But he couldn't. His mind couldn't turn off.

His mind inevitably went to her, no matter what. It was almost July, almost her birthday. How? How could it have been a year ago he held her? A year ago he'd told her he loved her in that quiet bunkhouse. He closed his eyes, holding the image of her sitting next to him on that bed. Her face as she'd told him that no, he wasn't the first, and how she'd been ashamed when she said it. He looked back at Gus and Patrick to be sure they were sleeping before reaching quietly into his pocket and retrieving her picture. The room was dark but for a small sliver of light showing through a window. He held the picture up, bringing it closer to his face to see.

She'd been so perfect that night. So free. Her wild blonde hair falling to the middle of her back and her lips smiling into his kiss. He hardly recognized himself in the picture, his cheeks red with embarrassment and his cowboy hat pushed back on his head so she could kiss him. He stared hard at the picture, committing it to memory once again.

"That her?" Patrick whispered, scaring Wyatt.

"Shit. Scared me," Wyatt said, putting the picture down.

"Naw, man. Lemme see," Patrick said gently, knowing his friend well enough to tread lightly.

Wyatt handed the picture to Patrick who squinted to see it, a slow smile spreading across his face.

"Look at you," he teased, "Look at that hair under your hat. No high and tight then."

"Nope. Pre-devil dog," he said nervously, his embarrassment making his cheeks go red for the first time in a long time.

"She's beautiful," Pat said.

Wyatt nodded once. "Never heard you call a girl that before."

Pat shrugged. "It's true, though. She why you don't like blondes now?"

Wyatt shrugged. "Don't know. Guess so."

Pat nodded slow, "You two look so–" he struggled to find the words, "I don't know. In love, I guess." He studied the foreign Wyatt in the picture, then looked back to his friend.

"It was a long time ago now," Wyatt said, taking the picture and tucking it back into his pocket.

"Sorry, man. I didn't mean to pry."

Wyatt shook his head. "You know everything about me anyway. No use hiding from you." He smiled.

"She's crazy if she don't want you. You're the best dude I've ever met," Pat said honestly.

Wyatt laughed for fear he might cry instead, Pat's words meaning more to him than he ever thought possible.

"Thanks, Pat," he whispered back. "You're not in love with me like Seth is, are you?" he joked.

Pat smiled back, the whites of his teeth flashing brightly. "Shit. The Marines keep me out here much longer I might be. Told you, you pretty as hell."

"Thought you were the pretty one," Wyatt said back.

"We both are. Shit, even Gus, too, but he's more cute than anything. Like a puppy or something."

Wyatt laughed, looking down at Gus, his long lashes curling above his full cheeks.

"Hey," Pat said, pausing for a moment. "We're gonna be alright. Hear me?"

Wyatt nodded to his friend and inhaled deeply.

"We're gonna be alright," Wyatt repeated back, knowing Pat needed to hear it just as bad as he did.

"Get some sleep, cowboy," Pat said quietly putting his head back against the wall.

He closed his eyes again, leaving Wyatt to his own thoughts. He listened to the sound of the men sleeping around him and closed his eyes to try to sleep.

Charlotte. He thought in his heart. *Charlotte, I need you.*

After breakfast Rose knew she couldn't leave yet. She knew her niece needed her and she simply couldn't bring herself to drive that long five hour drive home to the other side of the state, leaving her there by herself. And so she did what she did best, and made it seem like it was her own idea and that she was simply staying to get another day up in the cool weather. That way Charlotte wouldn't feel bad about it.

It was a Monday and Charlotte had a packed schedule. She finished her morning classes, then told Rose she'd meet her for a late lunch before she had to head to the bar. She'd considered taking the night off entirely, but she knew they were shorthanded with Barb still gone. Unable to let anyone down, she'd do it all, per usual.

Charlotte walked downtown, past the old brick buildings and the inviting smells of the cafes and coffee shops. Rose sat in the town square on a bench, her eyes closed under her Jackie O type sunglasses and her face pointing toward the sunshine. She wore a flowing floral skirt and a white tunic and looked every bit the Flagstaff local, but Charlotte wouldn't say that to her. Mostly because Rose thought the locals there were a bit strange. Too new-aged for her taste.

"Well, well, well, if it isn't Miss Bronte," Rose said sitting up and grinning at Charlotte. "How much time you got, babe?"

"Couple hours so we're good," Charlotte said, sitting down next to her.

"You look better today, how you feeling?"

"I'm ok. Working on it," Charlotte said, even though the first part wasn't true.

She'd gone out of her way to make herself look presentable since she knew Rose would be watching closely. She'd woken up early to wash and dry her hair and even put on makeup, all the while ignoring the pit in her stomach that would not go away. She put on her nicest lace tank top, the small straps exposing her lean tanned arms and her jeans hugging tight to her hips. She was beautiful, no doubt, but Rose saw through the act and felt her heaviness just the same as the day before that.

"You wanna go back to the Monte Vista for lunch? There's a daytime bartender there and you could bounce quarters off his ass. Might be fun." Rose grinned.

Charlotte laughed, finally cracking a smile for her aunt. "Your pick, perv. I'm up for anything."

"Anything, eh?" she said, putting her arm around her. "Funny you should say that. I have a little surprise for you."

"Oh, God," Charlotte laughed. "I have to be careful what I say to you."

Rose grinned wickedly and pulled Charlotte up from the bench, holding her hand as she walked her down the sidewalk, chattering on about the shops and the restaurants. Flagstaff, despite the stalling economy, was still booming. It was the biggest tourist town in northern Arizona and saw the benefits of its cool weather every summer when the citizens to the south flocked there to escape the unbearable summers in the desert.

Rose walked past the Monte Vista and down a small side street. "Come on, we gotta hustle. I'm starving!" Rose complained.

"Where are we going then? What's the surprise?"

Charlotte generally loved Rose's surprises so she couldn't understand why she was nervous what her aunt was going to show her. She knew, for some reason, that this would not be a small surprise. Rose finally stopped just outside the shop Buddha's Closet, where she'd made Charlotte get that ridiculous tarot card reading the summer before that. She turned and smiled mischievously at Charlotte.

"Oh no," Charlotte said firmly. "Hell no. Not this time," she said pulling her hand back from Rose.

Rose cackled loudly and went after Charlotte, grabbing her hand once again. She pulled her on a bench just outside the shop.

"No, no," she began. "It's not what you think, I promise. Sit down, babe."

She was still containing her laugher as Charlotte sat down next to her, a skeptical look on her face.

"Ok," she started. "Let me get serious now." She shook herself a bit and shifted her body to look at Charlotte.

"Did you know this place is closing?" Rose asked. "They aren't doing well."

Charlotte scoffed. "Shocker. Maybe because of those shit readings."

Rose laughed. "Right? They can't all be us, babe." She winked.

Rose took a deep breath, gathering her thoughts. "I want you to be honest with me, ok Charlotte? You won't hurt my feelings."

Charlotte furrowed her brow, confused. "Ok..."

"I miss you, babe. When you left Patagonia, I- I just felt lonely. And I've NEVER felt like that before. I've always been on my own and I've liked it that way. But you ruined that for me," she said, smiling into Charlotte's eyes. "I'm not tough anymore."

Charlotte scooted closer to her aunt. "Me either."

Rose laughed. "That's not true. You're the toughest person I've ever met and that's the damn truth."

Rose looked back at the building behind them, the two stories of brick quaint and formidable at the same time. It needed a sound saging, Rose thought, but overall, it was a lovely place.

"So, this is where I need you to be honest with me. I need you to tell me if you don't want this to happen. And it's ok if you don't, alright?"

"You know I will, Aunt Rose. Tell me what's going on. I don't understand."

"This place," Rose said, waving her hand at it. "It's for sale. And I could get it for a steal."

Charlotte looked at her a moment before processing the words, her jaw dropping just slightly.

"I was thinking I could move up here. Rent out the house in Patagonia, I own it free and clear. And I could buy this and we could go into business together. I know you have school and I really don't want to get in the way of your life here," she hurried on, "But I don't know, Char. It feels like the right move."

"Wait–" Charlotte started, "You wanna leave Patagonia?" She stared at her shocked. "For me?" she whispered after.

Rose nodded slowly, "Of course, my spirit baby." Her eyes welled under her sunglasses. "I can hardly live without you. I just want to make sure you want this, too. It's your life."

Charlotte was overcome. She looked back at the building, then to her aunt, still unable to believe she really meant it. That Rose, a fixture in her southern Arizona town, would even consider being somewhere else, and for Charlotte's benefit. Her heart swelled and she tried her hardest not to cry, not to show the relief that she felt at the prospect of having her close once again.

"Yes," she whispered as a tear streaked slowly down her cheek. "Thank you, Aunt Rose."

The days were long and the fighting unrelenting. Wyatt and his fellow Marines certainly looked worse for the wear, all sporting injuries of some kind, bandaged, bruised, and bloodied by days of constant engagements and no shower. Not even Pat complained about that, though; they all had a one track mind at that point, completely intent with ridding the city of the dangerous insurgents and nothing else.

That day's mission would be simple, much like the days before it. The Marines, along with patrols from the Army and air support, were to clear a small quadrant of the city, going door to door to check the houses and push their line up further. Wyatt sat next to the men in his platoon in another strange home, broken items littering the floor, waiting for the official word to push out. He studied his hands and his knuckles which were scraped and bloody from the past few days, one large gash on the inside of his hand that probably needed some attention. He brushed it off and made a mental note to deal with it later.

His own safety and wellbeing was of little importance lately. His men, his brothers on either side of him always came first. Especially after the news came that Alverez didn't make it. He'd succumbed to his injuries days later in the hospital and Wyatt had to force himself not to think of it, fighting the image of the bleeding Alverez lying on a door Wyatt had ripped from its hinges, there in that awful house soaked in blood. No, he wouldn't think of it. Couldn't think of it then.

"Bet this is it for us today," Pat said, adjusting his helmet on his head. "Heard the Lieutenant Colonel talking. Washington wants the Iraqi Army to take over. Says they gotta fight for themselves."

"What the fuck have we been doing, then?" Seth said, spitting over his shoulder.

"Now look, Casey. This might be the first time we agree!" He grinned at him. "Media is spinning it all crazy, man. We're the bad guys now. People forget too quickly."

Seth nodded, looking down at the ground. As much as the men would have liked to leave, it felt like a failure somehow. Leaving before the city was cleared would not be their preference, but they knew it was not their opinion which mattered.

"You got any chew, Wyatt?" Gus asked.

Wyatt nodded, getting into his pocket and removing the Skoal can. "You dipping now?" he asked grinning.

Gus nodded stoically. "Keeps me awake," he said, putting a large pinch in his lower lip.

Wyatt studied his profile, noting the bags under his eyes. Gus looked years older than when he'd met him, even though Wyatt knew that he was just shy of 19 years old. His birthday was the next month, just before they were scheduled to go home. Gus passed the can back to Wyatt, thanking him quietly.

"You ok, man?" Wyatt said, quiet enough so no one else could hear.

Gus nodded. "Yeah. I'm good. Ready to get this over with."

"Me too," Wyatt said, but part of him was lying. Leaving Fallujah without the job being completed would plague him, he knew. His thorough nature made anything less painful for him.

When the time came to push out, the men were ready, although much different from that first day. Seth didn't jump from foot to foot anymore, Pat didn't pray, and Gus no longer chewed his bottom lip nervously. Their combat cherries, as Stevens had put it, had been fully popped and there was no going back to the people they were before that.

The morning was quiet as they started patrol, a haze of clouds hanging over the town. Wyatt looked at the sky, hoping that it might rain, even sprinkle, something to break up the relentless heat they'd encountered every day. Even for him, it was trying.

"I want in first today," Seth said from behind Wyatt and Patrick.

Wyatt nodded. "You sure? Been working out solid this way."

Wyatt had been point man on every entry they'd made, his eyes steady and systematic each time he entered a building. He thought of himself as a wall that nothing could get through, protecting the men behind him. The prospect of giving that up panicked him in a way he couldn't explain.

Seth nodded, shifting his pack on his back. "I know how to clear a fucking house, Sterling," he spat.

Wyatt gripped his weapon in his hands but refused to engage with Seth, knowing that nothing productive would come from it.

"Fuck, relax, Casey. Here," Pat said, stepping to the side. "After you. You wanna go first? Go ahead!"

Casey and Griff pushed by them, leaving Harvey and Gus directly behind Wyatt and Pat. Marines lined the streets and Wyatt could already hear the tanks mobilizing in the distance, the commanders learning their lesson from that first engagement. They had underestimated the insurgents and they would not do that again. If they were going to be forced to leave the city, they would leave swinging.

"Wyatt and Pat, left. Harvey and Gus, right. Griff and I will breach and go straight, then we'll clear it."

"Copy," they mumbled back in unison.

Wyatt took a deep breath, his chin strap pulling tight to his stubbly face. He looked back at Gus and Harvey, nodding once before Seth kicked down the door and they entered. Everyone carried out their mission, moving the way they'd been instructed to. Wyatt and Pat kicked down bedroom doors searching the seemingly empty apartment.

"Clear," Pat said, turning back to the middle of the house.

"Clear here, too," Wyatt yelled from a neighboring bedroom.

Wyatt could hear movement going up the stairs and the unmistakable sound of Seth and his clown feet plopping around. Guns drawn, they walked back toward the middle of the house to go up the stairs, but were stopped short by the sound of bullets.

"Gus!" Harvey yelled, firing his M-16 rapidly after.

Wyatt ran to the other side of the house with Pat hot on his heels, his heart beating into his throat. Harvey was kneeling down next to Gus on the floor of the bedroom, blood pooling underneath him. Wyatt scanned the room with his weapon and saw the insurgent then. A young, dark boy, maybe not even 18 years old, slumped over with bullet holes in his head and chest, clearly dead.

"Just one," Harvey said, taking off his pack. "Pat, go check upstairs!"

Patrick took the stairs two at a time, calling after Seth and Griff as Wyatt knelt down to the side of Gus, trying to keep his face even. Gus was squirming, crying out in pain, trying to look down at his wounds.

Breathe. Act normal. Wyatt thought to himself. Harvey looked at Wyatt, his serious brown eyes saying what he couldn't say out loud. It was bad.

"Lay back, Barrett. Gonna get you patched up," Harvey said. "Wyatt, you got your pocket knife to cut that pant leg? Let me radio." Harvey took out his radio and walked out of the room, speaking in measured but intense tones. Wyatt set to work, taking off his pack to retrieve his knife.

"Is it bad?" Gus asked, his voice shaking.

"Naw, man. You're fine. Sit tight." He was amazed that his hands stayed steady as he cut his pant leg in a circular motion around Gus's wound, ripping a long piece of fabric off as he did. The wound was just below his pelvis and it was gushing so much blood that Wyatt couldn't tell how many entries there were.

"One hit my stomach, too," Gus said, panting.

Wyatt felt up his stomach, patting the Kevlar reassuringly.

"Vest, no worries." He wrapped the fabric around the top of his leg, moving it up as high as he could. He pulled it tight, trying to cut off the circulation and slow the bleeding. This was why he took those medic classes in basic. He would be ok, he told himself over and over.

"You're good, man. You're good. Stay calm, ok?" Wyatt put his face close to his, speaking soothingly to him. Just then he heard shots in the distance and the city come alive, once again, with fighting.

Harvey stormed back in, uncharacteristically frazzled looking. "Medevac can't come just yet. It's popping off out there."

More Marines joined them in the house, but none of them medics. The blood still poured from Gus's leg despite the tourniquet, so Wyatt tied another, then another, covering himself in blood. Pat and the others finally came downstairs, eyes wide looking at Gus on the floor. Wyatt looked up at them, shooting them a glare.

"He's fine. It's a fucking scratch, Gus. You're tough as hell," he said, stroking Gus's head.

It had been only minutes since he'd been hit, but it felt like hours that they waited there for help, Gus losing more and more blood every moment that went by. His color was fading and he began to shake uncontrollably.

"Wyatt," he said, chin shaking. "It doesn't hurt. That's bad isn't it?"

Wyatt looked at him, his blue eyes steady. "It doesn't hurt because you're a bad dude, Gus. So fucking tough. Remember when you beat Seth's ass in that wrestling match?"

Seth, eyes trained on his rifle pointed outside grinned, looking back at them. "It's true, man. I outweigh you by 50 pounds, too."

Gus mustered a small grin, his body still convulsing.

"Medic's here," Seth said, pulling open the front door, the sound of bullets peppering the street echoing through the house.

The medic, a clean-cut looking Navy kid, entered and didn't take his eyes off of Gus as he asked for a recounting of his injuries. He started an IV immediately and held his gloved hand over the gushing wound.

"How long?" he asked Wyatt, "How long has he been bleeding like this?" he said, the urgency in his voice obvious.

"I don't–" Wyatt stuttered, his hands covered in Gus's blood. "I don't know."

"15 minutes," Patrick said, kneeling down next to Gus and laying a hand on his shoulder. "We can carry him. Let us take him."

The medic exhaled, glancing out the door. "Call the armored ambulance. Tell them we have one critical that needs to go now."

Pat nodded and stood to complete the task. Gus reached for Wyatt and gripped his hand weakly. Wyatt squeezed his hand back, looking straight at him.

"You're gonna go now, Gus. They're gonna help you, ok?" Wyatt fought the tears he felt forming in his eyes, willing himself to be strong for his friend.

"Wyatt," he said weakly. "Thank you."

"For what?" Wyatt said smiling at him. "You don't have to thank me for anything, bud. You're gonna be ok. I'll see you real soon. Just be tough."

Gus smiled sadly. "I'm not as tough as you."

"You're tougher than me, Gus. There's no one tougher than you. Look he's giving you some medicine now so you're gonna feel better. You're gonna be ok," Wyatt said, talking intensely to his face.

Gus's eyes closed, fluttering open to look around the room listlessly. Wyatt slapped the side of his face briskly.

"Hey! You gotta stay awake, ok? Ambulance is coming right now. I'm gonna carry you there, ok?"

"No stretcher," the medic said. "You guys all grab a side of him."

The men didn't hesitate, all of them gathering around him and lifting him seamlessly from the floor. Blood dripped from his wound onto the tile as they shuffled toward the front of the house.

"We need some suppressive fire to get him outta here!" Seth yelled.

Harvey detached himself from Gus and stood out in front of the door, completely unfazed by the gunfire shooting every which way. The men carried Gus to the armored ambulance, setting him down on the stretcher and moving quickly back inside. Except Wyatt. He squatted down next to his friend, holding tight to his hand as the medics began working on him.

"I'm gonna see you soon, ok?" he said, gripping his hand. "Be tough, Gus."

"Wyatt," he said, pulling him closer. "You gotta tell my parents. You gotta tell them I did what I was supposed to."

"You're gonna tell them that. I don't need to tell them. You can tell them one day when you're telling your kids what a bad motherfucker you were. You hear me?"

"We gotta go!" one of the medics was yelling at Wyatt, "You gotta get out of here, Private."

Wyatt stood to go, giving Gus's hand a firm squeeze.

"Wyatt–" Gus mumbled. "Thanks for- for being my friend."

Wyatt smiled down at him but couldn't speak for fear of losing his composure. He turned and hopped out of the ambulance, running back inside the house where he found Patrick, gun in his hands and a tear streaking down his ebony cheek.

The fighting tapered off that day and Patrick was right, they headed back to camp that very evening. They would hand the city over to the Iraqi Army the following day and turn their attention to neighboring cities in country. They finally got a shower and Wyatt stayed in a long time, watching the blood wash off of him and down the drain, muted by the hot water he let burn his face and body.

He was in the barracks sitting on his bed with the rest of his men around him when Stevens walked in, still in uniform. The men were quiet but hopeful, and stood as he walked toward them. Wyatt crossed his arms, putting his hands under each bicep to hide the fact that he couldn't stop shaking. Stevens took off his hat and sighed deeply.

"Sit down, guys," he said, uncharacteristically gentle. Wyatt's stomach dropped as he sat down on his bunk, clasping his hands in front of him instead. Pat sat to his right, looking up at Stevens, his bottom lip already trembling.

"Gus didn't make it," he said shortly. "Bled out on the way to the hospital."

His words hung in the air and Wyatt felt the world drop out from underneath him. Gus Barrett, not even 19 years old, was gone. He thought of his plump face, still so childlike and innocent. No. Wyatt shook his head outwardly. No, it simply couldn't be. Why Gus? Why not him instead?

"I know you guys were tight. All of you," Stevens said, looking among the men. "He was lucky to die next to you guys. That he had you there."

Stevens put his hat on and turned on his heel, unable to look at the heartbroken faces anymore. There was silence among the men except for Harvey's crying. A strange, unrecognizable sob that shook the big man and the bunk he sat on. Wyatt still shook his head back and forth, as if somehow denying it entirely would make it impossible. He felt Pat's hand around his shoulder and leaned into his friend, his heart breaking in a new way that he didn't know existed.

III

"The woods are lovely, dark and deep,
But I have promises to keep,
And miles to go before I sleep,
And miles to go before I sleep."

~ Robert Frost

Charlotte sat at the window inside the new Spirit's Soul, gazing at the snow falling from the sky. It was the first snow of the year and the roads were quiet, hardly a person in sight. She pulled her knit sweater tight around her, sipping her coffee peacefully. Rose was in the back room with the door shut, performing a reading for a client who, despite the snow, kept her appointment time. Probably because she'd been waiting at least a month to get in with Rose who was, very suddenly, a hot commodity in town.

Charlotte, although thankful for the booming nature of the business, was grateful for the slow day at the shop. Since they opened the previous August, they'd hardly had a lull in the steady clientele through the shop doors looking for readings, spiritual literature, crystals, chakra candles, and more. There was no lack of people interested in what they had to offer, and Rose had to eat her words about all of the new-aged weirdos she couldn't stand. Flagstaff was, quite simply, the perfect place for Rose and Charlotte to do business. The spirit guides had been right, the answer had come and Charlotte was grateful.

They'd completely gutted the shop, saging every corner of it and redecorated the drab, spooky atmosphere with potted plants and art featuring landscapes from across Arizona. A large blown-up photograph of the San Xavier Mission hung in the middle of one of the brick walls, making Rose feel at home. There were shelves and displays taking up every space in the shop and a reading area in the front that doubled as a waiting room for Rose's readings. Charlotte stayed busy, always rearranging and finding new ways to maximize their profits. Customers came to love being in the space she created, coming back time after time and always saying how peaceful it was there.

Charlotte tilted her head toward the window to look up at the sky. She watched the silent, graceful way the snowflakes fell to the road below. It was so beautiful, almost poetic, that she felt her eyes well up with tears just to be near it. Just to encounter that stillness. And of course, she thought of him then. Prayed for his safety and sent him all the love she had in her heart, giving some of the stillness for to him to share. That summer it would be two years since she'd seen him and still he possessed the very essence of her being, taking hold of it and never letting go. She still felt him every day, that one thing she couldn't make right in the world.

"Every single day," Rose was saying, walking from the back room, "You need to meditate every single day. This is not just something you can do occasionally or just so people can *see* you doing it. Do it. And do it for yourself."

The young girl she was reading was still wiping her eyes, nodding to Rose as she walked to the register. Her dreadlocked hair peeked out from the bottom of a trendy knitted cap.

"I will," she said, a bit unconvincingly.

Charlotte got up from her place at the window and quietly rang up the client as Rose continued her recommendations. Finally, she hugged the girl and sent her on her way, out into the storm.

"Jesus," Rose said, sitting down hard in one of the armchairs at the front of the shop. "These kids are all so worried about how it looks on the outside. None of them give a shit how it feels on the inside."

Charlotte nodding knowingly, pouring a cup of tea for Rose and setting it down next to her as her aunt gazed out the window.

"I never did love the snow, but my god," Rose said, sighing. "This is goddamn majestic."

Charlotte nodded, sitting back down across from Rose. "It is. So beautiful."

Rose looked to Charlotte, noting her wet-rimmed eyes and quiet way. Her niece had bloomed before her very eyes in the last year and a half. Sometimes she couldn't believe the woman who sat in front of her. Beautiful, smart, intuitive, but also stoic. Part of her was impenetrable, even for Rose.

Charlotte had started to dress even plainer since they'd opened the shop, covering her body with chunky sweaters and braiding her long hair simply down her back. But it didn't matter. She was striking, her large green eyes framed by thick black lashes and her plump lips resting with her Mona Lisa half grin.

She only looked like her old self on Saturdays when she bartended at the Museum Club, which Rose had begged her to give up since the shop was going so well. But it was no use. Charlotte couldn't sit still anyway, unable to stop her momentum which had been so beneficial for both of them. Plus, her work at the bar helped her work at the shop; she met a bunch of people in town and was able to create a whole new clientele by getting to know the patrons there. The bartenders, even Willow, frequented the shop and continuously booked with Rose, tipping each time they did. Charlotte's hard work was paying off. The numbers were beyond solid and she'd been able to save up a few thousand dollars being as frugal as she was. She was distancing herself, all the time, from the way she grew up, from being like her mother, her greatest fear.

"I ordered more inventory today. Double from last month of those crystals and also those chakra books," she said, gesturing to the shop.

Rose sighed, throwing her head back against her chair. "Must we always work, babe? God, we aren't having any *fun* anymore! It's just work, work, work, all the time! And even worse for you. If you aren't here you're at school or that shitty old bar," she said, waving her hand in disgust.

Charlotte laughed, throwing up her hands. "Alright, alright. We don't have to talk business right now."

"Thank you!" Rose said, putting her hands around her tea cup and taking a long sip.

Quiet fell between them and they watched the snow coming down harder outside. The plows had finally come out and were slowly skimming up and down the roads, spraying snow up on the sidewalks. Charlotte closed her eyes, resting for a moment. She thought about all she had to do that evening. Her winter session course was intense, to say the least, and she'd been staying up until the wee hours of the morning trying to stay ahead of the curve, but she wouldn't say that to Rose. If she did, she knew Rose would insist on her cutting her hours and force her, finally, to quit her job at the bar.

"Well, shit!" Rose said. "I didn't say we couldn't talk at all!"

Charlotte opened her eyes, grinning at her aunt, her fickle ways ever-endearing to her.

"Ok, fine," Charlotte said, "What should we talk about then?"

"Boys maybe," Rose grinned. "Or men, I should say. Who has time for boys, right?"

Charlotte shifted in her chair and forced a smile for her aunt. "Ok, which *man* do you have in mind? You have so many I can't keep up."

Rose cackled. "It's true, isn't it? Well, you can't blame me, it's like a whole new barrel of fish up here and it's like I'm shooting them with a goddamn shotgun."

Charlotte laughed, putting her head back on her shoulders. "It's impressive, no doubt."

"But I don't wanna talk about any of them," Rose said, waving a hand. "What about any boys you know? Anyone striking your fancy these days?"

Charlotte shot her a glance, annoyed. "You know the answer, Aunt Rose. Don't act like you don't."

Rose shrugged. "If you're insinuating that I've looked into the matter magically, you're wrong. Even I have boundaries, you know," she said, putting her pinky up suggestively as she sipped her tea.

"Mmhmm," Charlotte said, sitting up in her chair, readying herself to do something, anything but sit there.

"Now, don't be mad at me, babe. I'm just saying. It's not normal for you to act like a nun. For Christ sakes, have you looked in a mirror? You need to be putting some miles on that perfect body you've got in this life, my dear. What I wouldn't do for it!"

"You sound like Willow," Charlotte said, rolling her eyes.

Rose widened her eyes, insulted. "Please. I didn't say to bang everything on two legs did I? But god help me, I do love that little hussy."

Charlotte smiled, nodding her head in agreement. "Hard not to like her for some reason."

"She told me, you know. That you've given out a few magical readings here and there at the bar," Rose said.

Charlotte looked out the window, trying to avoid the inevitable conversation. "Just a couple of small messages, really." She shrugged.

Rose laughed, taking another sip of her coffee. "Don't look so nervous. I'm not gonna force you to do anything, you know. All in your own time."

Charlotte smiled at her, hoping the conversation would be over. But in true Rose form, it wasn't.

"I just wonder why, Char. Why don't you want to use your gift? Are you afraid?"

Charlotte shook her head. "No, no. I'm not afraid. I just- I just don't know if I feel right about doing it. I- maybe I'm just meant to run the business side, you know? I'm happy doing that."

Rose nodded knowingly. "Yes, I know. Very happy to work yourself into the ground on a regular basis," she said sarcastically. "Just promise me that you won't reject the gifts you're given. Even if you don't use them the way I use them. I just want you to remember to listen to your gift. Even if it's only for you," Rose said as gently as she could.

"Ok, Aunt Rose. I promise I'll listen," Charlotte said quietly.

"That's my girl. Just let it come to you. This is how it comes," she said, sweeping her hand toward the front window. "Just like this," Rose said looking back to the snow falling gently from the sky.

Detroit in the wintertime was nothing to be trifled with. Patrick had warned Wyatt over and over again but Wyatt didn't quite grasp it, even after all of his insisting that it would be fine. The cold was unbearable, penetrating the layers of clothing he'd put on, icing him to the core. He walked down the sidewalk with Patrick to his right, grinning over at him.

"Not talking shit now, are you cowboy? I told you it was cold!" he laughed, pushing his friend's arm.

"Alright, alright, you were right," Wyatt conceded, pushing his hands deeper into his pockets. "So is this where you grew up? This same neighborhood, I mean?"

Patrick nodded. "Never lived in another house until I joined the Marine Corps. Shit, I'd never been on a plane until then, either."

"And look at you now," Wyatt said, grinning behind the collar of his winter jacket, "International traveler."

"Shiiiit," Patrick scoffed. "Does Iraq count as international travel?"

Wyatt shook his head, looking down to his feet scraping the icy sidewalk. "Not really. But maybe Florida does."

"Hell yeah, it does," Patrick said, smiling over to his friend.

They'd returned from that awful first tour in Iraq the summer before only to go back to Texas and sit around the base, wishing they were back over there. None of the men quite understood how it was that when they were in Iraq they wanted to be back in the states more than anything, but when they returned, all they could think about was going back. Even after losing Gus, they all wanted to be there, maybe moreso. At least then they could do something that felt productive. Wyatt hardly recognized the person he'd become. His need for the high intensity of the wartime atmosphere changed him forever.

And so when orders came for them to go back for a second tour after the holidays, Wyatt was relieved, excited even. He wanted to get back to that place where so much work needed to be done, to fight once again next to the people he could rely on most. Patrick was excited, too, even if he acted like he wasn't, already complaining about the dust and the lack of showers. He, too, needed it the way Wyatt did.

They had two weeks of R and R before they had to report for deployment and they intended to make the best of it, heading to Detroit to spend the holidays with Patrick's mom, then to Florida with Harvey and Seth, which was Patrick's idea since he'd never been on a real beach. Other than Lake Michigan, that is.

"Alright, listen," Patrick said stopping on the sidewalk and turning to Wyatt, "My aunties will eat you alive so don't be afraid to tell them to back off if they get to be too much."

Wyatt laughed. "Pat, I'm sure I can handle your aunties."

Patrick shook his head vehemently. "Nah, dude. You don't understand. They're gonna love you. Like, LOVE you. And it sure ain't gonna help that you wore your boots," Patrick said, waving his hands to Wyatt's cowboy boots.

Wyatt shrugged. "Why?"

"You never get it. That whole cowboy thing." Patrick kept walking down the sidewalk toward his childhood home. "It does something to the females, man. Especially round here, just wait. Sticking out like a goddamn John Wayne sore thumb." Patrick grinned.

Wyatt laughed and looked around at the street. Townhouses lined either side of the road, most of them kept clean and tidy out front, except for a few which were boarded up. Patrick's mom told him the neighborhood wasn't doing well since the recession started and she was right. In all his life, Patrick had ever seen his street look so unkempt and he told Wyatt that over and over as he walked, bordering on embarrassed for his childhood home. But Wyatt wasn't hard to impress and he liked the little neighborhood bustling with people and kids playing in the streets despite the bitter cold.

When they finally got to Patrick's house far up the road, Wyatt realized why he'd parked so far away. The neighborhood was packed with old cars, some that ran and some that clearly didn't, leaving little room to park. Snow covered the front lawn and walkway of his mother's home, which made Patrick frown immediately.

"She usually has this shoveled," he explained, thinking that it was normally him who did the shoveling.

"I can do it later," Wyatt offered.

Pat looked up at the porch as he walked the steps. His mother's normally tidy home had changed. There were papers littering the table out front and muddy shoes strewn about haphazardly. He bent over and straightened the shoes while Wyatt waited behind him, his large hand resting on the cold metal banister.

"Son of a bitch," Patrick said under his breath.

He wiped his feet on the rug and walked in without knocking.

"Mama!" he said loudly, walking through the small living room to the kitchen.

"My baby!" she yelled, laughing.

Wyatt shut the door behind him and watched as Patrick went to his mother. Karla McMurtry was a small woman, skin chocolate and beautiful, just like Patrick. He towered over her by almost a foot, but Wyatt had never seen him look as childlike as he did in that moment, going to her and holding her against his chest. Despite the height discrepancy, he seemed like a baby next to her. She laughed, rocking him back and forth in a swaying motion and patting his back.

"Look at you!" she said, holding him out at arm's length. "My god you look 10 years older." There was a hint of sadness in her voice and she embraced him again until Patrick finally pulled back and remembered Wyatt was standing just behind him.

"Mama, this is Wyatt," Patrick said, almost proudly.

Wyatt noticed that Patrick's eyes were watering just barely and he had to look away from him. The moment of intimacy was so personal between him and his mother, it made his stomach feel strange. A pang of something he hadn't felt in a long time hit him out of nowhere.

"You," Karla said, look Wyatt up and down. "THE Wyatt?"

Wyatt blushed just slightly and took his beanie off of his head, putting out his hand for her to shake. "Ma'am I–" he began, but he was stopped by the woman crossing the room and taking him into a tight embrace, her hands wrapping around his waist.

"You don't call me ma'am," she said into his chest. "You call me Karla, or Mama for that matter!" She pulled back from him and looked up into his eyes.

Her dark black eyes were so similar to Patrick's it was almost eerie. She was beautiful, hardly a wrinkle on her face. Only her graying hairline gave away her age.

"Thank you for taking care of my baby!" she said, holding his biceps tightly. "I can't thank you enough. But lord, Patrick. You never said he was so handsome!"

Patrick stood in the kitchen behind her, taking off his jacket. He grinned over her head at his friend's reddening face.

"Didn't I, Mama? Ladies love him almost as much as they love me," he teased, winking at Wyatt.

Karla detached herself from Wyatt and waved him into the kitchen, all the while talking to the boys about everything, the plane ride, where they parked, how long they were staying, church, and Patrick's fearsome aunties. She settled the boys at her small kitchen table, pouring them each a cup of coffee and slicing out homemade cherry cobbler in front of them, refiling their plates twice even though they'd both refused. Wyatt quickly realized why it was that

Patrick was intimidated by his mother. The woman was no-nonsense. But there was a softness to her, too, and it put him at ease sitting there with her. He felt like he'd known her for years, probably because of how much Patrick talked about her.

"Alright, Mama. No more questions! Dang! You worse than the colonel! We're on R and R! Rest and relaxation! You know what that means?" he teased.

Karla laughed, finally sitting down at the table with them, tiny hands around her coffee cup.

"I can relax, Patrick! I'm relaxing, look at me. I'm just sure happy to have you here. Both of you," she said, reaching out a hand to squeeze Wyatt's arm.

"What's up with the front walk? No one shoveling it for you?" Patrick asked.

Karla shifted in her seat, breaking eye contact with them. "I can do it, I'm just behind. Been working a lot with the holiday hours and all. They're talking about cutting hours so I've been grabbing them up quick."

Patrick frowned. "Well I'll do it while I'm here. But I'm gonna talk to the Johnson boys about doing it. I used to do it for them all the time. Least they can do."

Karla shook her head. "No, no. Rest and relaxation, remember?"

"Wyatt can't sit still. He's gonna do it whether or not you ask him," Patrick countered.

Wyatt smiled to her. "It's true. I like stuff like that."

Karla smiled and cut her eyes back to Patrick. "Well, baby. I didn't wanna tell you this right away, but I- I've gotta sell the house anyway. It's just falling apart and if my hours get cut and you're gone I- it might just be for the best."

Patrick looked like someone hit him in the stomach. "No," he said at first. "No, Mama. You can't do that. You bought it all by yourself. You can't- you can't just let it go now. I can get people over here to help," he said, his mind already crunching the numbers of how much she would need to make a difference.

Karla's face got serious, her lips forming a thin line. "No, sir. No. You're a grown man now off fighting a war and you're gonna mess with your mama getting help? Absolutely not!" she said, indignant.

Patrick started back, but Wyatt stopped him, standing from the table. "Pat, I'll go grab our bags. Excuse me, ma'am- Miss Karla," he said, quickly ducking out of the house.

He was relieved to hit the cool air, thinking, not for the first time, that it was a bad idea for him to be there. He should have let Patrick go on his own, but Pat had insisted, unwilling to let his friend spend Christmas alone on the base. But there he was, an awkward third wheel in a family debacle he shouldn't be in. He thought of his own family then. How long it had felt like since they'd all been together and normal. It felt like another life that he belonged somewhere that way, like Patrick did in his Detroit neighborhood. The place made an imprint on him that Wyatt felt as soon as he was there with him. The place was Patrick's and it made Wyatt miss home.

Patrick was waiting for him on the porch when he walked back up to the house, a duffle bag in each hand. He set them down on the icy porch and sat down next to his friend.

"Sorry, man," Patrick said

Wyatt shrugged. "No big deal, Pat. Everything ok?"

Patrick looked out at the street and the kids playing in the snow.

"No. Not really. She wasn't kidding. Place really is falling apart. Toilet's all jacked up, drywall molding in the bathroom." He shook his head. "Just some stuff I used to do that she can't."

Wyatt nodded. "I can help," he offered.

Pat smiled over at him. "I knew you'd say that. I appreciate it, man. Didn't bring you here to do all this work, I swear."

Wyatt smiled. "What else we gonna do? I can't just sit around and eat cobbler the whole time. I'll get fat."

Pat nodded, smiling. "I hate to even say this, but I-I don't think I should go to Florida. I should probably just give that money to my mom instead."

Wyatt looked away from his friend's embarrassed face. "Whatever you think, man. Up to you. But come show me what all needs to be fixed, ok? We can get moving right away," he said, standing out of his chair.

Patrick looked up at him and smiled. "Thanks, cowboy. No wonder my mom loves you. She made me call her ma'am until I left for the Marine Corps, by the way."

Charlotte laid in her bed, looking up at the ceiling. She had to spring for an extra blanket that winter and chose a down filled comforter. It was too oversized for her futon, but she loved it. Her little place was her sanctuary and even when Rose moved to town, they both thought it was best that Charlotte keep her own space. First, because Rose couldn't live inside the city with that many people crammed in, and also since Rose didn't want Charlotte to feel like she had to live with her. She wanted her to maintain her freedom.

Truth be told, if Rose did live closer in town and not on the very outskirts, she would have loved to live with her aunt again. It didn't bother her to spend all of her time with the woman and she certainly didn't have any social engagements which required privacy, but she knew her aunt did. Which was another reason why she kept her little apartment.

Charlotte could hear the train whistle in the distance and the familiar hum of people moving around the city below her. She shifted in her bed, flipping herself to the side, her naked body nestling into the thick covers around her. For as hard as she worked, still this was the way for her. Lying awake at night with her mind racing, thinking, worrying, praying. Even with all of the skills Rose had taught her, she couldn't help it.

And sometimes, the missing was so overwhelming, a tsunami washing over her, making her feel empty and hopeless no matter how many prayers she said for him. No matter how many times she looked at his picture, holding him close in her heart, it was never enough. Sometimes, the only way was to go back to that place. To afford herself that luxury of looking back.

She closed her eyes and remembered the quiet porch of the bunkhouse. It had rained that night, the water falling heavily from the clouds the whole time they were at dinner and then more when they drove home. But it was gone by the time she sat on the porch with her sundress draped over her naked body and the dark night surrounding her. The smell of it still hung thick in the air and she inhaled the scent of the wet dirt, the shower that had settled the dusty earth, once again making it fresh and clean.

She was sitting that way, on the front step in the dark, listening to the peaceful sounds of nature around her, when he walked out behind her.

"What are you doing, babe?" he asked quietly.

She turned to look at him. He was shirtless, only wearing his boxer briefs, leaning with his muscular arm supporting his weight in the doorframe. He wore the Michael medallion around his neck, the one she'd given him earlier in the night. She remembered how the soft light from the lamp inside hit his silhouette, framing him exquisitely. His hair was messy and his eyes tired, fresh from sleep. He was so perfect like that. The contrast of his hard muscles and boyish face making him all his own.

"I couldn't sleep." She smiled up at him. "Did you think I left or something?"

He smiled sleepily, "Kind of," he teased walking toward her. "You should have woken me up."

He sat down behind her, a step higher, putting his large muscular legs on either side of her. He wrapped his arms around her, pulling her into him.

"You ok?" he said, mumbling into her neck.

"Mmhmm," she said quietly, sinking into him. "Sometimes I just can't sleep."

He nodded his head into her, putting his lips to her neck, kissing her gently.

"I do that sometimes," he said against her skin. "Except when you're here. I sleep really good when you're here."

She smiled, turning her head around to look at him. "You don't sleep much when I'm here, though." She grinned.

"True. But when we sleep, I never sleep better," he said, brushing his lips against hers. "I wish you were here every night."

"Me, too," she said, turning and leaning her head on him.

He sighed, pulling his arms tighter around her body.

"I'm gonna miss you so much," he said quietly, breaking their unspoken rule of mentioning it.

"Me, too," she said, putting her hands over his.

"I love you," he said into her neck. "I've never- I've never felt like this about anyone, Charlotte."

She turned to face him again, shifting her body on the step in front of him.

"I haven't either," she said.

He was quiet, looking down into her eyes for a moment, and she saw that he wanted to say more, but he stopped himself. He'd surrendered to her in so many ways, much the same as she had, but there was still more, still things hidden that he wouldn't say.

"I want to–" he started. "I want to be with you." He stared down at her, boring a hole through her with his crystal blue eyes. "Always," he said after.

His face was serious, his brow furrowed, and she knew what he meant. She knew he wanted some kind of reassurance that they'd be together. That it would all work out, but she'd seen too much of the world to promise him that. Jaded over and over again by the harsh corners in her life. But she felt the same. Despite what she knew could happen, she felt the same.

"I do, too," she said quietly and kneeled on the step in front of him, lifting her face to meet him.

She kissed him softly, dropping her head to press her lips up his chest, stopping at the opening just below his throat. She took her time, brushing her plump lips along his jawline until she heard his breathing deepen and felt him stroking the sides of her body, running his hands up her ribcage to the sides of her breasts. She finally made her way back to his mouth and kissed him deeply, opening her mouth and pushing him back to the floor of the wood porch.

She moved astride him and he didn't hesitate, feeling up her muscular legs to her bottom, seated directly on top of him. She kissed him hard, pinning him down. He breathed deeply, already moving below her.

"You wanna go inside?" he said between kisses.

She shook her head, and kissed back down to his ear. "Here," she said, whispering to him.

"Ok," he panted, sitting up with her in his arms.

He ripped at the straps on her dress, pulling them briskly down her shoulders exposing her breasts. He moved one hand behind her head, tangling it in hair and pulling her face back to kiss her deeper. She moaned into his mouth when he entered her and he responded, placing his hand on her hip as she rocked back and forth on top of him.

"Charlotte," he panted. "Don't stop," he said, sucking on the side of her neck.

And she didn't, not until they finished together there on the porch. The quiet Arizona desert surrounding them.

Wyatt and Patrick worked on the house through the holidays, ripping out a bathroom wall and replacing it from the framing up. They tore out the toilet and replaced it with a brand new one in rose pink despite the fact that it was out of fashion. Karla clapped her hands together, jumping up and down when they carried it through the front door. Patrick's aunties were ever present, always lurking near and watching Wyatt work, t-shirts tight around his biceps. They'd fan themselves when he wasn't looking, constantly bringing him drinks and other treats until Patrick complained about being neglected.

They only stopped working for the delicious meals the women prepared for them and at the end of the night when they'd all sit in the living room and visit. Patrick marveled at all Wyatt knew how to do and repeated that over and over, but as usual, Wyatt acted like it wasn't that big of a deal. Most of it he'd learned from his dad's carpentry work, but the rest he'd learned from the ranch. From Luis's steady and patient ways. He'd tried to teach Patrick in the same way, by showing him and then letting him do it for himself with his own hands.

It was the day after Christmas and Wyatt was to leave the next day for Florida to join Harvey and Seth for a few days of debauchery before they had to deploy again. Patrick had yet to tell his mother that he wouldn't be going, mostly because he didn't want her to feel bad, but also because he was frightened she might slap the shit out of him for doing something against her wishes.

She was at the store that day, no doubt getting more food for them. Wyatt hadn't had that much homemade food in his entire life. She made them everything from barbeque to Mexican food, learning a recipe specifically to make him feel at home. Each night when she shuffled off to bed in her house slippers, she'd stop to kiss Patrick and then Wyatt on their foreheads, thanking them profusely for all of their help.

Wyatt realized how long it had been since he'd been touched by anyone like that, anything more than a slap on the arm from one of his Marine brothers. There were hugs only after Gus died and all bravados were dropped and they clung to each other. But nothing since then. He was embarrassed at how it made him feel when Patrick's beautiful mother would kiss him sweetly on his head. How it made his heart ache for any affection. Longing, once again for her.

"Can't thank you enough, man," Patrick was saying, painting the wall next to Wyatt. "This means a lot."

Wyatt didn't look away from the door handle he was fixing. "Stop saying that, Pat. I should be thanking your mom. I don't know if I've ever eaten this well." He grinned over at him.

Patrick laughed. "Yeah, it's how my family shows love, you know. Except for my aunties also show it in other ways, as you've seen."

Wyatt laughed thinking of the women. Blissfully, they'd all gone home the previous day and left the men to the projects rather than ask them a thousand questions an hour while they tried to work. Wyatt caught them all, with secret smiles, watching him reach up to change a lightbulb, his t-shirt lifting and exposing his lean torso. Pat had warned him, and he was right. But Wyatt couldn't help but enjoy the ladies, lingering hugs and all.

"All done." Pat sighed, cleaning up the painting materials. Wyatt joined in, helping him as he looked around at their work. They'd transformed the place in just a few days, repairing both crucial and cosmetic issues in the house, and they were both proud, looking over their work with a feeling of accomplishment.

"So you think you can go now?" Wyatt asked. He hadn't asked Pat about going to Florida since he told him he couldn't and Wyatt didn't want to push his friend. Instead he just helped him and hoped to hell that he would change his mind.

Patrick sighed, sitting down on the floral couch heavily. "Man, I don't think so. I mean- I, we did so much, but I- shouldn't." Patrick uncharacteristically faltered with his words.

"You don't think you should spend the money?" Wyatt finished for him, sitting down in a chair opposite him.

"Yep. You know me, huh? I just think I should give that extra money to my mom instead," Patrick said, looking to at the floor.

Wyatt sighed. "I know, Pat. I know how you help and send money to her. I get it."

There was quiet between them as Wyatt thought how to phrase his words.

"Listen, Pat. I want you to come to Florida. You deserve this trip. And we're- you know- we're going back over. You should be able to go," he started.

"No, I know- I just–"

"Just listen for a sec," Wyatt said assertively. "I knew you'd say you couldn't go. I knew you'd want to give that money to your mom." He met Pat's eyes. "I want to pay for your trip. And you can't say no, alright? I need you to be there. I can't deal with Seth on my own." He grinned to Patrick.

Patrick's face fell. "No. Wyatt, you can't pay for that. You worked hard for that money, just like I did!" He shook his head hard.

"Pat, I don't have what you have, alright?" He looked at him pleadingly. "I don't have anyone to send money to. What you do, how you help out your mom. It's amazing and I- I have no one to send money to. It's just me." Hearing the words out loud made him feel hollowed out inside. "You're my family, Pat. And I want you to go."

Pat look at his friend, his dark eyes beginning to water. "I don't want you to do that, Wyatt," he said, less forcefully.

"Let me, Pat," Wyatt said. "Please."

Patrick sighed and looked around the house for an answer, some other way he could refuse to take his money. But there was nothing. Wyatt stood and removed a check from his pocket before heading up the stairs to the shower.

"Give this to her," he said, dropping the check into his hands. "Don't tell her it's from me."

Patrick started to protest, but Wyatt kept walking.

"And pack your shit. Our flight's early tomorrow," Wyatt yelled over his shoulder, leaving Pat in the empty living room.

Charlotte walked on the icy sidewalk toward the shop. Since it was only two blocks from her apartment, she made a point to be there first each morning, watering the succulents, starting the coffee, and turning on the meditative music all before Rose would even walk through the door. It was almost a ritual to her and she loved it, being in that place that she and Rose built together. The booming success of it was second only to how it felt for her on the inside. That she had done something, been part of something wonderful.

The snowstorm was unrelenting and everyone in town was relieved the same way as the people in Patagonia rejoiced in the rain. It meant the ski resort would be open longer that season, which meant more people would come to Flagstaff. Charlotte knew that it meant more business for them, too, and she was constantly thinking about ways to capitalize on that, new ways to expand. She renovated the back two closets into smaller, peaceful rooms which she rented out to reiki specialists and massage therapists, sending the revenue soaring even higher. Rose was floored, telling her over and over again that not even she knew Charlotte would be as good as she was.

The snow continued to fall as Charlotte got close to the shop and she was surprised to see the lights already on and someone inside before her. She frowned, opening the door until she saw it was only Rose, and, surprisingly, Willow as well.

"Well, let's write this down in the damn history books!" Rose grinned at her from behind the counter. "This'll be the first and last time I'll ever beat you here."

Charlotte laughed, but she still felt uneasy as she looked over at Willow, sitting in one of the armchairs in front of the window. Charlotte didn't think she'd ever seen her out in daylight hours and it showed. Willow had dark circles under her eyes and her hair pulled up messily on her head.

"Hey," she said, hardly acknowledging Charlotte.

Charlotte stood, removing her jacket and scarf and placing her purse on the waiting hook.

"What are you doing up before noon?" she said coolly to Willow.

"Oh look, you made a joke," she said straight-faced. "I had a meeting with Rose."

Charlotte raised her eyebrows, shooting a look to Rose. She couldn't understand why, but she felt fiercely jealous about the prospect of the two of them speaking without her there.

"What kind of a meeting?" she asked placing her hands on the back of the chair opposite Willow.

Rose came from behind her, passing her a cup of coffee before sitting down in the chair.

"Willow got shit canned from the Museum Club," Rose said, not mincing words.

Charlotte's jaw dropped and she looked at Willow. She knew what it took to get fired from that place. There, the same place where she had ejected a regular from his chair on her very first night of work. Whatever Willow did, it had to be bad.

"Why?" Charlotte asked.

Willow looked away from her out the window. "I'd rather not get into details, but basically, you shouldn't fuck the owner of the place you work for. Especially if he's married with four kids."

Charlotte nodded, looking down to her aunt. She still had no idea what that had to do with Rose, why she needed to tell her aunt any of that. Unless it was for a reading. In which case she should have scheduled that through her. Charlotte stood straight and crossed her arms across her chest.

"So you needed some advice on what to do next?" Charlotte asked, still curious.

"Charlotte," Rose broke in, looking up at her niece, "Willow's asked me for a job here."

Charlotte's face remained even, though she felt a punch hit her stomach as clear as if had been real. Willow was her friend, had been since she'd moved to Flagstaff, but thinking about her in the shop, in that perfect environment she'd created with her aunt, scared her. She felt a pang in her stomach, her intuition shaking its head that no, it was not the right choice.

Willow looked pleadingly up to Charlotte, aware at how it must have come off. "Charlotte, listen, I'll be different from the bar. You can trust me and I'll work hard."

Charlotte leveled her eyes at her. "No I- I know. I just don't know if we have enough work–"

Rose stopped her, laughing heartily. "Charlotte, now come on. Are you afraid that you won't be able to work yourself to death here anymore? There's certainly enough work, Willow, and we will be happy to have you. But we have rules."

Charlotte closed her mouth, swallowing the fact that Rose hadn't talked to her privately about hiring Willow first. Wasn't she doing enough? Why did they need someone else's help?

"First, I'm going to drug test you. So you're going to cut that shit out right now," Rose said firmly.

Willow smiled. "Fuck, Rose. I thought you were some hippie psychic. Not even pot?"

Rose shook her head. "No. Not even pot. Shit clouds your aura and Charlotte and I can't be around it. Not in here."

Willow nodded slowly. "Ok, I can do that."

"You've got to cover this place when I take Charlotte on a trip this summer. It'll be a couple of weeks of back to back days, but we'd have to be able to trust you enough to put you in charge."

Charlotte looked at Rose, raising her brows. She knew nothing of any trip, but it was standard Rose procedure to spring things like that on her.

"And last. You've got to start meditating. It's required." Rose said, then looked closely at the girl in front of her. Charlotte knew she was reading her, but didn't say that out loud. "And never dabble. Never fuck around with psychic stuff. It is not a toy, it is a gift."

Willow nodded, her eyes still tired but now hopeful. "Ok, I promise."

"Good then," Rose said raising herself from her chair. "See Char? Asked the guides to find a way to get you to stop working yourself into the ground just yesterday and look what they made happen."

Charlotte forced a smile, thinking of how the alleged divine plan involved Willow being a homewrecker. "Yep, look at that," she said, and turned to work.

Florida was a dream compared to the icy cold of Detroit. The skies were clear and the surf was calm, and, best of all, the temperature hovered around 85 degrees, the nicest weather the boys had for as long as they could remember. Despite the fact it was December, Miami bustled, appearing more like Mexico than the US, at least to Wyatt, anyway. The food, the people, the culture, all of it reminded him of Tucson, except much bigger, and with a beach.

Patrick came, although not without protest. But Wyatt would have none of it. Plus, he'd told him over and over again, he'd saved more than enough money to do it easily, without making a dent in his bank account. Unlike the other guys in their platoon, Wyatt and Patrick didn't buy a brand new pickup when they arrived home from Iraq, Patrick since he had his mom to think about, and Wyatt because he was saving. For what, he didn't know but he found it easy to put his deployment money safely away and hardly touch it for everyday life. Yes, the Marines owned him, just like she'd told him, but they did provide.

They'd been drinking all day long, starting the morning off on the beach in a row of chairs facing the ocean, all shirtless with board shorts, eyes behind their sunglasses watching the girls who walked by them. Harvey and Wyatt stayed stoic while Seth and Patrick chatted up the beautiful women who walked by them. Patrick was charming and effortlessly smooth while Seth was decidedly less so, whistling and catcalling women more and more as the day went on. It made Wyatt nervous at first, his face growing red each time he did it, but it seemed that there were scarcely any rules in Miami, much the way there wasn't a dress code.

More than once the boys had to pick their jaws up off the floor because of the scantily clad women who walked by them. They'd seen a lot in their short time in the Marine Corps, but the Brazilian cut bikinis that were worn with little regard for modesty left little to the imagination.

"I'm never going home," Patrick yelled to Wyatt over the noise in a beachfront bar.

Wyatt smiled at his friend, taking a drink of his Corona. "What's home?" Wyatt yelled back, grinning.

"Exactly," Pat said, smoothing his shirt down over his chest.

Despite the fact that he'd ironed it in his hotel room, along with the other men's shirts, the humidity crinkled it unpleasantly and he couldn't stop fussing with it as they sat in the corner of the bar overlooking the boardwalk. Patrick and Seth had dressed in their nicest jeans and button downs, looking every bit the Miami tourists. But Harvey and Wyatt were hopeless, no matter the coaxing from the others, they'd both insisted on wearing jeans and boots to the bar.

Seth swayed back and forth in the booth, drunker than they'd ever seen him, which was saying a lot. The night was early still and Patrick had big plans for them. He promptly cut Seth off and passed him a glass of ice water so he'd be able to go the distance.

"Don't be fucking sloppy, Seth. Fuck. It's hardly ten o'clock. People don't even start going out here until midnight. You won't be worth a shit," Patrick said, pushing him his water.

Seth nodded, taking his cup in both hands and drinking like a child. The fact that he was too drunk to argue with Patrick was concerning.

"Look," Harvey said quietly, elbowing Wyatt in the ribs.

A group of young girls walked in, all wearing short dresses and giggling profusely. They all wore black except one who wore white.

"Bachelorette party," Patrick said, grinning. "Fish in a barrel."

Wyatt laughed and shook his head, looking toward the ground, then up again at the girls. They all wore heavy makeup and their hair meticulously combed and teased up around their faces. He looked them over as discreetly as he could. They certainly weren't his type at all, but his hormones, combined with the beer he'd been drinking all day, could see the appeal.

"Seth, pull your shit together. I need you on your game," Patrick said before getting up from the table and immersing himself within the group of women.

In true Patrick fashion, he had the women circled around him within minutes, all laughing at his jokes. Wyatt and the others sat and watched him from a distance, and laughed at how he worked them perfectly. He offered to take their picture and ordered a round for them and sure enough, returned to the table with all of the girls in tow, introducing them to the men. He named each girl by name, his seemingly photographic memory ever-handy. Wyatt and Harvey nodded to them, mumbling their hellos, and Seth delivered, pulling himself together enough to sit between a few girls and chat them up.

They sat in the corner booth, the men and the party of girls drinking and talking, Patrick leading the conversation. He captivated the women by retelling stories of Iraq in a watered-down, heroic way that didn't come close to describing what it was actually like, but that served its purpose. He didn't mention Gus or the other awful things they'd seen, but stuck to stories that were easy listening. Patrick always knew his audience.

He told them how Wyatt had punched the wife beater in the face in the middle of town that day, talking animatedly about the bad guy bleeding on the ground until Wyatt felt like climbing under the table. Instead, he kept his face even, cracking a smile when Patrick finally finished the story.

"Is that true?" the girl next to him said, batting her heavily mascaraed eyes at him.

"Mostly," Wyatt said, taking another drink of his beer.

"Wow," she said, scooting closer to him and talking into his ear over the loud music. "I'm really drunk, sorry."

She giggled at him and he smiled tightly as he looked her over. Her black dress was riding up her legs and she kept tugging at it. She had short brown hair and light brown eyes. She was pretty, but Wyatt thought she'd be even prettier without all of the makeup on her face.

"Where are you from?" she asked, slurring into his ear.

"Arizona," he said back, brushing his face to her cheek.

She nodded. "Figured somewhere like that," she gestured to his boots.

She moved closer to him, talking intimately into his ear. "You married?"

Wyatt shook his head, looking at the floor. "You?"

She shook her head. "I don't ever wanna get married. Not like this one," she said, waving her hand at the bride. "Her future husband is a dick."

Wyatt laughed and looked around the circle. Patrick had three girls surrounding him while Seth chatted up the bride and one other girl. Harvey sat next to Patrick, laughing but otherwise staying quiet. Wyatt knew that he didn't need to do much, though. He'd seen Harvey go an entire night without talking to anyone and still walk out with a beautiful girl at the end of it. His quiet, stoic way was irresistible the same way that Patrick's humor was.

The night wore on and the drinks continued flowing. The girl next to Wyatt was named Vicki. She was local to Miami and came from a big Cuban family that had lived there forever. She hardly took a breath telling him her life story, but Wyatt didn't mind, he didn't have the gift for talking to strangers the way Patrick did. When they decided to move to a new bar and walked down the boardwalk with the girls, Vicki clung to Wyatt's bicep as she teetered on her high heels. He was surprised at how much he liked the feel of her touching him and the more he had to drink, the bolder he got, touching the small of her back as he led her toward the rest of the party sitting in a dark corner of the club.

Wyatt looked around the new bar, checking for exits. He felt uneasy in the darkness with the loud music booming and checked around, looking at the other men. It seemed they were immune from worrying about it, either because of how much they had to drink or because of the women, but he held them all in his sight, accounting for them and checking their surroundings again. The club was starting to get crowded which gave him anxiety. He could feel his heart pounding in his chest but he took a deep breath and ordered a whiskey to take the edge off.

He shot Patrick a look and his friend grinned reassuringly back at him. Wyatt laughed at the fact that Patrick still juggled the same three girls from the previous bar, but would detach himself from them each time the waitress came by the table taking orders. She was petite and exotic looking, with wide-set brown eyes and a beautiful mouth. Best of all, Wyatt noticed, she hardly wore any makeup. The girls at the table flipped their hair and stuck out their breasts each time she came by, asserting their territory.

Vicki still chatted into Wyatt's ear, crossing her leg toward him, getting closer all the time. He tested the waters, placing his large hand on her thigh, and she responded, pulling his arm closer and talking flirtatiously to him. He was drunk, there was no doubt, but he maintained his steady appearance, unlike Seth who was singing at the top of his lungs, his top buttons undone on his shirt.

"Why are you so shy?" Vicki was asking, gripping his forearm.

Wyatt shook his head. "I'm not. Is it shy to sit with you like this?" He grinned, looking down at his hand on her leg.

"I guess not," she said, and before he knew what was happening she closed in on him and kissed him full on the lips.

Her friends were catcalling in the background and she was encouraged, full of liquid courage. She put her hands on either side of his face and opened her mouth, pushing her tongue into his mouth. If he hadn't been so drunk he would have been embarrassed at everyone watching, but he wasn't. He put his hand around her slim waist and kissed her back, unsure about the feeling in his stomach. It was something like longing, but mostly it was nature and the fact that he'd been deprived so long of being touched the way he needed. His body wanted only one thing: release. She smiled as she pulled away and he grinned back at her, placing his hand back on her thigh.

"I need to talk to you," Patrick said, pulling Wyatt to the side. "You drunk?"

Wyatt nodded, his eyes glazed over. "Yeah, aren't you?"

Patrick shook his head. "Nah, man. I stopped drinking. Don't wanna end up like this asshole," he said, waving his hand to Seth.

Wyatt laughed, coming closer to Patrick. "Which one?" he asked, looking to the three girls Patrick had been with all night.

Patrick ran his hand over his head, wiping the sweat away. "Man, none of them. Did you see that waitress?"

"Jesus, Pat," Wyatt said laughing. "Yeah, I saw her, but you've put in a lot of time here."

"Look, I know that, cowboy, but I gotta shake these girls now. You gotta do me a solid. I gotta talk to that waitress without them here."

Just then she appeared with a round of drinks and walked toward Wyatt and Patrick. Patrick was right to be smitten. She was tiny, barely 5 feet tall, but she had a curvy, beautiful body that was on full display in short black shorts and a midriff baring top. Her long black hair fell to the middle of her back and she had a quiet confidence that was in stark contrast to the girls from the bachelorette party.

"You need anything?" she said, looking up at them.

Patrick's mouth dropped open a bit and he looked uncharacteristically nervous. Wyatt looked to him and pushed his arm to get his attention.

"This is my friend Patrick," Wyatt said, introducing him stupidly.

The waitress smiled, picking up a few empty bottles from the table. "Oh, I know. He introduced himself already."

She readied herself to walk away, but Wyatt stepped up to help his friend, who had seemingly gone silent for the first time in front of a girl.

"What's your name?" Wyatt said loudly over the noise.

"Mia," she said, looking up into Wyatt's eyes.

Her eyes were black, almost as dark as Patrick's, and her skin was a dark caramel color that offset them beautifully. Wyatt couldn't blame Patrick. If he had seen her first, he might have ignored Vicki entirely.

"Mia, Patrick wants to buy you a drink. When do you get off of work?" Wyatt said boldly.

Patrick grinned at his friend and finally came to his senses. "Yes, Mia. He's right. When?" He locked eyes with her and she smiled, but shook her head.

"I don't think Patrick needs any more girls tonight. Looks like he's got his hands full." She winked and then walked away through the crowd.

Patrick looked at Wyatt wide-eyed. "Bro," he said shortly, looking after her. "I think I'm in love."

Wyatt laughed, slapping Patrick on the shoulder. "Alight man. Let's make the slip, then."

"Yeah, but what about you? Looks like you got a good thing going with that little Latina girl."

Wyatt shrugged. "Yeah, but I'm not in love like you. Come on."

It was like a military procedure in that the men all worked together toward a common goal. They left to a new bar several blocks away, getting the group settled and drinking, and left Seth and Harvey with the girls as Patrick and Wyatt slipped out the door back to Mia's bar. Wyatt didn't mind since Vicki had gotten sloppy drunk and he knew he wouldn't move any further with her that night because of that.

It was late in the evening when they got back to Mia's bar. They found a small high top table in her section and she smiled big when she walked up to them, her white straight teeth shining.

"Look who's back. What can I get you guys?" She smiled.

"We will have two of your best local beers please. And also a date with you," Patrick said, his earlier nervousness forgotten.

She rolled her eyes at him. "Come on. You were just in here with ten girls, and now you wanna go on a date with ME? Please."

"Where are those girls now?" he said, inching his face closer to hers. "I came back just to ask you. I'm only in town two more days and I want to take you out."

Wyatt looked back and forth between the two and was almost uncomfortable with what he saw. Mia was trying to resist, but her eyes said something different than her mouth. She couldn't look away from Patrick. Just sitting there, Wyatt could feel the attraction between them.

"Where are you leaving to? Back home?" she said, still not committing.

Patrick shook his head. "My bud and I are going back to war, ma'am. That's why you have to go out with me. Even if you don't like me, you should feel bad for me."

Mia looked to Wyatt. "Is that true?" she asked, raising her eyebrows.

Wyatt nodded solemnly, then looked away, no longer able to look at the two of them together. The familiarity of it was all too close to home.

"Ok, then. Tomorrow," she said shortly. "You can pick me up here. At eight."

A grin spread across Patrick's face. "Deal," he said to her.

Patrick watched her walk away through the crowd.

"I owe you, bud," he said, not taking his eyes off of her.

The next day in Miami was more of the same. Drinking by the beach, girl-watching. All except for

Patrick didn't chase girls like he had the day before that. Instead, he talked continuously about his impending date, Mia, what he should wear, and where he could take her, most of the time not even waiting for a response from his friends. Just looking out in the front of him, a glazed over look in his eye that Wyatt remembered well.

Seth had the roughest morning of all, nursing a fierce hangover that couldn't be cured by the greasy food he ate then promptly threw up. Not even a swim in the ocean could bring him back to life. Around noon, Harvey passed him a beer on the beach and instructed him to chug it. And just that quickly, Seth was back to his old self.

It was decided that while Pat was on his date the remaining three men would hit the bars again. Harvey had somehow kept it together enough to get one of the bachelorette girl's numbers from the night before, so their prospects of an enjoyable evening were looking fairly solid.

"Which one?" Patrick said to Wyatt in the hotel room.

He held two plaid shirts out in front of him and Wyatt couldn't even tell the difference between the two. They were both pale blue, by far Patrick's best color. Wyatt pointed to one of them and Patrick assessed it, brows furrowed.

"You sure?" he asked, concerned.

Wyatt lay back on the pillows, putting his hands behind his head. "Yeah, matches your eyes."

"Shiiit," Patrick said. "YOUR eyes maybe, not this ebony beauty." He winked at Wyatt, grinning wide. "Sorry I'm bailing."

Wyatt waved him off. "Naw, I get it. Plus, I'll be fine."

"Oh I have no doubt," Patrick said, grinning. "You should, you know." He widened his eyes at him. "You should probably have some fun tonight, cowboy. Sample the local cuisine."

Wyatt laughed. "That what you're doing?"

Patrick shook his head, pulling his shirt around his broad shoulders. "I don't think so, man. Not this time."

Wyatt nodded slowly in understanding. He looked at his friend in envy. Patrick's eyes all but sparkled since he woke up that morning. Wyatt had seen him with dozens of girls before that. He charmed them all. More than once he'd seen Patrick go home with random girls from a night out and he knew what probably happened on those nights. Only Patrick never talked about it. Not in detail anyway. For as perverted as his friend was, he was also a gentleman. But this time was different, that much was clear.

That second night out in Miami would be one they talked about over and over the next deployment. They met up with three girls from the night before that, one for each of them. Wyatt was not surprised to see Vicki back again, looking even better than he remembered. They bar-hopped and danced to salsa music, the local girls laughing at Harvey's immovable hips and concentrated face. They ended up on the beach in the early morning hours, then back to various hotel rooms just before the sun came up. The boys had come there seeking adventure and Miami delivered.

Patrick still wasn't home once all of the girls left that morning. He didn't return until almost lunchtime, collapsing onto the bed as soon as he walked in the room. Harvey and Seth were still sleeping in their adjoining room and Wyatt sat up from a nap when Patrick came back. Patrick laid with his face down on the mattress for a long time, not moving or saying anything until Wyatt threw a pillow at him.

"Private McMurtry!" Wyatt said laughing. "You alive?"

Patrick moved his head to the side so that he could look back at Wyatt. A huge smile stretched across his face as he looked at his friend. His eyes were glazed over and exhausted, but Wyatt was sure that he'd never seen him look so content.

"Barely," he said back to him.

Wyatt smiled, wiping a hand over his tired face. "How was it?" he asked, although he already knew.

"That's it for me, man. I want to marry that girl."

Patrick said it the way he said all things, trying to get a laugh from his audience. But Wyatt knew. He knew he really meant it. He felt his heart tighten, remembering that familiar feeling. He tried his hardest to be happy for his friend, to not be jealous of him instead. Most of all, he tried to forget how empty it had felt to push himself into Vicki the night before that, the release he felt second to the hollowness in his heart.

Business at Spirit's Soul soared through the winter months. Willow, for as lazy as she'd been at the bar, actually became helpful, checking out patrons, cleaning, and pushing sales, especially once Rose offered her commission for larger items. She didn't like to work, but but she did love money. She started to handle all of the day to day busy work which had consumed Charlotte before that.

And so, as usual, Rose had made the right decision hiring Willow. With her help at the shop, Charlotte was able to focus more on school and administrative duties of the business, finding more and more ways to grow the revenue. One day after meditation, she popped open her eyes and walked right out of the shop to the side of the building where a rickety wood staircase led to the roof. She climbed it, trying to keep herself from shaking. When she reached the top, she saw a perfect open rooftop with high edges creating a balcony. To most people all it would have looked like was a normal rooftop, but to Charlotte it was more. It was more space, more room to rent out.

She formed a plan immediately, hiring a contractor to come and bid out a new staircase and contacting the city to see if what she wanted to do was legal. And it was. Her newest plan for summer would be possible.

"We can do daytime yoga classes up here." Charlotte rattled on to Rose, who looked skeptically around the rooftop. "Then weddings, too. People would love that. Trendy, you know? Plus we have this killer view of the peaks behind us," Charlotte said, sweeping her hand to the San Francisco Peaks behind them.

Rose laughed. "What preacher is going to marry someone in our hippie shop, babe?" Rose grinned at her.

"Well, that brings me to my next point, actually," Charlotte said, ringing her hands, "Don't say no. But, I think you need to get ordained."

Rose spit her tea back into her cup in front of her.

"What in fresh hell are you talking about?" Rose gasped, looking at Charlotte, eyes wide.

Charlotte laughed, reaching out to put her arm around her aunt. "You have to trust me. You have a way with people. They all love you! Who wouldn't want to be married by you? For a price, that is."

Rose looked up at her, cracking a smile. "A price, you say? Hmmm." She squeezed her niece's small waist. "Depends on the price, babe. But you draw up a plan for it and if that price is right, you can whore me out for your weddings. But I'm not doing that obey bullshit line, you hear me?"

Charlotte laughed. "I promise. No obeying. Why start now?"

Charlotte's plans always came to her after meditation. That semester she'd been accepted to the business program at Northern Arizona University, but much of what she learned never seemed to apply to how she ran the shop and what she knew to be true about business. Her ideas always came from an unknown place, dropping into her head like a feather floats to earth. And the quieter she became, the more her thoughts grew.

She finally quit work at the bar that winter and was sometimes panicked at how much time she had on her hands. Never able to sit still, she'd often set out on her favorite trails, hiking despite the bitter cold and the snow on the ground. She liked the feel of the cold air burning her lungs as she panted, pushing herself higher and higher up the trail.

It was late February and there was still snow thick on the ground. Rose, desert rat that she was, had escaped off the mountain the day before to Phoenix. Charlotte knew she must be meeting her Phoenix lover since she didn't invite her, but she didn't mind. She knew that it was important for Rose to recharge in the sunshine. And in the company of a handsome man.

Charlotte stopped at the summit of Mt. Eldon, looking out onto the town below her. It looked a lot like a snow globe from that angle and Charlotte never tired of looking at it from that quiet perspective. The peace she felt all alone was a calming force for her. From that angle she only felt goodness. Not the bustle of the city, the arguments of her fellow students, the back and forth of the pro and anti-war protestors. She sat on a rock and pulled her jacket tight around her shoulders, breathing deeply.

She put a hand in her pocket feeling for the ribbon she brought, rubbing it between her gloved fingers. She pulled it out and ran her fingers over it, smoothing it out. It was satin, yellow in stark contrast to the white snow which covered the ground. For months she'd tied ribbon after ribbon to various trees in town, but invariably, they were always taken down.

The liberal community of Flagstaff was unwilling to support the war in any capacity. Charlotte didn't have a side, it seemed. She believed in peace. She believed in good. But she also believed in him. Knowing his heart more than she knew her own, she knew he was good to the core. And this she could do for him. Tie a ribbon around a tree, symbolizing his return. Something so small had become so important to her.

And so she stood with her ribbon and walked into the forest off the path. She looked up to a large pine tree in front of her, trunk thick and firm. She ran her hands down the side of it before wrapping the ribbon around it and tying it tightly in a knot that she knew wouldn't come out. She sighed heavily and placed her head against the tree, just above the ribbon.

"Come home," she commanded, planting her wish like the roots below the icy ground.

Iraq was bitterly cold the same way the desert in Arizona got cold. The lack of foliage or cloud cover gave nothing to offset the frigid temperatures. Wyatt, always the Arizona boy, would have much preferred to again suffer the sweltering summers of that foreign place over the conditions for that second deployment. Even Patrick was put off by it.

They were sitting just outside a group of Humvees, huddled together waiting for the rest of the platoon to return. They were going through villages one at a time to extract insurgents, which wasn't as easy as it sounded. So many times they came up empty since the townspeople hid them away among their own and there was no telling them apart. Except Wyatt always knew. He could look into the eyes of a man and know for sure if he was an insurgent or not. He didn't know how, but there was something about the bad ones that would strike him each time. An unexplainable recognition. But that didn't matter. Nothing could be done just on a feeling, anyway.

There had been more firefights, more carnage. More violence popped up suddenly, only to die down quickly after. But it was nothing like Fallujah. Nothing like the hell they'd endured going door to door in that huge city, attempting to take it back from the insurgents. The men realized as soon as they were back that during that deployment they'd been part of something bigger than they'd realized at first. Other Marines and servicemen would look at them in awe when they told them where they'd been. They'd proclaim their envy and ask endless questions about it until Wyatt and his friends realized that Fallujah would go down as one of the most challenging and epic engagements of the war itself.

But it didn't matter to Wyatt. He felt no glory or victory in that, because every time he heard the city's name all he saw was Gus's face. All he heard was his final words to him. Thanking him for being his friend. Whether or not the rest of the Marine Corps thought it was impressive or not, Gus remained gone.

"Mother fucker. If it would just snow it wouldn't be so bad. Swear to god this is the worst fucking place I've ever been," Patrick said.

Wyatt nodded in agreement, shifting his weapon on his lap as he moved around to keep warm. The sun was setting and they would be heading back to camp. They were three months into a six month deployment that was dragging by much slower than the last one, probably because of the lack of action.

"Man, I'm ready to get back! Might have mail call tonight." Patrick grinned over the brim of his jacket to Wyatt.

Wyatt smiled and shook his head. "Does she write to you every day, or what?"

Patrick nodded proudly. "Pretty sure she does. She loves me. Can you blame her?"

Wyatt laughed, rolling his eyes at Patrick. "Pretty sure you write to her just as much, man."

Patrick sat his head back on the Humvee behind him, looking up at the graying sky. "I know, man. I'm a goner."

Patrick had ended up spending the rest of the trip to Miami with Mia, almost missing the plane because he was busy meeting her large Puerto Rican family. They only had days left on the base in Texas before deploying, but despite that, Mia hopped on a flight to Texas to see him one last time and Wyatt had never seen his friend that way. His guard dropped entirely and all silly games he'd played with girls before that went out the window. He held her hand, opened doors for her, and kissed her sweetly in front of anyone, unembarrassed. Patrick was right. He was a goner from the jump and Wyatt couldn't blame him. When she came to Texas and he spent time with her, he could have fallen in love with her himself. She was warm, smart, and tough, but with a softness about her that was so welcoming. Mia was so much like

Charlotte that it was painful for Wyatt to be around them for very long.

Once they left on deployment, Patrick was sick missing her. He moped around, not entertaining the men like he usually did. He couldn't even read like he normally did; nothing could distract him from the emptiness he felt being away from her. His obsession with her came on hard and fast, like a sucker punch.

"You think we're coming back again, man? I mean, after this deployment?" Patrick asked, looking over at Wyatt.

"Oh, I'm sure we will," he said certainly. "I've still got three years left on, so I for sure will. How long do you have?"

"Two more years," Patrick said miserably. "So you're probably right."

Wyatt nodded, looking down at the dirt in front of him. "You gonna re-up?"

Patrick turned his body to look at him indignantly. "Hell no, dude. Why the fuck would I do that? Told you, I'm here for the G.I. Bill. Going straight to college after this," he said certainly.

Wyatt nodded and ignored the pang in his chest. He didn't know how he would be a Marine without Patrick by his side. He didn't even think it could be possible for him to be there without him, be who he was without Pat's steady, reassuring way always reminding him why he was there.

"What about you, man? What are you gonna do when you're done?" Patrick asked, his brow furrowed.

Wyatt shrugged and looked away from his probing gaze. "Don't know. Maybe re-up again? Might as well."

Patrick opened his mouth to speak, but then thought better of it and closed it, thinking for a moment.

"I don't think you should. You're smart, man. You could do anything you wanted to," Patrick said.

"What's wrong with the Marines? Marines need smart people, too," he said defensively.

Patrick laughed. "Oh, I know. Can you imagine how this operation would be run if they all had Seth's IQ? We'd be fucked."

Wyatt softened and laughed, but it still bothered him. That old opinion of his father's crept in on him once again. He often had to remind himself of the importance of what he was doing, but it always echoed in his mind that he was "only a Marine."

"I'm just sayin'," Patrick continued, "I'm just saying that I see you doing something different than this. I think you're meant for more. For something different."

Wyatt nodded, still not making eye contact with him. "You are, too. I have a feeling you might choose a Florida college, too," he teased, trying to lighten the mood.

"Man, you know me better than anyone." He grinned, eyes shining. "I'm thinking about it." Patrick sighed heavily. "I just can't figure out why I feel like shit all of the time, you know? Like, I know I'm at war and far away from her and everything, but I just-man, I don't know. I can't fucking stop thinking about her. It's ridiculous. Like a fucking sickness or something," he said running a hand over his shaved head.

Wyatt nodded and laughed quietly. "I know."

Patrick looked at his friend closely. His hair was growing out and a short beard sprinkled his cheeks. His crystal blue eyes were fierce-looking in contrast to his tanned face. He'd changed so much since Patrick met him in basic training, but there was still something about him that Patrick wanted to fix. Wanted to rescue. But his friend wouldn't ever let him in enough to do it.

"That how it was?" Patrick braved. "With her?"

Wyatt was quiet, looking out away from him. The sun was setting over the mountains in the distance, leaving a pale yellow glow on the horizon. He nodded slowly, thinking of her. Of how much it hurt even when things were good between them. Lovesick was a term he'd heard, but never understood until it happened to him.

"You think you'll ever see her again?" Patrick pushed.

Wyatt looked at his friend and smiled sadly. "I don't think so, man. Too much time gone by."

Patrick nodded and thought about leaving it there and not pushing him anymore. He knew, especially now, how much losing her had changed him. How much it had ripped him open.

"You never know, man. Look at me. In love, with a girl! ONE girl," he said laughing. "And you know, I almost didn't even go to Miami. Only went because of you." He shook his head, thinking of it. "Miracles happen."

IV

"My soul has grown deep like these rivers."

~ Langston Hughes

The spring semester in Flagstaff was always an exciting one. The impending graduation of thousands of students created a palpable energy for the whole town. Plus, it meant business. More business for the restaurants, hotels, and Spirit's Soul. The shop was booming with almost more business than they could handle. Spirit's Soul had become the premier place to throw a wedding downtown, especially since Charlotte had them catered by all local downtown restaurants and she handled everything for the brides.

Other companies started using her to throw private parties and luncheons, racking up the bottom line even more. Charlotte worked constantly to keep the momentum going, all the while maintaining Spirit's Soul as the most popular metaphysical shop with the best psychic. Rose was a celebrity in town much the way she was in Patagonia. Everyone who met her loved her and referred her out constantly. Her schedule was booked at least three months out and even though she'd begged Charlotte to take some of the readings herself, Charlotte refused, unwilling to take on the role just yet.

Charlotte briskly walked down the sidewalk of downtown toward the shop, her long floral dress blowing tight against her body. She'd been in Flagstaff almost four years, which was longer than she'd ever stayed anywhere. She felt it, too. That belonging. The place felt so much a part of her that she forgot how it used to feel as a gypsy, always new to a place. In this place, she'd found a home. She'd found people who loved and supported her. She couldn't ask for anything more, so she couldn't understand why her feet still sometimes itched to be somewhere else.

Charlotte pulled open the door to the shop and assessed her surroundings. The place was quiet, having only opened an hour before and with no one at the front desk. The meditative music floated gently through the speakers and sage burned on the front counter. Charlotte sighed heavily, inhaling the scent of the place. They'd expanded to the building next door, giving them more space to rent out for massage therapists, spiritual counselors, and the like. The place was open and airy with potted plants scattered over every surface.

"Hey, Char," Willow said, walking out from one of the back rooms with a box in her hands. She'd only gotten more beautiful over the years. Her long red hair stretched almost to her bottom and her face was free of the makeup that used to stay thick on her skin. She'd gone the "hippie route," as Rose called it, and it suited her. Her years working for Charlotte and Rose had calmed her a bit and actually made her into someone dependable.

"Hey Willow, Rose already in her reading?" Charlotte asked, hanging her purse on the hook.

"Yep. She's not happy about it either," Willow warned, unloading books to a shelf.

Charlotte sighed, looking through the mail. "Why? Only three readings today, right?"

Willow nodded, but avoided making eye contact. "Yeah, but she just doesn't want to work much this week since it's your graduation."

Charlotte laughed. "I'm the one graduating and I don't get any time off."

Willow shrugged. "I don't fucking know, Char. Talk to her about it. She wants you back here at three, too."

"I have finals today," Charlotte said back.

Willow put her hands up. "I'm just the messenger. All I know is that she wants you back here by three."

Charlotte checked her watch, crunching time. "Alright, fine. I'll see if I can take one early."

"She wanted me to tell you to dress nice," Willow said as Charlotte was starting out the door.

"Got it," Charlotte yelled back over her shoulder.

Charlotte knew that her last day of college should be more ceremonial, more significant, but it didn't feel that way. College had only gotten in the way of her business the entire time she'd been in Flagstaff.

She was the only business owner she knew of who was in college while running a successful company. Plus, a lot of the successful businessmen and women she knew never went to college at all. Which was why every semester she thought about quitting, only Rose would never let her, putting her foot down firmly if Charlotte even considered it.

"Trust me, babe. It doesn't feel important right now, but it's going to be important. And it's going to feel better than you could ever imagine to finish," Rose told her over and over again.

When she arrived on campus that day she still didn't feel any different. She took her last final exams, finishing before the majority of her class and shaking her professor's hand before walking out to the cool spring day with the wind blowing gently through the pine trees. She walked through campus toward downtown and looked up at the buildings. She stopped in front of the admissions building and looked at the tall white pillars contrasting with the old brick building behind it.

She remembered that day then. The day that had set it all in motion. She'd sat there with Rose so long ago when her only dream, her only wish was to finish college. To be able to do something she thought she'd never be able to do. She wanted it so badly, with all that she was. Charlotte felt her heart catch to think of it, to think of how her aunt had helped her, had pushed her all of these years to finish. Even though Charlotte had forgotten how important it was to her, Rose never had.

Charlotte continued walking back to the shop, her mind still back in that place. She placed her hand over the turquoise stone hanging close to her heart. He had been such a part of it all, too. So responsible for building her up and giving her the confidence to continue. Even after he was gone, far away from her, she would remember his words to her, telling her there was nothing she couldn't do. And anytime she had to do anything of importance with her business or school, she'd think of that. She'd think of him and how much he meant it. And she could believe it then. When she remembered it came from his mouth, from his heart, she could believe it.

When she arrived back to the shop promptly at three o'clock, she frowned to see the sign on the door which said it was closed early. She unlocked the door to find it vacant, all the while thinking of the lecture she'd give to Willow about losing revenue. She was looking through the numbers for the day when Rose walked out of the back room, her makeup and hair professionally done and her long maxi skirt hugging her curvy frame.

"Well, well," she said, holding a champagne glass in one hand and a bottle in the other. "If it isn't the graduate."

Charlotte smiled at her but furrowed her brow quickly after. "Why is the shop closed? Did Willow–"

Rose held up her hands with the bottle and champagne stopping her. "Nope. No business today. It's a rule. I closed the shop early. We're celebrating."

Charlotte started to protest, but Rose walked out the front door before she could get a word out.

Charlotte followed her to the side of the building and to the bottom of the stairs where Rose stopped and turned to her.

"You did it," Rose said, looking up at her. "Do you remember, babe? Do you remember how important it was to you?"

Charlotte smiled, looking down at her aunt. "I do, yeah. I remember."

Rose nodded. "I don't want this to pass you by without you feeling it. Without you knowing how important it is." Her eyes watered as she continued. "I don't want this to go by without me telling you how proud I am of you. I'm so damn proud." She beamed up at her.

Charlotte smiled back at her aunt, squinting up her eyes. She didn't have the words to give to her her. There was nothing she could say to make her realize how much she'd done for her. How much she'd healed her. "Thank you, Aunt Rose," she said, hugging her to her chest.

Rose pulled away a few moments later, wiping the corners of her eyes.

"And now, for the main attraction." Rose grinned. "Follow me."

Rose walked up the steps to the rooftop and Charlotte followed after her. When she arrived to the roof, she almost couldn't believe what she saw. Fresh flowers and candles were scattered across the tables with white starched linens below them. At least 30 people, Flower, Willow, friends, instructors, and fellow business owners, all sat at the tables, drinking and talking, turning to applaud Charlotte as she walked into the party. Her heart was overwhelmed as she greeted all of them, going from table to table to embrace them. She was overcome to see all of them in one place, all there for her. She made her way to the back of the rooftop to a table in the corner. Her breath caught when she saw the cowboy hat and the familiar face under it.

"Garrett!" Charlotte said, rushing to him like a child.

She threw her arms around him and hugged the man close to her, willing herself not to cry. Garrett, though, was not able to contain himself the same way. He patted her back and kissed her cheek fiercely.

"Miss Charlotte, look at you. My god, you're so beautiful. A woman!" he said, holding her out at arm's length. His smiling eyes welled and he brought her back in for another hug.

"I can't believe you're here!" she said, shocked. She looked around for Rose, who shot her a wink from across the party. "How are you? You look the exact same!" she said, laughing.

Garrett's hair was a bit grayer than she remembered, but other than that, he was all himself. His weather-beaten rancher's face was as handsome as ever.

"I couldn't miss this. Rose told me about it and I just- I had to be here." He grinned at her. "Rose tells me you finished that degree with your eyes closed." He smiled.

Charlotte rolled her eyes, laughing. "Not quite. You know Rose, though."

"Well, I can't believe this place you girls got here. And college on top of that." He shook his head. "You should be very proud. I'm very proud of you."

Charlotte felt her whole heart warm to be near Garrett, in part because he was who he was, one of the kindest people she'd ever met, but also because of him. Because being near Garrett, she felt closer to Wyatt than she had in years.

They talked more throughout the party even though Charlotte was distracted making sure she talked to all of her friends who were there. Rose spared no expense, hiring one of the nicest restaurants downtown to cater it and even a guitar player to come and sing a few songs as the night and the drinks wore on even after the sun sank behind the peaks in the distance. Charlotte found herself sitting at a table with only Garrett and Rose at the end of the night, looking out over the mess.

"How the hell did you do this without my help?" Charlotte laughed, sipping what was probably her tenth glass of champagne.

Rose shrugged. "I delegated that shit! Willow was pretty on top of it, I must say. We created a little monster in that one."

Charlotte nodded. "Well thank you, Aunt Rose. And thank you for inviting this guy, too," she said, placing a hand on Garrett's shoulder.

"Who says I invited him for you? I needed a proper date," Rose said, her eyes glazed over with alcohol. "I'm all burned out on these hippie men, Garrett. Sometimes you just need a cowboy. Right, Charlotte?"

Garrett blushed and laughed, and Charlotte was thankful he didn't look at her when Rose said that, worried once again that her face would give her away. She wanted so badly to ask him about Wyatt, if he'd heard anything about him, but she wouldn't let herself do that. Not even with all she'd had to drink. After all, she didn't really deserve to know anything about him after what she'd done to him all those years ago.

"Alright, babe. Willow says she's going to take you out for the rest of the night. You know, with the young people," Rose said, standing from the table.

"But- I'm out. This is enough. I'm tired," Charlotte whined.

Rose shook her head firmly. "Get your ass out to those bars. For god's sake, you've gone your whole college career with not one drunken night other than the ones you've had with your geriatric aunt! Come on, cowboy, take me home," Rose said, pulling Garrett up from his place at the table. She walked away, bidding goodnight to Willow and the other stragglers of the party, leaving Garrett standing next to Charlotte.

"Thank you for coming, Garrett. It really means a lot to me," she said, hugging him tight one last time.

"Wouldn't have missed it. Congratulations, really. You should be real proud." He held her at arm's length looking down into her beautiful face. His smile faded just barely before he spoke again. "Wyatt–" he started. "Wyatt's ok."

Charlotte closed her mouth and swallowed hard. “You’ve talked to him?” she said, her voice barely above a whisper.

Garrett nodded. “He’s had a rough go. Bout to leave on his fourth deployment over there,” he said shaking his head. “Just seems like this war’s never gonna end. I can’t believe it.”

Charlotte nodded, her heart aching to hear any news of him other than what came to her in her dreams.

“I know it’s been a long time and everything but- I don’t know- If you ever want to write him or anything. You let me know. I have his information and everything. I send him things from time to time especially when he’s gone. When he’s away...”

Charlotte said nothing, but gripped Garrett’s hands out in front of her, squeezing them tight.

Garrett smiled sadly down at her. “Rose told me you might not want to, but I wanted to offer, just in case. And if you can’t do that, maybe just say a prayer for him.”

“I will,” Charlotte said.

Garrett hugged her once more, then left her standing on the rooftop alone, feeling Wyatt there with her with all of her heart.

North Carolina wasn’t on his list of his favorite places he’d been, but it didn’t really matter. Life on the base was the same no matter where they were. And from what he’d seen, most bases were the same. Always half new with small sections of state of the art buildings and equipment while the other half was rundown, there for what looked like a hundred years. And being that Wyatt and Pat were in the infantry division for almost four years, they'd gotten used to the fact that their equipment was often the worst of anyone's. It didn't matter much to them, though. Marines were used to making do with that they had and after three deployments to Iraq, the men felt confident in pretty much anything. War will do that to a person.

Patrick was giddy. They were gearing up for what would be his final deployment that summer and it couldn't get over soon enough for him. By the grace of some unknown force, or maybe by the grace of Patrick's bargaining skills, they'd been able to remain together all of these years in the same platoon. Both sergeants now, they'd climbed the ranks together and relied on each other heavily. Theirs had not been an easy journey with the seemingly never-ending war in front of them, but they did it together, and that mattered.

"Last one, cowboy. Do you believe it?" Patrick grinned, packing his ruck on his bunk.

Despite the fact that most sergeants lived off of base, Patrick and Wyatt decided not to all of these years, instead pocketing the difference and saving more and more money. Wyatt nodded, folding his brown Marine issued t-shirts and placing them in his bag. "Last one for you," he said laughing. "Maybe not me."

Pat waved him off. "They can't send you back for a fifth, man. Plus embassy duty is gonna come calling again, and you better fucking take it this time."

Wyatt nodded, exasperated. Patrick had scolded him for almost a year straight since he turned down the prestigious embassy duty position he'd been offered. Head to toe and everywhere in between, Wyatt was the perfect Marine. He'd practically been cookie cut out to fit their mold and the powers that be always noticed.

"I'll take it, I'll take it. Shit. Did you want me to let you go to Iraq by yourself the last time? You would have been bored as hell. Would have been only you and Seth," Wyatt teased.

"That fucker," Patrick sighed. "You know I actually miss him? Really. That's what war will do to you, man. Makes you love an asshole like Seth."

All of their friends had scattered after the last couple deployments, all receiving new duty stations. Wyatt knew it was the right thing for all of them to do, to keep promoting and moving through the ranks, but he longed for those early days with his men, his original men he'd first set foot in country with. Harvey, Griff, Seth, Gabriel, Patrick, and, most of all, Gus, who he still thought of daily. He kept him in a small part of his heart he never mentioned to anyone else, much like the one he kept for her.

"What are you doing tonight? You wanna come to dinner with me and Mia?" Patrick asked.

"Naw, man. You guys go and have your time. I'll be fine," Wyatt said, thinking of which bar he could head to in order to find some company for the evening.

"Please don't go to Rooster's again," Patrick said, stopping his packing and looking straight at Wyatt. "Those girls are nasty."

Wyatt laughed. "What are you, my mother? Jesus, Pat from basic training would beat your ass, you know that?"

"I know, I know. I don't know what the fuck happened to me, but really, man. Why can't you find just a solid girl to actually date? You always tomcatting around those nasty bar flies." Patrick mock shuttered. "You too pretty for that."

Wyatt placed his packed ruck on the ground and laid down on his bunk with his hands behind his head. "When does Mia leave?" he said, changing the subject.

Patrick sighed. "Tomorrow, right after we do." He shook his head. "I thought this would get easier, but it doesn't. She takes it so hard."

Wyatt nodded, looking up at his friend. "But then you're done. As soon as you get back, Miami University awaits." He grinned, his heart already burning to think of his friend so far away.

Pat nodded, looking at him. "And you're gonna come visit, right? On R and R? Holidays?"

Wyatt nodded. "Of course. Unless your mama wants me to come to her house instead. She likes me better than she likes you, after all."

"Shiiiit. You think I don't know that? If you were darker she'd tell everyone you were hers," he said, rolling his eyes.

Mia walked into the doorway then, holding coffees and a bag of something that looked like pastries in her hand. Patrick stopped what he was doing and walked across the room to her.

"Baby!" he said, taking the coffees out of her hands and kissing her firmly on her plump lips.

Mia smiled. "Hi, babe. Don't spill that! That one's for Wyatt. Just black, right Wy?" she said, bringing Wyatt the steaming cup.

He sat up on his bed grinning at her. "Thank you, Mia. Pat, see? Your girlfriend *and* your mama love me more than they love you."

Mia reached her hand out and touched Wyatt's cheek sweetly, smiling at him.

"I do love you. If only I could get you to settle down!" she scolded.

Pat put his arm around her shoulders, looking down at her. "I was just telling him that, baby. He's always chasing those nasty bar girls."

She looked up at him, furrowing her dark brows together. "Mi amore, you met me at a bar. What's wrong with a bar?"

"No, no, baby. Not like that. I just mean- that... you know. He's not after those top shelf girls like you. You know?" Patrick said quickly.

"Top shelf?" she said, her face annoyed.

Wyatt watched them from the bed, grinning. He loved nothing more than watching Pat thrown off his game, a fear in his eyes that only showed around Mia or his mom.

"Wyatt, you know what I mean. Tell her what I mean," Patrick said, calling in reinforcement.

Wyatt shrugged, taking a sip of his coffee. "You're on your own, bud."

Mia hit Patrick playfully in his stomach and he wrapped his arm tighter around her shoulders.

"I used to think you were good with words until I got to know you," she said, rolling her eyes.

She put her hands on her hips, surveying the packing. She was a formidable presence even at five feet two inches tall. Her long brown hair curled around her face and her jeans and tank top hugged her ample curves. Wyatt often had to remind himself that Mia was Patrick's since she was so beautiful, it was hard not to look at her. Her striking features always demanded attention. Luckily, she was too much like family for him to look very long.

"Where do you guys want to go to dinner tonight? I would cook for you, but you have no kitchen," she said, raising her hands up around her.

"Wyatt won't go with us," Patrick said accusingly.

Mia kept her hands on her hips and spun her head to Wyatt on the bed. "Que? No, no, Wy. This is, what is that word you guys use all of the time? Mandatory," she said, articulating each syllable.

Wyatt smiled, shaking his head. "You guys just go have a nice date. I don't need to third wheel."

Mia exhaled heavily and sat down close to him on the bunk, wrapping her small arm across his sturdy back.

"You're coming with us. I'm going to miss both of my guys and I want you to come." She looked up into his eyes and he couldn't help but smile and agree. Her dark black lashes swept so innocently above her amber eyes. She was terrifying and had a way of making people say yes to her.

"Ok," he said, hugging her to his side as Patrick looked down on them.

"Shit, I'm gonna be the third wheel," he whined. "You're both supposed to love me the most, remember? Your best friend and your sexy boyfriend? God damn," he joked.

They continued packing and talking about the impending deployment. Mia chewed on her bottom lip nervously each time the men mentioned it. They were careful not to say too much in front of her. Not give her any information which would make her worry even more. Patrick regretted those times he'd returned from deployment only to fall into her and tell her everything that had happened. How dangerous it was. The carnage they'd seen. He didn't realize at the time how much damage it would do. How much it would make her worry. But this time would be different. They'd be going to Afghanistan which he promised her wouldn't be like Iraq, even though he knew it would be. Maybe even worse this time.

"I'll go get the rest of the laundry. Stay here with Wyatt, babe. Don't let him tell you any lies about me," he said, walking out the door.

Wyatt smiled at Mia who was meticulously checking the few comfort items Patrick was packing. Books, hard candy, pictures, and gum. She ran her hands over it all lovingly and looked up at Wyatt, her eyes sad.

Wyatt nodded at her knowingly. "We'll be back before you know it," he said, trying to comfort her.

She nodded slowly, looking back over the things on the bed. When she looked back at him, her eyes were watering, dangerously close to brimming over. Wyatt hadn't encountered a crying woman in years and the reality of being in a room with one he loved so dearly was terrifying to him.

"Please don't cry, Mia," he said quietly. "I won't know what to do."

Mia laughed, a tear spilling down her cheek. She wiped it away quickly with the back of her hand.

"Sorry, Wy. I'm just- I worry so much about you guys. I swear I won't sleep the whole time you're gone," she said, still looking into his eyes.

Wyatt nodded, looking away from her. "I know. I'm sorry-I–"

Mia laughed again, more tears spilling down her cheeks. "Only you would apologize for going to war."

She inhaled, trying to get ahold of her shaking breath.

Wyatt looked back at her and smiled. "We will be ok," he said, his voice steadier than he felt on the inside.

Mia nodded slowly, looking back up at him. "I believe you then," she said quietly. "Promise me that you'll bring him home."

Wyatt's heart tightened as he looked at her and saw the love she had in her eyes. How could he promise her that when he knew what could happen? He leveled his gaze steadily, his face not giving away the fear he felt on the inside.

"I promise," Wyatt said quietly.

After graduating, Charlotte didn't know what to do with herself. Since they'd hired Willow so long ago, much of the work was taken care of for her. At first she hated it, missing the simple tasks that the shop demanded of her- stocking shelves, dusting, and scheduling appointments. It was difficult for her to give it all over to Willow, especially when she felt like she wouldn't do as good of a job as Charlotte would have. But Willow had surprised them all, herself included, and was a dependable and hardworking employee at the shop. Much of that had to do with the fact that she had finally gotten clean and quit all of her vices except for booze and men, which Rose approved of and encouraged anyhow.

And so Charlotte's weeks were much less stressful that summer. No more papers to write or books to study, she had no excuse to continue running herself into the ground. She'd been showing up at the shop more frequently since it was summer and it would be busy season once again, but she often found herself without anything to do by midweek. Willow took care of all of the day to day odds and ends and Charlotte was generally ahead of the curve when it came to event planning and keeping the books. She was not used to the time she had on her hands and quickly decided that she didn't care for it. That she needed more. A new challenge.

She was hiking that summer morning in late June. It would be her birthday soon and it was weighing heavily on her that year. Twenty-three. She'd be 23 years old that summer and she never could have imagined how much her life had changed since hopping that Greyhound in the middle of the night all those years ago. She hated her birthday, and always had, really. Her aunt always tried to make it special for her- planning trips, dinners, anything she could to make it fun for her, but she knew that Charlotte was always somewhere else that day, her mind inevitably going back to Patagonia and the only birthday that had ever really mattered. If Rose had her way, they would've driven back there every July fourth and celebrated the proper way- with fireworks and a rodeo dance, but she knew Charlotte would never go back. They had an unspoken agreement that Charlotte didn't go farther south than Phoenix. Charlotte knew that as soon as she'd hit Tucson, he'd be the only thing she'd feel. So that year, also being Charlotte's graduation, Rose had big plans for them. A secret trip she'd refused to tell Charlotte about, only saying it required them to be gone a week, maybe more.

The air was fresh and clear that morning and the first of the summer storms was brewing in the distance. Charlotte loved that time of year on the mountain. She waited, just like everyone else, for the storms to roll in every afternoon, making the town dark and cozy. It was not as good as the smell of the desert after the rain, but it ran a close second. There was something comforting about the town being blanketed by clouds. Being encircled by the darkness.

Charlotte hiked up the back of Mt. Eldon to her favorite spot. She breathed heavily, the thin air burning her lungs like it did every time. Regardless of having lived there so long, it still got to her. She sat down on a large rock and took her backpack off, looking out across the skyline. She assessed the clouds and figured she had a good couple of hours before the rains started. Plenty of time to do what she'd come there to do.

She took a drink of water and pushed her long blonde braid to the other side of her neck, looking to the tree in front of her. Her ribbon had fallen off several times over the years but she always replaced it, each time saying a silent prayer for him.

The morning was quiet, only the breeze through the pine trees around her. She felt anxious, afraid even. She held out her hand in front of her and noticed it was shaking, just slightly. She laughed at herself and shook her head, trying hard to calm down. Crossing her legs on the rock, she closed her eyes gently and asked her guides for help.

"I am loved," she said to herself over and over, grounding herself into the earth. "Please help me. Help me do this right," she said in her head.

She sat there for a long time like that, letting the silence of the morning take her over and the peace wash over her. It never failed to focus her, never failed to bring her help, and this time was no exception. She blinked her eyes open and retrieved her pen and paper out of her bag, bringing it out on her lap.

It had been so long, so many years that she didn't even know if she had the right to contact him at all. What if it hadn't mattered to him like it had to her? What if he didn't feel the same way she did? If it hadn't broken him like it had her? She'd asked herself these questions and, more than ever since seeing Garrett, wondered what good it would even do at that point.

But then she remembered. She remembered how much he needed help through the hell that her dreams continuously told her he was going through. The visions that came unbidden into her mind over the years that showed her, yes, he needed something from her. Maybe not what he thought he did back then, but something. He needed to know he would return. That he would, one day, make it back home once again. And even if Charlotte didn't deserve to talk to him again, he deserved that, at least.

Charlotte closed her eyes once more before she began. She asked her guides once again to show her Wyatt. To show him as he would one day be, and there he was. Perfect and alive in her mind, and always in her heart. And then she began writing.

Afghanistan was different. They'd told them that in briefings and trainings before they deployed, but Patrick and Wyatt were unfazed. Having served three prior deployments in Iraq, they had confidence that they could handle whatever Afghanistan had for them as well. And so far they hadn't been wrong, they had been able to handle it, but it was a change of scenery from the small towns and cities in Iraq. Afghanistan was more rural by far with the Marines often passing through desolate villages and rocky mountainsides which made for dangerous firefights and ambushes.

Never did Wyatt think he'd prefer Fallujah over any other place, but at least there they knew there was trouble around every corner. In Afghanistan, years after the war had started, it was different. The violence popped up quickly and surprisingly after weeks of quiet and boredom. The hills of Afghanistan provided the perfect place for insurgents and Al Qaeda to hide.

The summer sun beat down on them as they walked through the hilly country toward the next village. Their mission for the day was simple: to interact with the people in the small village and attempt to get intel from them concerning the extremists who were constantly ducking out of view to live in caves and underground bunkers, keeping the Marines on the hunt. It was a lot like the work they did in those early days that first deployment, always trying like hell to make the citizens realize that they were there to help. It was an almost impossible feat at that point because of the sheer amount of time the war bad been going on. The distrust the people had of the Americans ran deep in them now, even in the children. And for the Marines, the feeling was mutual.

"Man, this is always such a mind fuck," Patrick said, walking alongside Wyatt. "People will look you straight in the eyes and lie to you. Cluster fuck."

Wyatt nodded, looking back at their men trailing behind them, all carrying M16s and looking around them into the trees.

"Vicious cycle, for sure," he said.

He adjusted his broad shoulders back and shifted the weapon in his hands. He could feel the sweat dripping down his back under his uniform and Kevlar, and he knew it wasn't because of the heat. The feeling of uneasiness had followed him throughout the morning since they'd left camp. He used to love the woods, walking through them looking for deer and other wild game with his father. But he was far from the mountains of Arizona then. This was a much different hunting trip than the ones of his youth and he'd thought more than once that hunting would likely be ruined for him forever because of it. He was thankful, though, for those skills and the steady way his father had taught him so many years ago. Despite everything, those skills made him an integral part of any team he was on, his sharp eyes making him an asset to his platoon.

"What's up, cowboy?" Patrick said, shrewdly assessing him.

Wyatt looked around into the trees. He hated feeling bogged down by the forest without being able to see the skyline. It was the desert rat in him that made him search for the steady sign of the horizon. Sometimes, he'd lose his breath when he couldn't see it for too long. Panicked that he couldn't find his way.

"I don't like it," he said, spitting chewing tobacco out in front of him.

Patrick nodded in agreement. He'd seen Wyatt sniff out danger dozens of times, always before there was any real sign of it. He was far from questioning his friend or second guessing his gut feeling.

"What you wanna do?" Patrick asked, looking back at the men again.

Wyatt stopped, putting up his hand to his side to signal the men behind him to do the same. He ducked down to get a look under the canopy of trees. He tilted his head, searching the ridge in front of them.

"I don't know, man," he said, shaking his head. "Don't like that ridge."

Patrick squatted next to him to get a good look.

"You wanna go the long way? Down the hill instead?" Patrick offered.

"Maybe. That doesn't make sense, though. Those valleys are always shit for firefights." Wyatt rubbed his gloved hand over his sweaty face, his crystal blue eyes sharp and hard.

"You call it, man," Patrick said.

Wyatt nodded looking back up the ridge. "Ok. I say valley."

Patrick nodded and stood, turning to face the platoon.

"Alright listen, we're gonna head down the long way through the valley. Don't fuck around. I want you guys flanked and ready, eyes up on the hills. Jackson, for fuck's sake, we're not stopping for you to shit this time so if you have to go, go now."

There was a rumble of laughter among the Marines and Patrick cracked a grin at them. Wyatt stayed with his back turned looking from the ridge and down to the valley below him. He couldn't shake the feeling in his stomach that told him it was coming again. And soon.

The men walked the long way down into the valley, quietly grumbling to each other about how much farther it was rather than making the summit at the ridge and going directly down into the village. The detour would add at least an hour each way and they weren't happy about it.

Wyatt walked along the dry creek bed, looking up into the hills, a large dip of tobacco in his bottom plump lip.

"Better?" Patrick asked, looking over at him.

Wyatt nodded briefly but unconvincingly. Patrick knew him well enough to feel his nerves. His senses were heightened even more than usual, so in tune with his friend that sometimes they felt like they were one person. Wyatt was reminded during that deployment, more than any other, of how important Patrick's presence was to him. He had no idea how he would do it without him there next to him.

Wyatt audibly exhaled when they finally reached the edge of the trees and the sky opened up around them. He didn't realize how suffocated he felt until he felt the sunshine hit his face. He could see the village in the distance and the ridge he'd refused to cross to the east of him. He looked behind him at his men once again before looking back to that ridge. He saw it almost immediately, his eyes always going to the part of the foliage that wasn't in place. Shapes with hard edges rather than the green flow of nature. The sun reflected off of the scope, shining directly at the Marines.

"Get the fuck down!" he yelled loudly.

Wyatt grabbed Patrick by the shoulder and threw him behind a boulder next to him. In the next instant, the firing started coming hard off of the mountain toward them. The men were down and covered quickly, ducking behind the boulders in the creek bed and aiming back at the mountain. They did not need permission to fire, and even the greenest among the young infantry Marines knew that once engaged, they were expected to engage back. And they did, eager to reciprocate.

Bullets bounced off the rocks around Patrick and Wyatt. Patrick chewed his gum hard, looking through his binoculars as Wyatt fired indiscriminately over the rocks.

"Looks like at least ten," Patrick said, smacking his gum nervously.

Wyatt nodded, turning his back to reload his weapon.

"Any RPGs?" he asked shortly.

Patrick shook his head, still looking through the binoculars.

"Not that I can see."

Wyatt looked out over the men to see one of them starting to stand from cover to get a better shot at the insurgents.

"Cortez, stay the fuck down! At least get some suppressive fire if you're gonna do that!" he shouted at him. The young private reminded him of other Marines he knew who seemingly valued their lives very little also.

The firefight went on for far too long for Wyatt's liking. His men's position was starting to make him nervous, being that they were open to the west and could be caught in a crossfire if the enemy had anyone to that side of them.

"Air support?" Patrick asked, reading his mind.

Wyatt nodded and gave the order to the radio operator, looking through his scope meticulously before finding a target. Once he found it, he didn't hesitate, squeezing the trigger. He watched through the scope as the man fell from his post at the machine gun and rolled down the hill. The Marines roared in approval, the primal place inside of them taking hold like it did in every battle.

"Nice shot, Sergeant!" Jackson said, laughing, giddy with the excitement of the battle.

Wyatt's face remained even as he turned back to check the progress of the air support that was coming. He looked to Patrick, patting his arm briefly. Sweat dripped from under Patrick's helmet and his face was drawn and serious. No longer exhilarated like the faces of the younger Marines. Not like it once was.

"You good, man?" Wyatt asked briefly.

Patrick nodding, shooting Wyatt an unconvincing smile. "Just another day at the office," he said, halfheartedly.

Wyatt watched as the Apache helicopter came from behind them and dipped low on the ridge where they'd given the coordinates. The missiles dropped into the side of the ridge and rumbled so loud that the men had to cover their ears at the last minute. The ground shook with impact and Wyatt could feel his heart pounding in his chest.

"You grabbed me," Patrick would say to him later that night, lying on his bunk. "You grabbed me before you ever heard a bullet," he said, shaking his head. "If we would've gone over the ridge we'd be dead," he said as Wyatt remained silent. "You always know."

Wyatt said nothing back to him but lied back on his own bunk and closed his eyes. Shirtless, he brought his hand and rested it over the St. Michael medallion around his neck, pushing it close to his hot skin.

The Georgia countryside was a lot like she remembered it, only greener. The thick foliage whipping by her window was a welcomed sight after being in airports and planes all morning long. Rose still hadn't told her exactly where they were going. Charlotte was frustrated enough to look into the matter magically although she never could trust what she felt.

Rose smiled happily as she drove, her large dark sunglasses perched on her nose as she hummed a tune. She patted the steering wheel, drumming along, and looked over to Charlotte and grinned. Charlotte stared out the window, exhausted from the day and already having anxiety about leaving the shop for a whole two weeks. She'd worked round the clock before they left to make sure everything was in order, leaving pages of typed notes for Willow and the other employees, but it wasn't enough. She hated the feeling of having to count on other people to do something for her and never was that feeling more prevalent as when she had to leave the shop.

"Would you calm the fuck down, please?" Rose asked sweetly. "I can *feel* you freaking out, you know. I can read your mind. The shop's fine!"

Charlotte sighed and sat up straight, looking out the front window. They'd landed in Atlanta that morning and Rose said nothing of their plans, only secured a rental car, upgraded to a luxury sedan of course, and told Charlotte to hop in, driving east on the highway like she'd done it dozens of times before that.

"Well, maybe you could tell me where we're going. That way I can get into this whole adventure you have planned," Charlotte said, as lightheartedly as she could.

Rose shook her head. "No chance, girl."

Charlotte smiled even though Rose was making her crazy. She'd become such a structured person over the years. The shop and the business made her into a creature of habit and one who had to have control over all situations. All of which Rose knew.

"Ok, fine, Aunt Rose. Why don't you tell me where you got this idea, anyway? You know I love your adventures. This one just feels... I don't know. Bigger?"

"Exactly!" Rose said, smile gleaming behind her red lipstick. "Some of those adventures are just sojourns. Small little getaways. This is more... I don't know... what did the guides call it? A quest? Journey?" She waved her hand. "Some shit like that."

Charlotte raised her brows, grinning at her aunt. "So this is your spirit guides' idea?" she asked, bordering on laughter.

Rose nodded like it should be obvious. "You know they've always got a plan, babe."

Charlotte laughed. "Oh I know, but I also know sometimes you just blame things on them if you feel like it."

Rose cackled. "Guilty. But not this time, I promise."

They drove for hours through the green countryside and Charlotte could feel herself detaching from her work back in Arizona. She didn't know if it was the beautiful sights around her or the fact that Rose had performed some kind of magic spell on her, but she finally started to feel like she could breathe again. And when they pulled into Savannah in the late afternoon hours, she felt even more at ease. The town was gorgeous with old cobblestone streets flanked by colonial buildings and large mossy trees that draped canopies over the roads.

Charlotte stepped out onto the sidewalk and felt a connection to the place immediately, much like the one she'd felt on that first trip to Flagstaff.

"Oh," she said audibly, placing her hand over her heart.

Rose looked over at her, retrieving the bags out of the car and smiling.

"Right? I like it. Great vibes."

She'd taken care of everything for them already, booking them a room at an old bed and breakfast in downtown Savannah that looked like something out of *Gone with the Wind*. Charlotte's feet creaked on the whitewashed porch, scattered with flowers and a front porch swing. She sat on the swing and waited for Rose to check in as she looked out around the town. The humidity was stifling compared to the dryness of Arizona. She wore jeans and a tank top, but debated changing into shorts right away since it was so hot.

"We're checked in. She brought the bags to the room. Come on, let's go. Cocktail time," Rose said, expertly reapplying her lipstick.

Despite having traveled all day long, Rose looked beautiful as ever. Her brown hair was effortlessly piled on top of her head and her clothes remained unwrinkled and flowing off of her as always. Charlotte started to protest leaving already before she could change, or get a nap, but Rose was too excited, holding out her hand for Charlotte to hold as they walked down the street together.

Rose talked excitedly about the town, pointing out the gorgeous architecture and the lushness of the trees and grass which grew everywhere, even out of the sidewalk cracks.

"I haven't been here in years!" she said as they walked. "I came here for a conference years ago. Lots of metaphysical folks in this community. You're gonna love it. Magical, just like us."

Rose led them down a side street that opened up to the Riverwalk. The Savannah River was huge compared to the rivers Charlotte had seen in her life, and the beauty of the sun sinking behind it that first night in Savannah almost took her breath away. She loved the contrast of the river flowing quietly next to the bustling storefronts.

River Street was packed with tourists and locals alike, all walking and looking through the shops and frequenting bars and restaurants. Charlotte was famished and readily agreed when Rose found a riverfront bar with outdoor seating facing the river. Rose ordered her standard white wine while Charlotte opted for a beer, the waiter looking at her a bit sideways when she asked about the Mexican beers they had available.

The night was perfect, and as soon as the sun set, the heat that had overtaken her when they landed in Georgia dissipated and gave way to the cool wind which floated off the surface of the river. Rose ordered appetizers and round after round of drinks, talking with everyone who sat down around them as Charlotte remained quiet, sipping her beers and looking out to the river walk and the flowing water behind it.

"Alright, babe. Ready? I bit off more than I could chew," Rose said, widening her eyes to focus on the receipt she was signing.

Charlotte laughed and took it out of her hands, signing it for her.

"Now that you're drunk, tell me why we're here," Charlotte teased.

Rose wagged her finger at her niece. "No, no, no. I'm not that easy." She cocked her head. "Actually I'm really easy, but not about secrets." She cackled.

Charlotte shrugged, her head spinning after the beer. "I'll just figure it out magically then," she said, letting it slip out.

Rose swung her head around to her, catching her. "A-ha!" She clapped triumphantly. "I knew it! So tell me then! Why are we here?"

Charlotte shook her head and covered her face, immediately regretting her words. "No, I was kidding. Never mind!"

Rose pulled her hands from her face and grinned up at her. "You know! Protégé! She's my protégé," Rose explained to a drunk group next to them.

They laughed drunkenly together until Rose pulled herself together to get serious again. "Listen, I'll make you a deal," she said, standing and pulling Charlotte up next to her. "You tell me what your magical mind told you and I'll show you why we're here."

Charlotte considered her offer, linking her arm with her aunt, walking down the Riverwalk. The night was alive with people, a younger crowd headed out to the bars. Large steamboats continued paddling up and down the river, loaded down with tourists.

"Ok fine. But you have to follow through if I'm right!" Charlotte said, still laughing. "Wait, isn't the bed and breakfast that way?" she asked, pointing behind her.

"Well, do you want me to tell you or not?!" Rose quipped. "We gotta go this way."

"Ok fine," Charlotte said still walking next to her. "Me first?"

"Wait," Rose said, hustling them along a ways longer. "Ok, now," she said, stopping in a quiet place toward a row of closed stores.

Rose faced her niece and placed her hands on her arms, holding her still so she would stop spinning. Her face was giddy with excitement and Charlotte couldn't help but laugh.

"I thought you said never to do drunk psychic work," Charlotte mock scolded.

"Do as I say not as I do!" Rose said, cackling again. "Ok really. Out with it!"

Charlotte shifted on her feet and felt her cheeks hot with embarrassment. She didn't know what she feared more, being right or being wrong.

"I don't know... the shop. I saw the shop," Charlotte said quietly.

Rose threw her head back and laughed from her belly, still holding onto Charlotte for security. She looked back at her after a few laughing fits and tears streaked out of the corners of her eyes.

"It's official. You're magical," she said, hugging her niece to her tightly.

"Wait, wait, wait!" Charlotte said, laughing. "You have to tell me what that means! I mean, I love Savannah. There's something about it, but why here?"

Rose composed herself, but couldn't wipe the huge smile off of her face.

"You don't know already, babe?" she asked seriously.

"No!" Charlotte laughed. "I just saw our shop, but different. I have no idea!"

Rose grabbed Charlotte's shoulders and spun her around to face the building behind her. It was two stories tall with a large sweeping front porch and balcony that overlooked the Riverwalk. Built in stone, it looked different from the buildings on either side of it, or any of the others they'd seen that day, really. There was a huge mossy tree out front and an iron gate that fenced in the grassy yard. Charlotte looked at it from top to bottom where the for sale sign was posted. She felt the pang hit her gut almost immediately.

"Oh," she said, losing her breath.

And Rose was beside her, looking at the place the same way.

"Oh, is right," she said quietly. "The Holt girls take the world."

They were only a month away from heading back home. For Patrick, it would be his last time at war. It was his last time fighting next to Wyatt and even though part of him was relieved, the other part of him wasn't. The other part of him didn't quite remember who he was on the inside before he was a Marine. Before all of his worth had been found in his ability to do his job and do it well. Who he really was when that was gone, when he wasn't standing next to his best friend, he didn't really know. And it scared him more than he would say out loud.

They lay on their bunks quietly that night. The perk of their promotions meant they had a little more privacy, sharing their dumpy little room with two other sergeants rather than dozens of Marines. But they both missed being out with the men, even if it meant they slept better and weren't interrupted by wrestling matches and silly debates over which swimsuit model was hotter. It made them feel like the old guys to be removed from it, but that's what they were now. They were seasoned, their cherries popped so long ago that they didn't even remember what it felt like to be as green as their men were.

Patrick lay on his back in his silkies reading a Stephen King novel one of the other Marines had discarded. It didn't matter what type of book it was, Patrick would read it, especially on deployment. He read so fast that he'd blow through books his mom and Mia sent him in a matter of days, even when they had to work the majority of the time.

"Man, this dude's head is fucked up," Patrick said, putting the book down. "He writes about the creepiest shit."

Wyatt smiled, keeping his eyes slightly closed. "You're still gonna finish it."

Patrick sat up, facing toward Wyatt's bunk. He wiped his hand over his tired face. "Only cause there ain't shit else to do at night. It's boring as hell sometimes."

Wyatt opened his eyes, keeping his hands on his bare chest. "I'm not fun enough for you anymore?" He grinned.

"Naw, you're alright. I mean, you're not like Miami Wyatt. That dude is fun as hell. He'll drink all the whiskey in a bar and dance with every girl in the joint!" Patrick laughed.

Wyatt grinned and closed his eyes again. "Don't know who you're talking about."

"Mmm-hmm," he said, smirking at him. "Mama Karla hasn't met that Wyatt. That's why she still loves you."

Wyatt laughed. "Don't you dare tell her about him. I'm afraid of her just like you are."

He sat up in his bunk and faced his friend. Patrick looked exhausted. Dark bags hung under his bloodshot eyes and his face was drawn and serious, even when he smiled. The small bit of baby fat he had on his cheeks when Wyatt had met him in basic training was gone, giving way to a chiseled jawline that rippled when he clenched his teeth. Wyatt looked at his friend and, for the first time, felt worried for him.

"Only a month left, man. Piece of cake," Wyatt said steadily.

Patrick nodded slowly, looking at the ground. "I know, crazy," he said, pausing a moment. "Then I'm done." He looked back at Wyatt. "Feels weird."

Wyatt forced a smile, ignoring the feeling in his stomach. "You're gonna do great, man. College won't be a problem for you at all for as much as you read."

Patrick smiled and nodded. "Hope so."

They were quiet then, both avoiding eye contact. There was so much to be said about this time. Wyatt had dreaded it since they became friends, knowing that Patrick's last day would not be his. And the truth about that was that Wyatt was heartbroken. He loved all of his fellow Marines, they were his brothers, all, but none were as close to him as Patrick. None understood his heart the way Patrick did. Patrick always knew what to say to him, and what not to say to him. There wasn't a person in the world as close to him as Patrick. Except maybe her. But she didn't even exist anymore. So far away, so long ago that she may as well have been a dream.

"Wyatt," Patrick said, breaking the silence. "I've never told you thank you. I've never told you thank you for being there for me." Patrick's eyes brimmed the slightest bit but he blinked his tears away quickly. "You're–" he started, "You're the best friend I've ever had."

Before Wyatt could answer, Patrick stood from his bunk and grabbed his towel, heading for the showers. Wyatt laid back down on his bunk and placed his hand over his heart, trying to ignore the unsettled feeling in his stomach.

That night Wyatt dreamt he was drowning and there, out of the dark water, she came. A mermaid, her forlorn face yelling something into his as she tried to pull him to the surface to no avail.

Charlotte could hardly bring herself to get on the plane back. She hated flying and thought more than once about telling Rose they should rent a car and road trip home. But that would take even more time away from the shop.

"Jesus, we aren't going to crash!" Rose said as they buckled in for the long flight.

She was on her second glass of champagne and the plane hadn't even left the terminal yet. She showed no signs of slowing down, either, referring to herself as "Vacation Rose" each time Charlotte mentioned it to her.

"Vacation Rose self-medicates," she said, grinning wickedly over at her niece seated next to her in first class. "She also curses more than regular Rose and is wildly promiscuous."

Charlotte exhaled audibly. "She sounds exactly like regular Rose to me," she said, looking out the window to the tarmac below.

Rose cackled loudly, unfazed by the other first class flyers who looked at her sideways.

"For fuck's sake, Char, you've gotta calm down," Rose said, flagging a flight attendant.

The woman was beautiful, with her hair tied back severely making her face tight and serious. Rose read her name tag as she approached.

"Agnes? Yes, I need a whiskey for my niece immediately, please. She won't survive without one."

"Ma'am, we'll be coming back around again–" Agnes started.

"Listen, Agnes, I'm gonna tip the shit outta you. I'm begging you. Look at this girl," she said waving her champagne glass in Charlotte's direction. "She's a wreck."

Charlotte smiled tightly at Agnes, pulling at the ends of her long blonde hair nervously.

"Yes ma'am. I'll get that for you," Agnes said, actually cracking a small smile.

"And you can keep these coming," Rose said, raising her glass up. "Who the fuck has ever heard of naming a baby Agnes. Can you imagine?" Rose said before swigging her champagne down in one gulp.

Charlotte laughed nervously and checked her seatbelt again.

"I checked the flight," Rose said again, "We're fine. Just relax."

Charlotte couldn't understand why she was so worked up. Something was off, but she couldn't pinpoint it. Maybe it was just anxiety from being gone too long. Or maybe it was because their plane was going to crash. She couldn't figure it out since she was in her head, completely ungrounded to the point that even cleaning her energy and a 30-minute meditation that morning couldn't even help. Something was wrong. She felt it in her very bones, but she had no idea what it was.

Agnes quickly returned with the drinks, at which point Rose ordered another one for Charlotte, demanding that she drink the first one down immediately. Charlotte complied and felt the whiskey shoot through her veins, making her feel warm all over. She didn't drink much, but Vacation Rose wouldn't take no for an answer. Once her next drink came she was finally able to relax as Rose launched into a story Charlotte had heard a thousand times before about the time Rose shot out her cheating boyfriend's car window with a shotgun. Charlotte loved the story, but mostly she loved how Rose told it and how every time she heard it, new details emerged making it even better.

"And now look," Rose said, leaning over Charlotte to point out the window. "We're already over the clouds and you're fine," she said, patting her arm.

Rose was magical, that much was clear, especially since she had the ability to distract Charlotte enough for the plane to take off and be at cruising altitude before she realized they'd left.

"How did you do that?" She laughed quietly, looking out over the scattered clouds. "Did you just cast a spell or something?"

She turned to Rose, her green eyes lined with a smile. Rose reclined her chair, pulling her colorful shawl around her shoulders.

"Not me, my dear. Whiskey is even more magical than I am." She winked at her and closed her eyes gently, putting herself down for her afternoon nap.

Charlotte laughed to herself, looking back out the window. She took a deep breath and exhaled, calling in her guides to watch over them before leaning her chair back to go to sleep.

Charlotte had a hard time sleeping on planes, or anywhere except her little apartment actually, but there was no other choice. The flight would be over four hours and Charlotte was fairly certain there wasn't enough whiskey on the plane to keep her calm for that amount of time. Sleep would have to suffice. She closed her eyes, feeling her head spin the slightest bit. She shifted in her seat, pulling her sweater around her shoulders.

It started like it always did. Just the thought of him creeping in and taking hold of her, bringing her back to that place. And suddenly she was there. The grass was green and high, the storms having already started and mercifully ending the drought of winter. He was in a field near his truck, on his knees fixing a barbed wire fence. He was so focused on the job in front of him, he didn't even hear her approaching.

She stood watching him for several moments before she said anything at all. He was in his work jeans and boots, his filthy cowboy hat pulled down low over his ears. His t-shirt was covered in dirt and grime and she could see the sweat dripping down the middle of his back to where she knew he had two dimples in his lower back, just above the top of his jeans. He cursed under his breath, twisting the wire around, and Charlotte smiled to herself.

"You need some help, Mr. Earp?" she said, walking up behind him.

Wyatt jumped, dropping the fence line in his hands.

"Jesus Christ!" he said, spinning toward her, his expression changing as soon as he saw her. A wide grin spread across his face and he looked down at the ground, embarrassed at how scared he'd been.

She stood by his truck, grinning at him. She wore her boots and jeans low on her hips, her tanned stomach peeking out from the bottom of her tank top. Her hair was wild around her face the way he liked it, even messier than usual with the humidity from the rains.

"You're like a little Indian. So quiet," he said, walking toward her. "What are you doing here?"

He moved his hands tight around her waist and lifted her into an embrace, nuzzling his face into her hair.

"Garrett said you were out here. He told me and Rose to come over when we saw him in town earlier. Didn't he tell you?"

Wyatt pulled his head back and looked at her grinning. "No, but we can add that to reasons I love Garrett." He kissed her full on the lips before realizing how sweaty he was.

He pulled back and set her on the ground. "I'm sorry, I'm so dirty. I probably taste like salt." He grinned down at her, keeping hold of her hand.

Charlotte smiled up at him and stood on her toes to kiss him again, placing her soft lips over his.

"I don't care," she said quietly.

Wyatt smiled at her and looked around him. There was no one near them, they were at least a half mile from the main house and the vaqueros were already gone for the weekend.

"Where are Rose and Garrett?" he asked, eyes focused on her lips.

Charlotte shrugged. "They're having happy hour on the porch. Garrett told me where you were and that you could be done for the day."

Wyatt smiled. "So you got me off early, too? How do you always make people do what you want them to do?" he said, wrapping his arm around her waist and pulling her back to him.

"Magic," she whispered into his ear, giggling as he kissed the side of her neck.

"Why do you smell so good?" he said, smelling the side of her neck and hair. "How am I going to finish this fence with you standing here?"

He pulled his head back and lowered his face to hers again, kissing her slowly at first until she answered back, sucking gently on his bottom lip and running her hands down his sweaty back to the top of his jeans, pulling him toward her. He kissed her harder then, pushing his hat off of his head so he could get closer as he walked her backwards. He moved her back until her head rested on the side of his truck. His hands roamed down the side of her body to her bottom where he gripped her tightly, pushing himself against her. He lifted her then, pushing her up against the side of the truck as he held her tight. He kissed her deeply, breathing hard into her mouth between kisses.

"My god," he said into her mouth. "This is why you can't come see me at work anymore."

She sighed into his mouth and pulled back to look into his pained face, running her hands through his messy black hair. She looked into his crystal blue eyes then, and he pinned her down with them until she was unable to look away. She stared back, committing the moment to memory, the feeling of his large sturdy hands supporting her as she floated above the earth, embedded in her mind forever.

Wyatt woke with a sense of uneasiness just the same as he had gone to bed with the night before that. The same one that had plagued his dreams, her face haunting him even after he woke. It was not uncommon for him to feel uneasy, especially since they were at war. He'd been there so many times before that. He was seasoned, a Marine through and through, but he was not yet immune to the feeling. But this was different. He caught himself breathing shallow and short as he dressed and had to stop and remind himself to breathe deeply, to try and calm himself.

"You alright, man?" Patrick asked as they dressed. "You been making those sex noises all morning," he teased.

Wyatt cracked a sideways smile at him, leaning to finish packing his ruck for the day.

"How do you know what kind of noises I make?" he quipped back.

"Maaaaannn, I know you well enough. Plus I've been there when you've brought those bar flies home." He shivered. "I know all your moves."

Wyatt blushed, despite himself, turning around so Patrick couldn't see him. "You're so full of shit, Pat."

Patrick grinned and sat down heavily on his bunk. "So what's the plan? We gonna split up so we can cover the whole village?"

Wyatt nodded, sitting down opposite Patrick and checking his watch. "Yep. I'll start west, you can start east."

"Naturally." Patrick grinned. "Basically, Tupac and Biggie. Except I'm the prettier one so I should get to be Tupac."

Wyatt grinned. "I told you I don't know who the hell that is anyway. So fine, you be Tupac."

Patrick nodded once and stood. "Alright then. Let's do this, cowboy."

That final deployment was dragging out. As devastated as Wyatt was about Patrick leaving the Marine Corps once they got home, even he was eager to get out of there. There was something so unsettling about that place, more so than Iraq, but Wyatt couldn't decide what it was. The contrast of the beautiful scenery and the treachery around every corner made for a strange combination. In short, Wyatt hated it there. The whole place just felt wrong. Plus, he was eager to keep his promise to Mia, to return Patrick to her safely even though he knew that meant she was going to take him away. He knew that nothing would be the same once they got home. Not ever again.

They rode in the Humvees with their men, separated until they pulled up to the edge of the village. They stopped there and Patrick and Wyatt got out of the vehicles to speak before heading to their respective locations. Patrick chewed a wad of gum, his dark sunglasses covering his tired eyes. Wyatt kept chewing tobacco in his lower lip and assessed the edge of the village. It was a small place, probably only 300 people total, but it looked deserted from their vantage point, no one on the roads and minimal noise. The homes were rugged to say the least, some of them with only plywood for siding. Colorful tapestries often hung over the windows instead of glass.

"Quiet," Patrick noted, chewing his gum nervously. "What you think?"

Wyatt shook his head, looking to the rooftops of the buildings near them. “Not my favorite. But it never is.”

They reiterated the plan: Wyatt and his unit would start from the west and Patrick and his from the east. They decided on a rendezvous point where they could meet and compare notes before heading back to the Humvees. The task of the day was to ask after a known insurgent who had recently disappeared from the area. Army intelligence needed to speak to him regarding several issues, so the Marines were to deliver.

“So zip cuff him if we find him and then radio, right?” Patrick said.

Wyatt nodded, still not looking directly at Patrick. “Yeah, let’s double time if we find him. No need to stick around.”

Patrick nodded back. “For sure, let’s beat feet the fuck outta here after that.”

Wyatt looked at his friend and smiled. “Alright, Biggie. Let’s go.”

Patrick grinned wildly at him, walking backwards toward the Humvee. “I’m Tupac, remember? Look at this smile,” he said, raising his hands to his mouth. “Pretty as Tupac.”

Wyatt got back in the Humvee, ordering his private where to go as Patrick’s caravan drove in the opposite direction. He took a deep breath and gripped his rifle tight in front of him, tapping his finger on the side of it steadily. Once they parked they set right to work with the interpreter in step with them and doing what the Marines referred to as “knocking and talking," although that day it seemed that the Marines were doing all of the talking. Doors were closed quickly after they opened and even when the Marines asked to search the buildings, they were hurried along quickly, the townspeople not offering any information regardless of what the Marines told them.

They were only an hour into the search when Wyatt's nerves started to get the better of him. He walked the streets with his unit, but kept his eyes on the rooftops to either side of them, looking for anything out of the ordinary. The place was nothing like Fallujah, smaller and more rural by far, but something about it was reminding him of that day. He knew, just like he always did, that something was about to happen.

He held up his Marines on a corner and looked down the empty dirt road that headed to the east where Patrick and his unit were. He looked back the other way and noticed a woman and her children scurrying down the street before ducking into a small house.

"Alright, listen. Change of plans. We're gonna rendezvous with Sergeant McMurtry's unit earlier than expected. Jackson, radio and tell them we're coming."

"10-4," Jackson said, as they started down the street.

Jackson leaned his head down to his shoulder, speaking into his radio. A few moments later, Patrick's voice came through.

"Tell Sergeant Sterling, Tupac says affirmative, Biggie."

The men chuckled and Wyatt cracked a small grin, easing his nerves the slightest bit. He'd feel better when the units were together, clearing the town in one swoop rather than individually. Something just wasn't sitting right.

The men were only a few blocks from Patrick's unit when they heard the shots starting. Wyatt's men threw themselves against the side of the building before they realized the shots weren't close enough to get to them. It was not them who was being fired at, it was Patrick and his men. Wyatt, heart pounding in his chest, remained outwardly calm as he gave orders to his men.

"Stay back behind me!" he yelled firmly. "Jackson, ask where the fire's coming from!"

Jackson obliged, speaking into his radio as the men continued down the road with rifles set out in front of them. The shooting persisted in the distance and Wyatt could feel the sweat dripping down his face and into his eyes. It was several moments before Patrick's platoon came back with an answer.

"They got us pinned down here, we got one hit. Coming from a rooftop!" The radio crackled and the Marine came back on and rattled off the coordinates.

Wyatt took out his satellite phone, speaking intently into it, telling command they needed backup before ordering his Marines down a side street where they knew they would find Patrick and his unit. The men jogged with rifles trained and ready for action. When they reached the road where the shooting was happening, Wyatt couldn't see Patrick and his men at first, only the shooters on the opposite roof firing down into the street below. He ordered his men behind a cement barricade, setting his rifle on the side of it and aiming toward the roof in front of him.

Once they fired, Wyatt knew the insurgents' focus would be taken off of Patrick and put on them instead, which was what he wanted. He put his best riflemen next to him and commanded them to fire.

"Jackson, you're coming with me to get Sergeant McMurtry's unit outta there. I want the rest of you trained on that fucking rooftop, you hear me?" He looked into the eyes of his young privates, knowing their intensity, their need for battle. "I want you to fucking kill them, right now. Do you hear me?" he spit out, his ice blue eyes terrifying in contrast to his tanned skin.

"Yes, sergeant!" they roared back before firing.

It worked just as he planned. The insurgents turned and began firing at Wyatt's unit and they fired back as Wyatt and Jackson slipped behind a building heading to where they knew Patrick and his men would be pinned down. When they reached the back of the building, Wyatt looked around and noted that the windows were boarded up entirely.

"Kick this through!" he demanded of Jackson, both men raising their feet to kick through the wood nailed haphazardly into the doorframe. It only took a few kicks each to loosen the boards enough for them to bust through using their shoulders. The building was quiet and looked deserted. Wyatt cleared the room in front of him, listening hard for signs of Patrick.

"Pat!" he screamed loudly. There was a desperation in his voice that he hoped Jackson didn't hear.

Jackson and Wyatt kicked through several walls, listening for the shots and voices before they finally heard them.

"Marines!" Jackson yelled before kicking through a flimsy wall that led to them.

Wyatt busted through the door and assessed the scene. Several Marines had their rifles pointed through the front window, firing up to the insurgents on the rooftop across the street. Some assisted, handing them ammo. Wyatt searched the room and looked at the scared Marines' faces.

"Where's Sergeant McMurtry?" he screamed above the firing.

One of the Marines helping with ammo looked toward the back of the room, eyes wide and frightened.

"There," he said back to him.

Patrick lay on the floor at the back of the room with one of his young Marines next to him. Wyatt rushed to him, taking off his pack and discarding his rifle on top of it. Patrick shook uncontrollably with blood gushing from his arm and neck, but he mustered a grin looking up at Wyatt.

"My mom's gonna be pissed," he said, his teeth clanging together.

Wyatt put his hands on him immediately, looking for the wound.

"Where is it?" he demanded of the young medic. "Where's he hit?"

"Arm and neck, sergeant," he said, as steadily as he could. "I called for support," he said before Wyatt could ask him.

Wyatt looked back to Patrick's arm. He couldn't believe the amount of blood that was coming from the wound. He'd seen some extreme injuries during his deployments, but there'd only been one other time he'd seen that kind of blood.

"Get another fucking bandage on this," Wyatt commanded, turning his attention to Patrick's neck which was likewise bleeding profusely.

Patrick grinned. "He used to be nice, Paulson," Patrick explained to the young private. "Just a mean ol' Marine, now." He closed his eyes lightly.

"You better keep your fucking eyes open, Pat. I swear to God. You look at me, right fucking now. You see me?" Wyatt grabbed both sides of Patrick's face, looking intensely into this eyes.

"Don't fuck around. You're fine. I need you to stay here. I need you with me. Stop fucking around," Wyatt said, trying to keep his voice steady.

"Sergeant Sterling," Jackson said, sitting down next to Wyatt. "Sergeant, we have reinforcements waiting next to our unit. Medevac is ten minutes out."

Wyatt looked over at Jackson, willing himself to keep hold of his emotions. He nodded once. "Good. We'll bring these guys out the way we came. I need at least four to carry Sergeant McMurtry."

"Yes, Sergeant," Jackson said, looking down at Patrick and the blood that soaked the floor around him. "Is he gonna make it?"

Wyatt had to stop himself from punching Jackson across the jaw, opening his mouth to speak before closing it hard, the muscles in his cheek rippling fiercely.

"Get the fuck away from me and get these men ready to go," he seethed.

"Yes, Sergeant," he said, scurrying away.

Wyatt sat back down next to Patrick, wrapping his bandages tight again, and Patrick moaned in pain.

"We're going right now. Pat! Pat, listen hang tight. I'm getting you outta here. Don't fuck around, man. I need you here, alright?"

"Mia," Patrick moaned.

Wyatt's heart tightened, and he felt like he was going to vomit. How many times had he seen someone like this, this way? Thinking, as they drifted out of consciousness, about the people they loved most.

"Pat, you listen to me, are you listening?" he said, speaking into his face again. "I promised her I'd bring you home. I'm going to fucking bring you home."

Wyatt choked on his last word before swallowing hard and looking up to the young Marines staring down at the sergeants with wide, shocked eyes.

"Help me carry him!" Wyatt commanded.

They brought him out the labyrinth that he and Jackson had kicked down only a short while ago, reaching the back of the building and finally emerging into the hot summer's day with the sun high in the sky. They could still hear firing in the distance, but it had dissipated quite a bit, Wyatt knew, because of the reinforcements who had been called to crush the insurgents. That alone was the only thing stopping him from storming the rooftop and killing them all with his bare hands.

They sat on the side of the building, Wyatt squatting down next to Patrick who continued to slip in and out of consciousness. When he heard the medevac in the distance he turned back to Patrick and gripped his hand.

"Pat! Medevac is here. You're gonna go now," Wyatt said, a lump forming in his throat.

Patrick nodded slow and fluttered his eyes open to look at his friend. "Wy..." he started, unable to keep speaking.

Tears came to Wyatt's eyes as hard as he tried to fight them. He nodded down at Patrick. "You're my brother," he said quietly into his ear. "You're my brother and I need you, ok? I need you, Pat."

Patrick tried to respond, his mouth opening the slightest bit before closing. The last thing Wyatt saw before he put him on the helicopter was the slight smile resting on his lips.

The barracks in Afghanistan were crude even by Marine standards. Thrown together years ago now, they had to be continuously added onto. Since Marines normally built them themselves, the workmanship was less than stellar. But, as they'd been told since boot camp, real Marines needed nothing more than what was on their bodies to survive.

Wyatt sat on a rickety picnic table toward the edge of camp where he and Patrick normally had coffee in the morning. It had been over 24 hours since they lifted Patrick away in the helicopter and there was still no word of him. Wyatt had asked his commanding officers hourly if they'd heard anything, bordering on aggressive when they wouldn't tell him anything. Only that he was in route to Germany where all wounded servicemen went.

The sun was setting in the distance and Wyatt sat with his head in his hands, his stomach pitted out with an awful empty feeling. All he could think of was Gus. And Patrick. How he'd said goodbye to them both the same way, praying hard when they left that they would return. Only Gus never did. And now Patrick. A loss that he didn't know that he would survive.

He rubbed his hands over his shaved head down to his face. His heart ached, but there was something else there this time, too. Something different from when he'd lost Gus. There was anger. A fire that he felt growing in himself so much so that he was afraid what he might do. He couldn't go back into his room since Patrick's stuff was too much for him to be around. The picture of both Patrick and Wyatt standing next to Mia taped to the wood siding of the wall alone would push him over the edge. What would he tell Patrick's mom? What would he tell Mia? He'd made a promise and he'd broken it. What was worse, he knew there was something wrong and didn't follow his gut feeling. Had he done that, maybe it would be him flying to Germany on a plane. Maybe dying, but who would care? He had no one counting on him, not like Patrick did.

"Sergeant Sterling?" Jackson said quietly, slowly approaching Wyatt.

Wyatt spun around and stood, looking at Jackson with haunted eyes. "News?"

Jackson looked down at the ground, shaking his head slowly. "No, Sergeant. I'm sorry."

Wyatt exhaled and sat back down, placing his elbows on his knees.

"What do you need, Private?" he asked shortly.

Jackson shifted the envelopes in his hands. "Mail call, sergeant. I brought- I thought you would want Sergeant McMurtry's mail, too."

Wyatt looked back up to him, then at the mail in his hands. He rarely got mail, sometimes from Garrett, but Patrick was always getting something from his mom or Mia, often addressed to him, as well. He put his hands out and Jackson handed them over before walking silently away. Wyatt looked at the letters in his hands, the first several to Patrick from Mia. He looked at her beautiful handwriting written lovingly across the envelope and felt the lump forming in his throat. The heartbreaking truth that she probably wrote the letter weeks ago, before ever knowing that Patrick wouldn't be there to get it.

Wyatt moved Mia's letters in a pile and looked at the last, larger envelope in the stack. It was a large manila envelope addressed to him. There was no return address but it was postmarked from Arizona. The handwriting looked nothing like Garrett's, but he opened it without thinking much about it. He dumped it to the side and a book came out, a Louis L'amour he hadn't read in years. He rubbed his thumb over the title, *Law of the Desert Born,* before placing it down on the table. His brow furrowed in thought, he pulled out a thick letter inside a smaller envelope.

His heart pounded as he read the words scrawled across it. "Wyatt Earp." He looked at it a long time, making sure he was seeing what was actually in front of him and this wasn't some type of hallucination brought on by stress and grief. His hands started to shake as it finally set in. It was her. After all of these years, she'd written to him. She'd contacted him.

He put the letter down carefully on the table in front of him and looked up at the sky. He couldn't stop himself from shaking, so much so that he was rattling the old table. He stood up and paced, looking down at it. Wyatt Earp. It'd been years since he'd heard that. Years since he'd seen her or heard any word from her. And now, after all of this time, she wanted to contact him. For as many times as he dreamt of it, he never imagined it would feel like this.

Red hot anger seethed inside of him. Losing Patrick, being alone all of this time with no one but him to turn to, war. All of it had irrevocably changed him from the person he was back then. From the person she knew. He was not that boy anymore. He was a Marine now. He'd killed men and not regretted it, not for a second. She didn't even know who that person was. And she never would, he thought.

Wyatt rubbed his hand through his hair again and could feel the sweat collecting near his temples. She'd always told him about the timing of the universe. How things never happened by mistake. That there were no coincidences. And maybe she was right. Maybe it wasn't a coincidence that he would get her letter on that day, with his heart so full of sadness and anger that he could see nothing else.

He picked the letter up off of the table, holding it in his hands for a moment and thinking. His heart wanted to open it. The person he once was wanted to hear what she had to say. But he would never be that person again. That person was gone. His eyes dry and cold, he tore through the letter, ripping it in small pieces and throwing it out into the dust, giving her back to the desert.

V

"Yet it would be your duty to bear it, if you could not avoid it: it is weak and silly to say you cannot bear what it is your fate to be required to bear."
~ Charlotte Brontë, *Jane Eyre*

Charlotte was surprised at how quickly she adjusted to life in Savannah. Her gypsy roots were still intact it seemed since as much as she loved her life in Flagstaff, she felt a sense of relief that was almost palpable when they left. She thought the shop would be much harder to leave, but it wasn't. Probably because it wasn't shutting down like Rose's tiny little Patagonia shop had all of those years ago. It would live on, doors still open, business plan intact except Charlotte would be running it from afar now, leaving the daily management entirely to Willow, who had proven herself hungry and capable of the task.

A few of Rose's psychic friends from Sedona had agreed to commute to Flagstaff a couple days a week for readings and even if they weren't Rose, they'd still bring the seekers coming back. Before they left Georgia they had put in an offer on the Savannah building and headed back to Arizona to finalize their plans and move forward. After Charlotte's tireless work getting it ready, Spirit's Soul Savannah would open its doors just before Christmas that next year. And it was easier that time. Much easier than in Flagstaff when she felt like she was faking it. Like she didn't belong as a businesswoman.

She had a formula now and she knew exactly how to execute it. Her vision for the shop came together the first time she walked the gorgeous old building. The space was a dream compared to the congested quarters of the Flagstaff shop. The old house was three stories tall, leaving room for private offices for Rose and Charlotte on the top floor complete with Rose's favorite, a reading and lounge room where they had their morning meetings and Rose caught her afternoon naps. The middle floors were all dedicated to separate rooms for massage therapists, reiki specialists, and spiritual teachers. The bottom floor was the only one that needed much remodeling. The kitchen was converted into a small coffee shop with a bar and small seating area for patrons. Charlotte had walls torn down, opening up the floor to create room for the shop itself along with a separate room for yoga, which was also offered on the back lawn on nice days.

The shop had been open just over six months and was already the talk of the town. Rose was right, there was a huge metaphysical following in Savannah. Much like Flagstaff, there was a built-in clientele that wanted and needed their services. As usual, Rose quickly made a name for herself and Charlotte marveled how fast Rose made the right friends. She insisted on eating out almost every day, always chatting up the waiters or waitresses, inevitably passing out her card at the end of the encounter.

"Drunk Gorilla marketing," she'd say to Charlotte. "Bet you didn't learn that in your fancy college classes."

And she was effective. The buzz around the shop was infectious and the yoga classes, along with the different services on the second floor, attracted more and more people. People inevitably wanted to buy something, get a reading, or simply sit in the shop and read peacefully with a cup of coffee. The calm environment the women had created was irresistible for patrons.

It was May, a year since she'd graduated college at NAU, and she could hardly believe how much had happened in that one year. She sat in her office that morning, going over their numbers for the previous month and ordering more inventory. Charlotte hardly resembled that girl who showed up in Patagonia all of those years ago. Her long blonde hair was seldom wild around her face anymore and she wore it braided or twisted up in a bun on top of her head, her face warm but serious, not giving anything away. She wore black slacks that hung over high heels, complemented by a silk gray blouse that stuck suggestively to her curvy breasts. She'd taken to dressing more professionally since they arrived there, learning quickly that the businessmen of Savannah were not like those hippie businessmen in Flagstaff who did business in birkenstocks and would have taken her seriously if she showed up to meetings in cutoffs. No, not the southern gentlemen of Savannah. Charlotte learned quickly that to make up for being so young, she'd have to look the part and act it, as well.

"Charlotte!" she heard Rose yell from their adjoining lounge room. "Stop working and come talk to me. I need some motivation!"

Charlotte didn't take her eyes off of her work, but smiled at her aunt's voice. Rose had recently developed a distaste for work in general. Charlotte practically had to beg her to do readings three days a week, and the rest of the time Rose walked around the shop talking to employees and patrons alike, taking yoga classes, and begging Charlotte to stop working so they could go shopping or to lunch.

Charlotte walked into the lounge with her coffee cup in her hand and smiled down at Rose, who sat cross-legged on one of the pillowed floral couches they'd purchased for the room. Despite the fact that Charlotte didn't get to enjoy it much, the room was her favorite in the whole house. The bay window overlooked the river and Rose had spared no expense making the room comfortable with cozy couches, bookshelves, plants, and that picture of the San Xavier Mission hanging proudly on the wall.

"You've only got three readings today. Plus, I have a new plan to make it easier on you," Charlotte said, knowing how much Rose wanted to sit in the quiet room and read a book instead. Rose flung herself over the couch dramatically, flinging her colorful open blouse out to the side of her.

"I'm sick. I can't work today. Call me in sick," she said, covering her eyes with her arm.

Charlotte laughed and sat down opposite her, crossing one long leg over the other.

"No dice, old lady. I need you today. Three readings. Three readings at $150 a pop. Not a bad way to make a living. You could be out on a street corner instead, you know?" Charlotte grinned.

"Is that supposed to be a threat? Sex for money? Jesus, doesn't sound half bad right now," Rose said, sitting up and taking her tea cup in her hands.

Rose liked Savannah alright, but she had yet to hit her stride on the dating market since she hated the way southern men talked in a sugary sweet way, words dripping off their lips thick in accent.

"All these southern gentlemen," she lamented, "and not one Rhett Butler."

Charlotte, a pro at wrangling her aunt, redirected her attention promising that they could go to her favorite restaurant for lunch between readings, even writing it down in her calendar for good measure.

"And it's Friday," Charlotte coaxed her. "I won't even work tomorrow."

Rose lifted her eyebrows at her niece. "So we can go to the beach then? I think there's networking to be done there, so technically we will be working."

Charlotte sighed, checking her watch before looking back at Rose. "Ok, fine. But if you're going to try and whore me out again and call it networking, count me out."

Rose waved her hand at Charlotte and set her head back on the couch, closing her eyes for meditation. "I gave up on you a long time ago. You might as well be a nun."

Turkey was different from any other place he'd been. Even after his time in Iraq and Afghanistan, he'd never experienced anything quite like it. The city was bustling, a far cry from his Arizona hometown. The place was jammed with people and cars so much so that he often found himself overwhelmed and short of breath, on the verge of panic because of all of the people around him. It was the Marine in him, the warrior inside that made him assess every person he encountered, evaluating the threat just like any good Marine would.

The people were mostly friendly, although Wyatt often encountered those just like he'd seen in the Middle East. That skeptical look, shifting eyes, and scrutinizing foreheads that no amount of smiling or friendliness could alleviate. Not that there was much time for him to interact with the citizens of Ankara anyway since he spent most of his time inside the thick cement walls of the embassy itself, planning security details, completing paperwork, and scheduling his Marines to their posts. A staff sergeant now, he'd received several meritorious promotions to get to where he was, sought out by his superiors for embassy duty.

The job was considered by many to be prestigious, but for the life of him, Wyatt couldn't figure out why.

He knew there must be something wrong with him that he was so bored, even in a position that was still considered to be quite dangerous. Embassy attacks, both historic and contemporary, were something all Marines knew about from the time they entered basic training. But it wasn't war. This, being within the walls of the sturdy fortress, was nothing like the heart-pumping things he'd had to do next to his brothers. Next to Patrick. Maybe that was why he was so bored, he'd thought more than once. The fact that this was his first assignment without Patrick next to him changed everything.

It had been a year since he'd put Patrick on that helicopter. A year since he'd felt the world get ripped out from underneath him. A year since he'd made that decision to be done with Charlotte for good, ripping all she had to say into shreds. All that time and still he would wake in the barracks of the embassy in a cold sweat, panicked that Patrick didn't make it out alive. But he had, Wyatt would have to remind himself. He would breathe deeply and remember that day, days after Patrick had been shot when Wyatt finally got that satellite phone call with Mia crying on the other end.

"Wy!" she cried through the phone.

Wyatt stood in the command center and had to put his hand against the wall to steady himself. Hearing her voice, he thought Patrick was gone, until the line crackled again and her small sobbing voice came through again.

"He's going to be ok," she said, her voice shaking.

His knees had weakened upon hearing it, a sense of relief like a wave washing over him. He crouched down, putting his hand over his face to avoid the stares of the other Marines in the room.

"Wy? Wy, are you there?" she said, still crying.

"I'm here, Mia. I heard you," he said, his voice cracking into the phone.

Mia laughed and cried at the same time, talking rapidly into the phone. "I'm here with him. He's going to be ok. He wants to talk to you, but he's not allowed to talk too long."

"Ok Mia. Ok. Thank you," Wyatt said, longing for his friends with every fiber of his being.

"Wy, come home safe to us. Ok?" Mia choked on her words and Wyatt felt his heart strain to think of her and how terrified she must have been.

"I promise," he said quietly.

The phone rustled around a bit before Wyatt heard Patrick croak into the phone.

"Cowboy," he said, a smile in his voice.

Wyatt rubbed his hand over his tearing eyes, and grinned widely.

"Pat. You fucker. You scared the hell outta me," he said, stopping before he sobbed into the phone worse than Mia.

"My dick still works," Patrick croaked, and Wyatt could hear Mia scolding him in the background.

Wyatt laughed, his eyes still brimming with tears. "You got shot in the arm and neck. Why wouldn't it?"

"I'm just telling you. I always wonder if people's dicks still work when they get hurt. Just didn't want you to have to wonder," he said laughing painfully into the phone.

"Alright, good to know, man. I know you can't talk long," Wyatt said.

There were so many things that he wanted to tell him. How awful it was without him there. How no one, even his Marine brothers he loved, could understand him like Patrick could. How he didn't know if he could do it there without him. But he couldn't say any of it. Men, Marines, didn't say things like that. Especially not to someone who was wounded in combat.

"Cowboy? Thank you," Patrick said, the line crackling. Wyatt could hear his unsteady voice on the other end. "Come home safe, brother."

Wyatt nodded, unable to speak back to him for a moment before responding.

"I will, Pat. I'll see you soon," he said quietly back.

And with that, Wyatt finished the rest of his tour on his own. He had to learn how to function without Patrick right next to him. He felt like his arm was missing without him there anytime he wanted to bounce something off of someone, often catching himself opening his mouth to ask him something only to realize, once again, that he wasn't there. But perspective is everything and Wyatt didn't grieve it as much as he once would have, mostly because he knew what it would've meant to lose him for good.

Wyatt looked out of his office window that overlooked a small cement courtyard with a couple of trees and benches interspersed to make the place seem at least a little bit hospitable. He sighed heavily, pulling at the collar of his dress blues, tight around his neck. Catching a glimpse of himself in the reflection of the window he almost couldn't believe what he saw. A tall, sturdy man with a crew cut stared back at him, his eyes sharp and cold.

Spirit's Soul Savannah was booming that summer. Charlotte had a plan and she executed it, making sure that she avoided any mistakes she'd made in Flagstaff. The place ran smoothly from the jump. Soon, the community of Savannah jumped onboard. Yoga classes brought in new people daily and they inevitably utilized more of what the shop had to offer, thus growing the business exponentially. Tourist season was high and the shop became a must-see for folks passing through town, as did Rose's readings.

She was booked out for months and even though she'd begged Charlotte to take on some of the readings, Charlotte had still refused, citing the insane amount of work that came from operating both the Savannah and Flagstaff locations. And Rose couldn't argue that. Charlotte worked constantly, even from home. She and Rose had purchased a quaint Victorian home in downtown Savannah just blocks from the shop, complete with a small guest house on the side where Charlotte volunteered to live. It was her compromise with Rose since her aunt still insisted they shouldn't live together like "dried up old spinsters."

On weekends Rose would come to her door with a fresh espresso in hand for Charlotte who was inevitably working on her laptop or on her phone speaking sternly to vendors or employees of both shops. Rose would sit impatiently and wait for her to finish so they could meditate together in the grass or sitting on the porch side by side with the hum of the city around them, surprisingly comforting. There were a lot of things that Charlotte had given up to build the businesses to what they were, but meditation was not one of them. It was such an important part of her life, of who she was, that it gave her the idea for Rose to teach classes at the shop.

Rose was skeptical at first, but after the first couple of workshops, she was sold on the idea. Charging by the head, Charlotte organized a Saturday every month for workshops, and a day of yoga, meditation, and lunch followed by class with Rose. She knew her aunt well enough to know that she couldn't give the woman an itinerary on what to teach, but would instead make a suggestion to her like, "How about talk about energy cleaning?", and that would be all it took. Rose came alive speaking in front of people, feeding off of the energy and the laughter of the crowd so much that Charlotte often thought her aunt may have missed her calling as a standup comedienne.

At the end of class, which was always informative and entertaining, Rose would do a gallery reading, picking out random people to read, always to the oohs and ahhs of the audience, alive with the magic of being in the same room with Rose. Charlotte often sat in on her class, watching her aunt in awe and always learning more from her even though she'd technically been her student for years. Her perspective on the world never grew old to Charlotte, and every time she heard Rose speak she wished she could be more like her. That she, too, could see the world in the way her aunt did. But there was no way to change who she really was inside, she knew that. The edges in her life always kept her hard. Kept her tough.

It was nearing the end of summer and Rose's classes were steadily more packed. Charlotte stood at the back of the room watching Rose at the front of the class finishing up her gallery reading for the day, her small, hourglass frame commanding the audience.

"Students, I want to thank you so much for coming today. Wasn't it a beautiful day?" she said, smiling out into the audience, her floral dress sweeping the floor as she paced comfortably around the front of the room.

"I want to leave you all with something to think about. Something to take with you as you go," Rose stood still and sighed, closing her eyes briefly before she continued.

"In the spiritual world, people talk a lot about miracles. About big miraculous things that are supposed to happen in our lives. Every religion, every faith speaks of miracles, and if you think about it, they all have something in common: they're all earth-shattering, unbelievable things that are so otherworldly that they've become myths. They've become something that we think is impossible. Something we will never encounter."

The room was quiet as she spoke, every eye on her.

"I want to tell you a secret, ok? I want to tell you something that most people simply cannot understand about this beautiful world we live in. Miracles are not what we think they are. They aren't these unreachable, unbelievable things. Miracles happen to us every day. Only we don't notice. We can't see it."

Rose stopped again and leveled her eyes at Charlotte in the back of the room.

"I don't know everything about this crazy universe, I would never claim to. But I can tell you this: look for miracles, and you will find them."

Charlotte locked eyes with her aunt and couldn't look away. She couldn't understand why her heart pounded hearing her words echo through the room.

"God grants miracles. God grants miracles if we only know where to look."

After months in Turkey, Wyatt came to the realization that he hated it there. There was nothing wrong with country itself, he was just bored. He was constantly second-guessing his decision to agree to embassy duty. The war was still going strong and every day he would wake to read the reports from the day before and feel the pull to be back in that place with his men, doing something, anything but being in that cold embassy building, pushing paper and polishing his shoes. He looked every bit the put together Marine, but his heart wasn't in it, missing the dirt and the grime, his unshaven face and dusty boots of the Middle East.

He'd told Patrick this each time he'd written to him or spoken to him on the phone, teasing him that Patrick should have stayed active and been the one to be on embassy duty since he loved being clean so much. That would have suited him better than the rough conditions of Iraq or Afghanistan any day. But Patrick was a long ways away from him now and that was part of the reason he felt like he didn't belong. Not only because he was used to Patrick being there, but because his friend had moved on, he was no longer a Marine, and, what's more, he didn't seem to really care. He adapted as he always did to his new life as a college student in Miami with Mia.

The truth was, Wyatt was jealous of him. Only, he checked himself every time he felt that envy hit his heart. Reminding himself how much Patrick deserved it. How he'd almost not made it out at all. Wyatt had to remind himself that he should stop being so selfish and be happy for his friend instead. And he was. Ultimately, he knew he was afraid that he wouldn't adapt like Patrick did when he left the Marines.

Wyatt's time was coming. He would have to decide soon what he was doing. He'd spent almost six years in the Marine Corps and he had one more to go. Soon he'd get the call, get the formal letter. The one that asked what he wanted to do, sign the re-upping paperwork or sign the discharge paperwork. And he didn't know what to do. What's more, he didn't have anyone to ask about it other than Patrick, and he already knew his opinion. He'd mentioned it to Garrett the last time they spoke on the phone, but the old man was non-committal, telling Wyatt that God would put him right where he belonged anyway, so he should just pray.

Wyatt didn't have the heart to tell his old friend that he didn't pray, didn't know if he believed in a God anyhow, not after what he'd seen. So he stayed quiet on the other end of the phone and allowed Garrett to change the subject to the weather, which Wyatt found oddly comforting. He loved hearing anything about Arizona, about the ranch, even though it'd been years since he'd been there. Years since he'd set foot in the desert of his home. He'd never felt farther from Arizona than he did in Turkey with the skyscrapers and congestion of the city all around him. Mostly he stuck to the embassy on his days off and read or worked out, but sometimes he had to leave, feeling like the walls were closing in on him.

It was recommended that Marines never left the embassy alone, so Wyatt adhered to that even though he felt like being alone most of the time. That Saturday, a young private named Scott Hubble came with him to walk through a local marketplace. He was a foot shorter than Wyatt and talked constantly about his Louisiana home, his thick accent making it difficult for Wyatt to understand him.

Fall came fast in Turkey and the men walked down the busy streets with their hands tucked in their pockets, their civilian jeans still making them stick out among the locals.

"Why they all look at us like that?" Hubble complained, looking around at vendors they passed by. "Always scowling and shit."

Wyatt shrugged. "Could be worse. They're not shooting at us."

Hubble nodded. "Yeah, that's right. I forget- how many deployments you got?" He grinned up at Wyatt's serious face. "What, three?"

"Four," Wyatt said briefly, not looking back at him.

Hubble whistled. "I hope I get to go after this. Bet I am. You were in Fallujah, right? Fuck, man, you're so lucky."

Wyatt looked down at his feet moving through the street, taking a deep breath so he didn't say something he regretted. He thought of his feet slipping on the blood on the floor inside that house in Fallujah. He thought of Gus's face, of the faint squeeze of his hand.

"Yeah," Wyatt said.

The men walked through several shops, buying up local jerky and fruits they could bring back to the embassy. Hubble bought gifts for his family, talking incessantly the whole time about his sisters, his mom who he called Mother, and his dad who he called Daddy. Even though Wyatt couldn't stand the kid, he couldn't deny Hubble had a good heart, taking the time to pick out things for even extended members of his family.

"Here, let's go in here. They have fabric and Mother loves to sew things. Been asking me to find something so she can enter it in the fair."

They ducked into the small shop tucked away on the busy city sidewalk. The shop was quiet and peaceful and smelled of incense and essential oils. Wyatt looked around at the merchandise and found some dangly handmade earrings he knew Mia would love. He ran his hand over the fabric, finding something familiar about the colorful pattern. He looked up and looked directly into the eyes of an older Turkish woman. She wore a gray hijab and had striking green eyes that stared back at Wyatt.

"Hello," he said quietly before remembering himself. "Merhaba."

"Hello," she said, her face remaining even. "You're here."

Wyatt looked around, suddenly uncomfortable with her probing gaze shooting through him.

"I- I'd like to buy these earrings." He said, holding them up to her.

"I'm gonna go next door, man," Hubble said, walking out.

"Ok, be right there," Wyatt said after him.

The woman stared at Wyatt a moment longer before turning to the back of the shop and disappearing. Wyatt looked around, confused, and thought about putting the earrings down and leaving.

"You drink this." The woman came back and walked in front of him, coming within inches of him. She held a small cup of Turkish coffee in her hand.

"Oh, no. No, thank you," Wyatt said, starting to refuse.

"Drink," she said, grabbing his hand and placing the cup in it. "Come."

The woman turned and walked to the room she'd just come from and Wyatt reluctantly followed. The room was the size of a walk-in closet. Colorful tapestries hung from every corner and pillows littered the floor.

"Sit," she said, choosing a pillow of her own.

Wyatt squatted down and sat awkwardly on one of the pillows. He crossed his feet in front of him, his cumbersome cowboy boots making it difficult to sit comfortably.

"I just want to buy these," he said, holding up the earrings again.

She nodded. "Forty," she said, taking them from him and wrapping them in tissue.

Wyatt handed over the money and took a sip of his drink. Turkish coffee was by far his favorite thing about the country. It was thick and rich just the way Garrett used to make coffee at the ranch. Only this was stronger.

"Thank you," Wyatt said, sipping it and looking at her. She still scrutinized him, her sharp green eyes wrinkled in concentration.

"I dreamt of you last night," she said matter-of-factly. "I knew you'd come."

Wyatt could feel his heart pound in his chest. His palms started to sweat and he laughed nervously.

"Me? But I don't know you," he said, laughing nervously.

"Finish that," she demanded.

Wyatt gulped down what was left of the small cup, hoping that would get him out of there faster. No sooner did he finish then the old woman grabbed the cup from his hands and put it close in front of her face. She looked down into the grounds and finally cracked a smile, looking up at him.

"So much light. So much light," she said to Wyatt's stoic face. "You don't know, do you? You don't know how special you are."

Wyatt opened his mouth to speak, but closed it soon after. It had been years since he'd sat across from Rose and she'd told him the same thing. How he could do anything. Years since Rose sat there and told him, as natural as anything, about Patrick coming into his life. But despite that, he still couldn't believe. He wouldn't let himself believe in something like that. Something so impossible. His mind always brought him back to the logical reasons for things.

"Your journey here. It's almost over. You must go home."

Wyatt stayed quiet, his mind growing skeptical. Every American this woman encountered was on a journey that would end at some point. Tourists, military people, everyone. He was almost relieved that she was a fake, that he could find a reason to write off what she said to him. The possibility of it being real was dangerous for him on a lot of levels. As if sensing his skepticism, the woman looked up into his eyes once again, leveling him with her eyes that were so much like Charlotte's it was eerie.

"The woman from the desert. The woman from the desert still prays for you. Every day she prays for you."

Wyatt could feel the lump forming in his throat and he couldn't respond or smile. His heart clenched inside of him, giving way to her even though his mind told him not to. Wyatt stood to leave, cutting the woman off as she began to speak again.

"My friend's waiting for me. I have to go. Thank you–"

"No," she said standing and blocking him from the door with her tiny body. Wyatt towered over her, looking down, terrified at what she might say next.

"Pray for her. Pray for a miracle," she said, tears forming in her green eyes.

"I'm dying!" Rose cried, holding her hand to the side of her face. "My fucking tooth feels like it's falling out!"

Charlotte frowned over at her in the dentist chair. She knew her aunt had a flair for the dramatic, but she could tell Rose was in pain. She'd banged on her door early that morning, begging Charlotte to take her to the dentist. Half of one of her molars fell out when Rose was brushing her teeth that morning.

"It didn't even hurt, for God's sake! Just fell out of my head out of nowhere!"

"Shhh, Rose. Keep your voice down. They said they'd be in soon." Charlotte scooted her chair closer to her aunt and held her hand, trying to send her any peace she could muster in the cold office.

"Great, now you wanna believe in magical shit? I have to be dying for you to use your powers?" Rose said, still holding her face.

Charlotte laughed, shushing her again. "What are you talking about?"

"I feel what you're doing, kid, but it's no use. I feel like someone took a baseball bat to my face." She cringed. "Fuck, me, what is taking so long?"

"Here I am, I'm sorry about the wait, Ms. Holt," the dentist said, walking into the room.

Charlotte looked up at him and was immediately uncomfortable with the way she felt. He was tall, at least six feet with a solid muscular build that was prevalent even under his white doctor's coat. His short dark hair was neatly trimmed and his face cleanly shaven, exposing a wide dazzling smile. His light brown eyes looked down at Rose, then to Charlotte sitting next to her. He stared at her a moment, losing his footing before looking back to Rose.

"Ms. Holt, I'm Dr. Russo," he said, holding out his hand for her to shake.

"Hi, I'm fucking dying," Rose said, shaking it briefly, then falling back to the chair dramatically.

Dr. Russo grinned out of the side of his mouth, trying to suppress a laugh.

"I'm sorry, we'll get you feeling better fast," he said, settling in his chair and looking back to Charlotte. "And are you a- friend? Or?"

"I'm her niece," she said, trying not to make eye contact with him.

He extended his hand across Rose's body to her. "Dr. Russo," he said, looking her square in the face and grinning widely at her.

"Charlotte," she said taking his large hand in hers.

"Nice to meet you, Charlotte," he said, holding her in his sights for a moment scrutinizing her face.

He set to work asking Rose about her tooth, how long she'd been feeling pain, and a little about her medical history. Rose gave her dramatic, profanity-laced responses which he took in stride, smiling and laughing at her. Charlotte noticed that he patted her arm before asking her to lay back so he could take a look. Mask over his face, he set to work, poking around Rose's mouth while he spoke in code to the hygienist next to him, referencing all of her teeth by number.

Charlotte still sat close to Rose, holding her hand as he worked. She tried not to notice how beautifully his hands moved. They were large and manly, but there was something elegant about them, as well. His eyes were sharp and scrutinizing behind his safety glasses. More than once, Charlotte caught herself looking at him and the way his brow stayed furrowed, concentrated with work.

"Alright, Ms. Holt. Let's sit you up," he said, moving back and removing his glasses and mask.

The chair moved up and the hygienist left the room, leaving the three of them together. Dr. Russo rolled his chair close to Rose and looked down at her while removing his gloves.

"So what happened is, you basically had a cavity deep in there that you couldn't feel for a long time. And you said you haven't been to the dentist in how long?"

"Fucking 20 years! I floss!" she said in defense of herself.

Dr. Russo looked to Charlotte and back to Rose again. "I know, I know. You have really great teeth, but if you would have come in for a checkup we would have seen this in an X-ray," he said as gently as he could. "But obviously it's too late for that now, so, I'm sorry to say, we're going to have to do a root canal on this."

Rose cried out, holding her face, her eyes wide like a child in fear. Charlotte took a firm hold on her hand, sensing her fear.

"Dr. Russo," Charlotte started, "Could you- could you give her something for the pain? Or just to calm down? She's not usually like this."

"Of course. Yes. We will do that right away." Dr. Russo pried his eyes off of Charlotte and back to Rose. "I'm going to get you feeling better fast, ok, Ms. Holt?"

"It would make me feel better if you didn't call me that. Makes me feel old. It's Rose," she said grumpily.

Dr. Russo set his head back on his shoulders, laughing.

"Feisty, I like it." He grinned. "Then you call me Tony," he said, looking to Charlotte. To her surprise, he extended his hand again.

"Tony," he said, taking her hand and shaking it firmly.

"Charlotte," she said stupidly back.

"I remember," he said lower, looking back to Rose who was squirming in the chair again. "Ok, Rose. Let's get this party started. How do you react to happy gas?"

"Fucking beautifully. I don't care what it is. Give me two," Rose said.

Soon the hygienist was back, getting Rose prepped for the procedure. Charlotte had to make room for her so she moved to a chair closer to Dr. Russo, looking over at Rose with her eyes closed in the chair.

"So what do you ladies do?" he said, putting a fresh set of gloves on and turning to Charlotte for an answer.

Charlotte opened her mouth to speak, but then closed it again, thinking better of telling him the whole truth. Rose was always so much better at explaining it to people, but being that she was unable at the moment, it fell to Charlotte. She sat a bit taller in her chair, her long blonde braid moving off her shoulder as she did.

"We have a- a metaphysical shop here in town. Yoga classes- things like that," Charlotte said, looking anywhere except back into his eyes.

Tony raised his eyebrows at her, his face giving way to an interested smile.

"Really? Whoa, that's cool. What's it called?"

"It's called Spirit's Soul. It's- it's down on the Riverwalk."

He nodded, listening intently. "Nice. Ok, I'm new here so I don't know where much is. Just moved here last month."

Charlotte nodded. "We're pretty new, too. Only been here a year."

"Where are you from?" he said, unfazed by the hygienists seemingly doing all of the work to ready themselves for the procedure.

"Arizona," Charlotte said, feeling the pull for what she now considered to be her home state.

"Way out west. I'm from Long Island. Feels like a long way from home, here," he said, smiling at her.

Charlotte smiled shyly, ignoring her stomach which suddenly felt like it was churning. "I know what you mean."

"Yoga shop, Charlotte?" Rose said, pulling the mask off of her face. She grinned drunkenly, giggling loudly. "She's trying to make us sound normal, Doc. We're psychics."

Tony swung his head back to Charlotte, his eyes wide and his mouth agape.

"Psychics?" he said, shocked.

Charlotte smiled nervously and waved her hand. "My aunt is. I'm not. She just says that."

"What a crock of shit," Rose said, flapping herself back down to the chair. "She has no idea how good she is."

"What about you, Rose? Are you good?" he teased.

"Pfft. I thought I was, but I sure didn't see this bullshit coming. She's the one with the gift."

Tony grinned at Charlotte. She may as well have been naked for how she felt. So exposed and stripped bare in front of him. The way he looked at her made her feel strange and nervous.

"Well," he said, still looking at her before he began, "I'll have to come and get a reading then."

Charlotte looked back at Rose and felt her face flush through. The procedure took over an hour and Charlotte stayed put the entire time. Listening intently to the aftercare directions since Rose was not to be bothered, laying with her eyes shut in the reclined chair.

"And please bring her back in two weeks so I can check it out. That crown was tricky just because of where it was so I'll need to- I'll need to check it," he said, smiling over at Charlotte.

"Ok, thank you, Dr. Russo," Charlotte said, standing.

He stood at the same time and Charlotte noticed the sheer size of him. His chest was broad and his biceps busted from under his lab coat.

"It's Tony," he said, staring back into her eyes.

"Yes, Tony–" she said, collecting her belongings. "I'll make sure she comes back for her checkup."

"Very nice to meet you, Charlotte," he said, shooting her one last smile before leaving the room.

The barracks were cold and lonely on embassy duty. Wyatt separated himself from the men intentionally. His quarters were separate, but he purposely limited the amount of time he interacted with the others. In part because he was the supervisor of most of them, but also because he didn't feel like any of them understood him the way his other Marines had. Those who stood beside him and fought in combat understood the things that couldn't be spoken. It was something that these Marines, most of them fresh off of basic training and a brief tour in the U.S., couldn't possibly comprehend.

And so a lot of time was spent in his sparsely decorated room, his cot impeccably made and only a picture of his unit from Fallujah sitting on the nightstand. He sat on his bed, shirtless in only his boxer briefs. The day's work was over and he was only months from leaving that place. He still hadn't made up his mind what he was going to do with his life and, in true form, he was inwardly ripping himself apart over the decision, either way seemingly a failure in his eyes.

Wyatt sighed, lying back in his bunk and looking up at the ceiling. He knew nights like this were dangerous for him. All of that time to think. It was the exact reason why back home he'd entertained himself going out to bars and chasing all of those women that Patrick disapproved of so. But there would be none of that here even though there were female Marines on base. Wyatt learned early on what his recruiters had told him, "Don't shit where you eat." And so it was loneliness instead. And quiet. And time to think of all of the mistakes he'd made.

Wyatt turned to his side and pulled out the drawer on his bedside table, removing the book. The day after Wyatt had ripped up her letter, Jackson showed up in his room with the Louis L'amour book in his hands, returning it to his sergeant, since everyone knew he was the only one who read books like that. Wyatt took it, mumbling a thank you and tucking it away in his things, forgetting about it completely because of Patrick and the remainder of the deployment. It was only once he was home that he unpacked it, holding it in his hands there in the barracks.

He cracked it open and the prayer card fell out onto the floor. He picked it up and ran his thumb over the faded picture of St. Michael, reading the words over and over again.

St. Michael the Archangel,
defend us in battle.
Be our defense against the wickedness and snares of the Devil.
May God rebuke him, we humbly pray,
and do thou,
O Prince of the heavenly hosts,
by the power of God,
thrust into hell Satan,
and all the evil spirits,
who prowl about the world
seeking the ruin of souls. Amen.

He put the card back in the book, promising himself he'd get rid of it. Put it somewhere. Only he didn't. He put it away in his closet only to pack it in his bag at the last minute before leaving for embassy duty where he brought it out on nights like this. Nights when there was no other place for his heart to go.

He held the book in his hands, running his fingers over the title again, thinking of how she probably had done the same. How her hands had once cradled the same book he was touching. Wyatt closed his eyes, trying to fight what he felt happening inside of himself. That Wyatt was gone, and so was she, he reminded himself over and over again as he fell asleep, dreaming only of her, and a soft Arizona breeze running through her long hair.

It was workshop day at the shop that fall weekend and as Charlotte hustled around the shop getting everything ready, she silently thanked her guides that Rose had recovered from her tooth ailment in time for the day. She'd moped around for a few days after the procedure, but gone back to her follow-up appointment without Charlotte and returned in a much better mood, talking animatedly about the Italian Stallion Dentist, as she dubbed him. Charlotte knew that if she had finally noticed how good-looking he was, she was certainly on the mend.

The workshops had grown so much that Charlotte couldn't avoid teaching in some capacity any longer. She still refused to do readings, but agreed to lead the guided meditation class instead. Thankfully Willow was visiting that weekend, so Charlotte put her to work teaching a yoga class and wrangling the patrons in general.

The women stood around the front desk as the customers filed in for the day, Charlotte trying to focus both Rose and Willow on the itinerary of the day.

"So yoga first, Willow. Then we'll split up into smaller meditation groups, then lunch, then Rose will take them for the final class and gallery reading. Got it?" Charlotte said, looking over at her.

Willow's hair was even longer than when Charlotte had first met her, falling almost to her bottom. Years without drugs had only enhanced her beauty, her skin pale and clear and her eyes as piercing as ever. One habit she never shook was dressing provocatively, always wearing form-fitting clothes with her breasts spilling out of her top. She leaned on the counter nonchalantly, her white breasts peeking out.

"Got it, General," she said, grinning over at Rose conspiratorially.

"It's not so bad," Rose said, stretching her arms over her head, "She usually has me done in time for a nap." She winked.

Charlotte looked over the papers stacked in front of her, laughing and shaking her head. "Yes, Aunt Rose. I received the nap memo. I will have you done in time, I promise–"

"What the fuck is that?" Willow said, straightening up and looking toward the door.

Tony Russo sauntered through the front door wearing loose black sweatpants and a white t-shirt hugging his biceps. His dark hair was gelled, perfectly in place, and a slow smile spread across his face as he walked toward the front desk, locking eyes with Charlotte.

"Dr. Tony!" Rose said, separating herself and walking to him enthusiastically. "I hoped you'd come! Welcome, welcome," she said, standing on her toes to give him the standard Rose welcome for good-looking men, hugging him tight against her.

Charlotte's heart pounded in her chest and she reminded herself to take a deep breath, getting a hold of herself to give him a friendly, but not too friendly, smile.

"Fuck me running," Willow said under her breath to Charlotte.

"Now, Dr. Tony, you remember Charlotte, of course. And this is Willow. She'll be teaching your yoga class today, actually!"

"Hello, Charlotte. Nice to meet you, Willow," Tony said, holding out a hand for Willow to shake.

"A doctor! Oh, Rose. You always know where to find them, don't you?" Willow said, looking up into his eyes and smiling seductively at him.

Tony laughed nervously, breaking eye contact with her and looking at the other ladies. "I'm a dentist. Rose's dentist actually."

"Oh my!" Willow said, her entire demeanor changing. "So nice of you to come!"

"Rose invited me. I had to see what you ladies had going on in here," he said, looking back to Charlotte again.

Charlotte looked back to her paperwork, staying quiet in the exchange. Rose and Willow chatted him up enough so that it didn't matter, though, both fawning over him and placing their hands on his biceps as they laughed at his jokes.

"Ok, doc, class is about to start. Head right down this hallway and Willow will be down soon. You enjoy yourself! I'll see you at lunch, then at class afterwards," Rose said, smiling at him.

"Ok, thank you," Tony said, looking back again at Charlotte who kept herself absorbed in her paperwork.

"Dibs," Willow said as he walked away.

Rose laughed, "Oh no, you little hussy. That's for Charlotte. He's in love. Damn near cried when I didn't bring her to the follow-up appointment."

Charlotte sighed and looked up at Rose, cocking her head to the side. "So you invited him to the workshop? I didn't even have a spot for him. You could have let me know."

"Why? So you could fake a fucking heart attack and get out of it? No, thank you. He's a customer. You better be nice!" Rose said, then found her way upstairs before she had to be back downstairs for lunch.

"What's up with Rose? She looks so skinny," Willow said looking after her.

Charlotte shrugged. "All she does is yoga. Says she's bored here, doesn't care for southern gentlemen. She might be a little depressed."

Willow grinned, "I get that. I'm not one for that sugary-sweet bullshit either. Except for that yummy dentist," she said fanning herself. "If you don't go for this one, you really are a lesbian. Maybe I still have a chance with you after all," she said, winking as she started off to teach her class.

The day was progressing the way Charlotte had planned with all of the students rotating in and out of the meditation and yoga classes. All except for the fact that she'd not planned on him being there. She didn't like to speak in front of other people to begin with, and the fact that he'd be there, watching her with his dark eyes, made her uncomfortable.

When it was his turn to rotate into her class, Charlotte had to make a conscious effort to ground herself and remember what she was there to do. She sat cross-legged in the front of the class with the lights dimmed and candles burning in the corners of the room. The room was filling up when he finally walked into the silent environment. Looking over at her and giving her a timid smile, he sat toward the back of the class where he could see her through a zigzag of people.

Charlotte wore loose-fitting black yoga pants and a tank top with a lotus flower blooming across her chest. Her hair was down, long and wavy and hanging over her breasts. Tony sat and crossed his legs with surprising dexterity. He emulated those around him, putting his hands, palms up, on his thighs. He watched Charlotte closely as she began to speak.

"Good morning," she began, "Many of you might be familiar with meditation and for some of you, this might be your first time. For those of you who are new, I will tell you what my teacher told me the first time I tried to do this: there is no wrong way to meditate. All you have to do is sit quietly with your own thoughts. The goal is to empty your mind of everything that weighs you down, but if you can't do that, it's ok, too," Charlotte said, looking around at the friendly faces in front of her. She tried to avoid looking at Tony for too long, but each time her eyes swept by him, he was there, boring a hole through her with his stare.

"And so to begin, I ask that you choose an intention today. Choose some place for your energy to go. This intention could be big, it could be small. It could even be a dedication to someone else. Listen to your heart and you will find one," Charlotte said gently. "Now gently close your eyes and we will begin."

Charlotte guided the group into a deep meditation, her steady, gentle voice lulling them into a relaxed state until she could feel the energy of the room shift. She closed her eyes then, too, and joined them in meditation. It never failed to reset her. Never failed to clear her mind. She felt as she always did, like she was floating. When her mind came back to her, she knew it was time to end the meditation. She blinked her eyes open and looked out at the students all with their eyes softly closed, some with smiles on their faces.

She scanned the room and stopped when she got to Tony. His hands were still facing upwards on his muscular thighs, but his eyes were open and sparkling as she looked at him. He didn't smile at her, but held her in his gaze so that she could not look away, nothing but the quiet room and dozens of unknowing people surrounding them.

Wyatt returned to the states in time for the New Year, but didn't go back to his base. Instead, he flew directly to Miami in time for Patrick's and Mia's wedding, which they had planned around his return.

"Can't get married without you there, cowboy," Patrick said to him on a phone call to Turkey months ago. "I need my best man. Shit, if Mia had her way, you'd be her maid of honor, too."

And so Wyatt went directly to his friends, fighting back tears as he embraced them at the airport. The Marine Corps was lonely without Patrick there with him, and it was maybe one of the biggest reasons he finally made the decision not to re-up. He had no idea what he would do instead, but after embassy duty, he knew his time in the military needed to be over. There would be no recreating what it had been in those early days with his brothers fighting beside him.

The war was still on, but not like it once was. They were even offering bonuses to people to leave the Marine Corps, a reality that was both attractive and heartbreaking to Wyatt. Was it so long ago that he sat in that recruiter's office and listened to how much he was needed, how someone had to fight for their country? And now they were paying him to leave? He knew logically why it had to be that way, but it didn't change the way it felt to him on the inside.

"Cheers, cowboy," Patrick said, raising his Corona to meet Wyatt's.

They sat on the beach side by side in Miami, not far from where they'd sat years ago on their first trip there, the one that had changed the course of Patrick's life forever.

"Cheers, Pat," Wyatt said, smiling over at his friend and taking a long drink of his beer.

He sat back in his chair and tried his hardest to relax instead of watching all of the people walking by, sizing each of them up as a threat. He looked over at his friend, his eyes landing on the scars on his neck and arm. He looked quickly away so Patrick wouldn't notice. Patrick leaned his head back on his chair and turned his face to look over at Wyatt.

"You ok, man? You seem tense."

"Sorry, man. Just a culture shock, I guess," Wyatt smiled, taking another drink. "Think I've spent more time out of country in the last few years than I have here."

Patrick nodded. "You have, man. Did you decide yet? I mean, if you're gonna re-up?" he asked carefully.

Wyatt nodded and looked out at the ocean. "I'm not going to re-up."

Patrick leaned his body to the other side of his chair and gaped over at Wyatt. "You're fucking kidding me."

Wyatt frowned, furrowing his brow. "Nah, why? I thought you wanted me to quit?"

Patrick laughed and took a swig of his beer. "It's not quitting, cowboy. Shit. You did your time. I'm just shocked you're not going back. I'm happy, man. Shit, Mia's gonna be over the moon about this. Can you tell her?"

Wyatt smiled thinking of her. "I'll tell her tonight at the rehearsal dinner."

Patrick grinned, his white teeth sparkling in the Florida sunshine. "Goddamn, that makes me happy." He stuck out his hand for Wyatt to shake. "Congratulations, man. You'll do great."

Wyatt shook his hand, but his face cringed the slightest bit. "Well, I don't know what the hell I'm gonna do yet, so don't speak too soon."

Patrick waved him off. "Anything. You can do anything you want, man. Look at me, not even done with college yet and the Army wants me for all of these contracting jobs. Shit, man. Making more money than I ever thought I could."

Wyatt nodded, looking down at the sand in front of him. He knew that Patrick had found almost immediate success as a military contractor, but he also knew that life wasn't for him. After the paper pushing he did on embassy duty, he knew himself well enough to know that was not the way for him.

"But it doesn't need to be something like that," Patrick said, reading his thoughts as always, "You could do anything. Really, man. It's gonna be good," he said, putting his hand out on his friend's shoulder and gripping him tightly.

Wyatt looked at his watch. "We better get back and get you ready, groom. I'm not answering to Mia's dad and brothers if you're late," he said, wide-eyed.

Patrick took another long drink, putting his head back on the chair. "Should have eloped. Just had you come along," he said, sighing. "Listen," Patrick said, sitting back up and looking at Wyatt. "I wanna tell you something. We're telling everyone tonight, but I just don't feel right not telling you now."

Wyatt squinted up his eyes at Patrick. "Oh shit, what did you do now?"

Patrick grinned slowly, looking down at the sand and then back at Wyatt again before he began.

"Mia was worried you would be gone again, that's why she'll be so happy you'll be stateside." He took a deep breath. "I'm gonna be a daddy."

Wyatt looked at him and his jaw dropped the slightest bit. Patrick's eyes brimmed as Wyatt stared blankly back at him.

"No," Wyatt said, disbelievingly. "Pat..." Wyatt stood, as did Patrick, and they embraced there on the beach, passersby watching them curiously. Wyatt patted his back hard before pulling away and smiling at him, holding him at arm's length.

"Baby is due July 4th, man. Do you believe it? How do you get more American than that?" Patrick said, grinning back at him.

Wyatt smiled, congratulating him over and over as his heart ached inside of him.

Tony came to every workshop for months, always trying and failing to get Charlotte alone so he could ask her out. It seemed like something always got in the way- mostly, Charlotte making excuses to run off and help a customer or do something for the shop. Anything so she didn't have to sit there and look back into his two dark pools of eyes that always seemed to be on her.

So one day, he changed his tactics. Instead, he made an appointment with Rose for a reading, so that he could talk with Charlotte alone afterwards. When he finally cornered her, he confidently told her that he was taking her to dinner that Saturday and that Rose had already told him that she had no other plans so she couldn't say no. And he was right, she couldn't.

And so, Charlotte found herself dressed and ready to go, sitting on her couch in a long flowing sundress with thin straps accentuating her lean arms and ample breasts. She looked at the clock, sighing before pouring herself a whiskey neat and downing it in one gulp. When he knocked on her door, she felt as ready as she could be, with the whiskey numbing her just the slightest bit.

“Hi,” she said, swinging open the door.

He wore slacks and a button-up white shirt, neatly starched and tucked in, showing off his flat center. A wide smile stretched across his face as he looked her up and down unabashedly.

“You look gorgeous,” he said, leaning in to kiss her on the cheek.

Charlotte mumbled a thank you before grabbing her purse and walking out her front door so he couldn’t look around her little place anymore. Hardly anyone had been there and it felt odd for him to be standing there.

“I thought I’d take you to a great Italian place. You like Italian?” he said, grinning over at her suggestively.

“I do, yes,” she said, fighting the urge to smile. When they got to his car, she wished she’d had another drink before they left. He drove a two-door BMW sports car which made Charlotte gag inwardly. There was nothing she and her Aunt Rose hated more than a man in a fancy sports car. Years of Arizona men in pickup trucks made them averse to anything else.

He opened the door for her and drove them to dinner, all the while keeping the conversation going by asking her about work and telling her funny stories about his week at the office. The restaurant was small and dark with brick walls and candles pouring over the Chianti bottles on each table. He talked all through dinner, telling her about his huge New York Italian family, trying to make her feel comfortable. He finally succeeded after her third whiskey. Charlotte laughed at his jokes and put her guard down just the slightest bit, still trying not to look in his eyes for very long. When dessert came, he ordered them two espressos with Bailey's Irish Cream mixed in.

"So Charlotte, tell me about your family. I've told you all about mine. What about yours?"

Charlotte shrugged, taking a slice off of the cake. "Just me and Aunt Rose. No one else."

He raised his brows, taking a slice of his cake. "Really?" he said, not wanting to pry too much. "Well, she's enough, isn't she?"

Charlotte laughed, feeling her head spin with alcohol. "She is. She just loves you."

"Is that so?" He grinned over at her, the candles reflecting in his eyes. "Well, she's not the one I'm after."

Charlotte took a sip of her coffee and looked away from him.

"Why do you always do that?" he asked candidly.

"What?"

"You always look away from me," he said, staring back at her.

"No, I don't," she argued, smiling slightly.

"You do," he said, his voice low. "Look at me, then. Don't look away."

"Fine," she said jokingly. She leaned her arms on the table and put her face closer to his, a smirk resting on her face.

Tony smiled back, staring into her eyes for what felt like minutes. His smile melted away and there was something else there instead. Something that made Charlotte look away and shift in her chair.

"I win," he whispered to her before the waiter arrived with the check.

The drive home was quieter, mostly because Charlotte felt too buzzed to talk much, afraid of what she might say. When he pulled up to the curb, Charlotte turned to look at him.

"Thank you for dinner," she said politely. "I had fun."

Tony turned off the car and looked over at her, running his hand through his hair. "Did you? I don't know. I can't ever tell if you're telling the truth."

Charlotte balked, looking back at him with a furrowed brow.

"What the fuck does that mean?" she said shortly.

Tony laughed, his jaw dropping a bit.

"No, no. I just meant. I don't know, I feel like you're holding back or something," Tony said, scrambling.

Charlotte could feel her head spinning and the whiskey in her veins, her temper triggered.

"Is that right?" she said sarcastically. "Ok then. This car is stupid and men who drive sports cars are usually overcompensating for something," she said, swinging the door open to get out.

She walked briskly down the long path to her guest house and she could hear him behind her laughing.

"Charlotte, wait!" he said, catching up with her on her front porch. "I didn't mean to be rude. I'm sorry. Shit," he said, squaring his shoulders to her. "I just- I want to get to know you. I really like you. Even if you think my car is stupid." He grinned down at her.

Charlotte sighed, digging through her purse for her keys.

"No, I'm sorry. I had too many drinks. This was probably a bad idea anyway. I don't really date much."

"I know. Rose told me. But Charlotte–" he started, "I wanted to find a way to tell you this. I- Rose- she told me about you in my reading. That you're important for me for some reason. And I- I know it sounds crazy, but I just felt a connection with you that first day I saw you and I- I want to be around you. That's why I come to the workshops."

"Tony, I–" Charlotte started, looking up at him. He was beautiful, his large, slightly droopy eyes looking back at her as she spoke. "I don't know if this is a good idea. I don't really- I don't know. I don't know if I want a relationship," she said, more bluntly than she anticipated.

"I'm just asking to spend some time with you. Maybe you'll like me back if you get to know me," he said, shooting her that smile again. "I even set my intention to take you on a date and look!" he said, putting his arms up to his sides, "it worked."

Charlotte smiled and looked down at the floor.

"I'm sure you have lots of women after you, Tony," she said, trying to make excuses.

"But I'm here," he said, not denying it. He stared down at her, taking a slow step closer to her.

"I'm not good at this," she said quietly, looking away from him.

He brought his hand up to the side of her face, making her look back at him again.

"I'm not, either," he said, and, to her surprise, he lowered his face to hers and kissed her softly on the lips, starting off gently before he wrapped one strong arm around her waist and pulled her tight against his hard body. He put his other hand on the back of her head, tilting her head back and taking her over. When he finally pulled back, Charlotte was out of breath, a moan escaping her lips. Her body was responding to him, regardless of what her head told it to do.

"Can I come in?" he whispered into her mouth.

She nodded as he kissed her again and backed her through the front door. The place was small with only one bedroom to go to and he found it quickly, kicking the door shut behind him and pushing her back through the bedroom door and onto her bed. It was either the whiskey or Tony himself that made her lose herself the way she did, all caution gone. He lay her on the bed and kissed her relentlessly, skilled mouth working its way down the side of her neck to the top of her dress. He pulled the straps down expertly and shimmied the dress off of her, revealing only a pair of lace panties.

He balled up the dress and threw it to the side, sitting back on his heels to unbutton his shirt as he watched her on the bed, scooting herself back to the pillows. He said nothing as he looked at the length of her body on the bed. When he came back down on top of her, Charlotte could feel him pressing against her. He stopped briefly, pulling away from her and looking down and her.

"Was I overcompensating?" he said, a smile in his voice.

Charlotte giggled as he lowered his head back down to kiss her again. He took his time with her, kissing her stomach and moving his tongue on the inside of her thighs before finally removing her underwear and deftly putting on a condom. Charlotte was surprised at how quickly her body had come alive. How it remembered exactly what to do and what it needed.

As he pushed slowly into her and kissed her neck, she tried not to think about how long it had been, how many years it had been since she'd felt the need for this the way she had then. Mostly she tried to push away the fact that it was not Wyatt there in her room like she had dreamed thousands of times before that.

VI

"Awakened by voices that whisper my name
How I'm alone in the night
How can a place so empty and cold
Be filled with such glorious light"

~ *Mirage,* Willy Braun

That October brought more changes than any October before it. All but that one when he left Patagonia all of those years ago. It was eight years since he got on that plane, heartbroken and lost, and left for basic training. It was hard to remember who he even was then. Before he was a Marine. Before he was really a man. Wyatt looked back on that poor kid with both embarrassment and pity for how broken he was- that time, losing her, and the sweet sting that comes along with being baptized into a warrior. It was so much, and somehow he knew it all had to happen that way to make him into the man he was now.

It was impossible not to think of that time of his life as he left the Marine base for the last time. Months of paperwork and hoop-jumping. Now, he was only a Marine in his heart, bound by blood and loyalty to the Marine Corps he loved so. Everyone told him that once he was a Marine, he would always be one. He knew that that was partly true, but he couldn't help but feel that he didn't fully belong with them anymore. That he never would again. His time as a warrior was over.

Unlike other men he knew who left the Corps, he didn't make any big purchases with his money. He'd been meticulous about it the same way he had about his deployment compensations, and in turn, he had quite the nest egg. Only he didn't know what to do with it. Or where to go. He bought an older Chevy truck from an aging South Carolina farmer and hopped on the freeway headed south to Patrick. There was nowhere else to go. Plus, Mia wouldn't hear of anything else, insisting he come and see the baby anyhow.

He arrived to find Patrick on the front porch, cradling his son in one muscular arm, grinning at Wyatt as he parked and walked toward them. Patrick looked much different as a father, but something about it suited him. His eyes were tired and his demeanor was softer. His chubby son, with caramel skin and dark eyes, looked up at Wyatt as he approached. Patrick grinned at Wyatt without saying anything at first.

"Go to your godfather, Michael," he cooed down to the baby as he handed him to Wyatt.

A surprised Wyatt took the baby, looking down at his soft body cradled in his arms. The baby smiled up at him with jet black eyes, the same as Patrick and his mother had. He shifted him in his arms, afraid he might drop him at first, then rocked him back and forth a bit. He smiled down at the baby, fighting the urge to tear up.

"He's a big boy," Wyatt said quietly, looking him over. "So solid."

"That's because he's mine," Patrick boasted. "Also, cause he's got a good middle name," Patrick said, looking back into Wyatt's face.

Wyatt nodded and smiled a sad smile. "Michael Gus McMurtry," he said softly. "Good name." He looked back at Patrick, raising an arm to hug him, taking care not to crush the baby between them.

"Wy!" Mia said, flying out of the front door of their small bungalow. "You're here!"

She inserted herself in between them and hugged Wyatt tight around the neck, pulling him down to her height. She wore a form fitting sundress with her milky breasts spilling from the top, her middle just as tiny as it was before the baby. Wyatt looked down at her and smiled widely.

"Jesus, Mia. You look amazing," he said honestly. "Didn't you just have a baby?"

"Bless you, Wy," she said, standing on her toes to kiss him on the cheek fiercely. "You finally get to meet baby Michael!" she said, touching her baby's head in his arms. "He's been waiting to meet you," she said, her eyes tearing.

Wyatt looked down at the baby who still sat content in his arms. He was so soft and not at all what Wyatt assumed he would be like. He'd always been terrified of babies, shrinking away quickly if anyone ever asked him to hold one. But that wasn't the case with Michael. He was so calm and happy that Wyatt didn't want to put him down at all. Or run away.

"He's–" Wyatt started, looking down at him. "He's perfect," he said.

A tear ran down Mia's cheek as she looked back and forth between Patrick, Wyatt, and the baby. She wiped it away, laughing and grinning.

"I cry all of the time now. God, I must drive Patrick crazy. I'm just happy," she said, dissolving into a fit of tears as Patrick put his arm around his wife, bringing her close to his side.

"We're all happy to have you here, cowboy. Now come in. Let's have a drink and celebrate," Patrick said.

The house was old and small, but Mia made it beautiful. Green succulents were scattered over every surface and colorful fabrics hung over their old couches. The whole place smelled of Puerto Rican food, making Wyatt salivate immediately. He'd visited enough that he knew what kind of food he was in for that trip and that alone was enough to get him down to Florida.

Wyatt and Patrick sat on the couch talking as Mia fussed over them, cooking and bringing them drinks while Wyatt still cradled baby Michael who stared up at Wyatt's bearded face as he spoke. Patrick told him all about college, which was much easier than Patrick imagined it would be- nothing compared with the stress level of being in the Marine Corps. It was secondary to his contracting work which was still profitable, although it didn't seem like it in the high-priced city of Miami.

"Damn place is so expensive, man. You pay a price for wearing flip-flops in winter, that's for sure," Patrick complained. "What about you?" Patrick asked, not wanting to push too hard. "Where do you think you're gonna go?'

Wyatt shrugged, taking another drink of his beer. He'd had time to think about where he would go, what he would do, but uncharacteristically, still hadn't made a decision. Plenty of his fellow Marines talked of going back as a contractor or joining local police forces, but none of it felt right to him. None of it felt like the turn he should take.

"Don't know, man. Thought I'd take a trip cross country. See what places I like," Wyatt said, hoping Patrick wouldn't ask much more than that.

Patrick nodded. "Well, if you want a job as a nanny, you got it. Baby Mike loves you." He smiled, looking at his friend holding his baby.

Mia came out of the kitchen and cooed, looking at her baby in Wyatt's arms. "You put him to sleep!" she said, a surprised smile on her face. "Uncle Wy is good at this," she said, leaning to scoop the baby up.

Wyatt shifted his body, still cradling baby Michael next to his large bicep. Mia took him gently out of the crook of his arm and it felt empty when he was gone, the warmth of him still sticking to Wyatt.

"That looks good on you, man," Patrick said, smiling at Wyatt as Mia carried the baby away. "That's what you should do. Be a daddy."

Wyatt laughed, changing the subject, but couldn't fight the tug in his stomach that made him wonder if anything had ever felt as natural or as beautiful as holding that baby close to his chest.

Tony Russo wore her down. After that night in January he pursued her aggressively, turning up on her doorstep on random weeknights with bottles of wine, sending flowers to the shop, and leaving notes on her car. He came on hard and fast and although normally that would have driven her crazy, she was surprised to find that she actually loved the attention, catching herself constantly thinking of him and his sturdy body pressed against her throughout the day. He had something that stuck, that much was true, and according to Rose, Charlotte was much easier to deal with since he came around.

"This is why I've been begging you to date all of these years," she said to her one day in the lounge. "You're a hell of a lot easier to deal with when you're getting laid." She grinned.

Charlotte blushed, avoiding eye contact with her aunt, but she couldn't deny that something inside of her had changed. She was thinking about more than just work now, more than just numbers, spreadsheets, and marketing campaigns. Now, there was more. There was Tony and his strong and sure hands that eagerly touched her whenever they were together.

"Ok, Aunt Rose. You're just saying that because I'm not making you do the workshop this weekend. So where are you going, anyway?" Charlotte said, changing the subject so she could stop thinking about him for a moment.

Rose shrugged. "Don't know yet. I just gotta get the fuck outta here for a couple of days. You sure you don't want to come?"

"Can't. Gotta work," she said, raising her head to wink at her aunt before looking back at the paperwork on her lap.

"Suit yourself," Rose said, swinging her feet around to hit the ground in front of her. "My reading is probably here. Lunch today before I go?"

Charlotte nodded. "It's a date."

Rose smiled at her niece, her eyes tired. "That's my girl," she said, patting her arm before she left the room.

Charlotte glanced down at her calendar, organizing the next week. Wedding season was seemingly constant in Savannah, picking up in the fall and staying steady until the holidays hit when there was a brief respite, filled by holiday parties hosted at the shop instead. Then in the spring, it picked back up again, the brides relentless, booking years in advance. She was so absorbed in her calendar that she didn't hear Tony walk in the room and stand behind her. Suddenly, she felt his breath on the back of her neck.

"Can I make an appointment?" he said, opening his mouth to kiss the side of her neck.

Charlotte jumped, then laughed, leaning her body back against the couch to look back at him. He was dressed for work in slacks and a starched shirt tucked neatly into his belted waist.

"What are you doing here?" she said, standing off the couch to walk around and greet him.

"I had the morning off. I wanted to see you," he said, looking her up and down as she walked to him.

Charlotte wore a long maxi skirt that hugged her curvy hips and a black v-neck blouse that barely exposed the tops of her breasts pushed up by the lace bra underneath, her hair piled on top of head. He stepped toward her, wrapping his arms around her waist and moving them over her bottom. He gripped her hard before kissing her breathlessly on the mouth, pushing her back to the wall.

"Wait, Tony. Stop," she said, pulling away, flustered. "Rose is right here doing a reading." She nodded to Rose's adjoining door.

Tony looked at Rose's side of the room and back to Charlotte. "Let's go in your office," he said, all but panting. He grabbed her hand and pulled her through the door to her office and locked the door behind him, crossing the room to lock the other one that entered the room. Charlotte collected herself, smoothing her hands over her body, trying to calm herself.

She put her hands up to stop him as he came back to her. "You need to calm down," she said, laughing at him. "I have to work right now. And plus, I just saw you last night!"

Tony grinned at her, his perfect teeth shining as he approached her again, looking down at her hips hungrily.

“Not enough,” he said bluntly. “I need to have you one more time.”

Charlotte looked to the doors and felt her pulse start to quicken. She hated the way he demanded things of her, always showing up at inconvenient times, asserting himself into every situation then defending himself saying it was the New Yorker in him, the Italian man who made him like that. And despite herself, he could melt her every time. All it took was for him to place his expert hands on her body and all else was lost.

“Tony,” she started, backing herself up to her desk. “You should go to work.” But he could tell that’s not what she wanted to say.

“Hmmm?” he said, pushing himself against her again, rubbing his hands up and down the sides of her body. “Where do you want me to go?” he whispered into the skin just behind her ear.

“I said–” she started, short of breath. “I said–” He stopped her, kissing her again and lifting her to sit on her desk.

He lifted her skirt to her hips, moving his hand between her legs.

“You were lying,” he accused. “You want me to stay.”

When he pushed into her, he covered her mouth with his hand, thrusting hard into her as she lost herself. Thinking of nothing.

As hard as it was to leave Patrick, Mia, and baby Michael behind, Wyatt was relieved when he finally left after a week of visiting. He loved them all dearly, they were his family, but he knew he didn't belong there with them. That familiar feeling of being the third wheel was emphasized even more since they'd become their own little family unit. He couldn't have been happier for his friend, but it was hard to watch him like that, grown seemingly overnight into a husband and father with his beautiful wife and son dependent on him. He wore it well, like he did anything, adapting into what he needed to be for them. Each morning he woke to hold his baby and kiss his wife sweetly on the back of the neck as she made breakfast for them. It was these small expressions of love and intimacy that reminded Wyatt that he needed to go.

Wyatt decided to wind his way up the Florida coast on the way out, driving Highway 6 with the Atlantic to his right and the open road stretching ahead of him. He stopped when he reached Savannah, remembering all of the stories his Georgia friends had told him about the old, haunted town. And it was just as they described. Victorian buildings flanked the overgrown streets, the sidewalks alive with tourists. He found a hotel room on the Riverwalk and stood on the balcony looking out over the water. The sun was sinking behind the river in the distance, silhouetting the bridge in the glowing sunset.

He sat stiffly on the old wooden chair on the porch, placing his hands on his jeans and taking a deep breath. There were people everywhere on the Riverwalk, shopping, laughing, and taking pictures of the sunset. It was overwhelming after being in the quiet of Patrick's home for the whole week before that, nothing but the occasional whimpering of baby Michael or Patrick's laughter to disturb him. He took a long drink of whiskey and looked back at the sunset. Something about it made him think of Arizona, although he didn't know what it was. The place was nothing like his desert home. The air was thick with humidity and the distant smell of the beach instead of the dust and creosote he loved.

And that's how she came back to him. That was all it took. He tried to ignore it when he heard the voice whisper in his ear. More than that, he tried to ignore the fact that it was her voice, just like he'd heard in his ear anytime he needed her.

Go home, Wyatt. She whispered.

Charlotte shot up out of her sleep, gasping for breath. She gripped the sheet around her naked body and looked around the room.

"What?" Tony said from beside her on the bed, placing his head back on the pillow tiredly.

Charlotte breathed deeply, feeling her heart pound inside her chest. She could feel the sweat collecting near her temples and her mouth drying up in nervousness.

"Nothing. Nothing," she said, swinging her feet over the side of the bed and standing to put her robe on. "Go back to sleep," she said quietly, even though he already had, the sound of his faint snore already starting back up.

Charlotte hugged her silk robe around her shoulders and went to the kitchen for a glass of water, gulping it down only to still feel weak. Her dream was different than it normally was. He always came to her in the night, but never like this. She opened the front door quietly and walked out onto the lawn in the cool night's air. She put her bare feet into the grass, trying to ground herself into the earth.

She took a deep breath and looked up to the full moon above her. But all she could see, all she could feel, was his hand reaching out for her. The desert sun sinking low behind him.

He left Savannah the morning after he arrived. Anxious to keep moving, he drove without aim across the country he had fought to protect the last seven years. It was funny to him that he hadn't seen much of it. His travel in country was limited to short trips like Michigan and Florida, and the bases that he only temporarily occupied before being deployed over and over again. Most of what he knew about the parts of his country weren't from traveling, like recruiters had promised him he would, knowing the U.S. in and out by the time he'd be done serving in the Marines. Most of it he learned from the men he served with over the years, all of them yearning for their homes so fiercely that they talked endless hours about them on deployments.

He was through Arkansas by the time he realized where he was going. Gus had never stopped talking about his Oklahoma home. How the green grass rolled on for miles, how the ice would cover it in the winter, sheets of slick ice that seemingly came out of nowhere. So frigid that everyone would want to complain, only they didn't, because it was the same as rain. Just as good. And no good Oklahomans ever complained about rain, he'd told Wyatt. They only prayed for it. Out loud at the dinner table, at night before bed, at church on Sundays.

Rain was life, just as it was in Arizona. He liked listening to Gus talk about his home, how much he loved it. About his parents who had him later in life. Gus, their only child who they lost that day, right there in front of Wyatt. There wasn't a day that went by that Wyatt didn't think of him or feel him around him. He had made Gus a promise, and he was a man of his word. As much as he didn't want to go there, he knew he had to.

Hennessey, Oklahoma was a speck, really. A small farming community outside of Stillwater with only one stoplight and no landmarks to speak of. Wyatt had gotten an early start that morning and made it to town just after the sun came up, stopping at the only open establishment, a gas station. He parked his truck and got out, shoving his hands into his pockets. The fall chill in the air was a stark contrast from the Florida sun.

An older man with discerning, crows-feet ridden eyes stood at the counter, nodding skeptically at him as Wyatt's large frame walked through the door.

"Mornin', sir," Wyatt said, nodding at him.

"Mornin'," he mumbled, busying himself stocking cigarettes.

Wyatt poured a cup of black coffee and walked back toward the register, thinking about how to phrase his words.

"One-fifty," the man said shortly.

Wyatt nodded, taking a five dollar bill from his wallet and passing it to the man.

"I was wondering if you could help me with something," Wyatt started politely, aware of the man's discomfort with him. "I- I'm wondering if you could give me directions to the Barrett place."

The man looked up to meet Wyatt's eyes as he handed his change back to him.

"Who's askin'?" he said, crossing his hands over his chest.

Wyatt hated telling anyone anything personal, but he didn't see a way around it in this instance.

"My name is Wyatt Sterling. I- I was in the Marine Corps with Gus Barrett," Wyatt said quietly.

The man's face fell a bit. He uncrossed his arms and reached a hand over the counter to Wyatt.

"Oh- I'm sorry. I just- oh, wow. Gus," The man said shaking his head and looking Wyatt in the eye sadly. "Thank you for your service, son."

Wyatt cringed inwardly, hating when people felt like they needed to thank him.

"Thank you, sir," he said awkwardly. "So you know his parents? Could you help me to find their place?"

The man looked back down at the counter, nodding his head slowly. "Yes, I can tell ya. I'm sorry to say that Mr. Barrett passed away a year ago this fall." The man sighed, taking out a sheet of paper to write down directions. "Just don't think he could ever get over losing Gus."

Wyatt's heart ached in his chest, but he worked to keep his emotions off of his face, nodding stoically.

"Sorry to hear that. And Mrs. Barrett?" Wyatt asked.

The man smiled sadly. "She'll be happy to see you. If she's not home, head to the Baptist Church. No other place she'll be."

After thanking the man and going over the directions, Wyatt drove through the small town, in awe at how much he recognized it already. The water tower with the town's name sat proudly behind the small high school, the one Wyatt knew Gus had attended as the star wrestler of the nearest three counties. He wound his way down the small dirt road to the Barrett place, feeling his hands sweat on the steering wheel despite the cold weather. He was no good at this, he knew. No good at comforting people when they needed it or talking to them about sad things.

What could he possibly say to Gus's mother? She was a woman who had lost it all that day in Fallujah, not knowing for a whole day after he was killed that he was even gone. And now this, now her husband gone, as well. Wyatt was second guessing his decision to go there at all until he saw the small farm house come into view. He couldn't help but smile when he saw it. He remembered a picture Gus had of himself standing with his mother on the those very steps, her arms wrapped around the waist of his dress blues. Yes, he reminded himself, he should be there.

He parked his truck and walked swiftly to the front door before he changed his mind, taking a deep breath after he knocked. She opened the door wearing a dirty apron and her gray hair piled on top of her head. She opened the screen door and smiled up at Wyatt.

"Hello." She smiled wiping her hands on her apron. "Can I help you?"

Wyatt looked down at the petite woman, so much like Gus that he had to remind himself that Gus was gone and not standing in front of him. He was silent for a moment, opening his mouth to speak before closing it and shoving his hand out for her to shake.

"Ma'am, I'm Wyatt Sterling and I–"

"Wyatt? My Gus's Wyatt?" she all but yelled, her face stretching into a huge smile.

Wyatt smiled. "Yes, ma'am," he said.

Sara Barrett flew out of the door and wrapped her arms around Wyatt, gripping him tightly.

"I can't believe it's you," she sniffed into his chest, pushing back and holding him at arm's length. "Gosh, you look so different from the pictures from way back then." She wiped her eyes and got a hold of herself, taking a deep breath. "Come in here right now, out of the chill."

The house was immaculate and sparsely decorated the same way Garrett's ranch house was. Nothing was there that didn't serve a purpose. A handmade quilt hung on the back of the couch and reminded Wyatt of the one Gus had in the barracks. He looked closer at it as he sat as he was instructed to do.

"That was his," she said, reading his mind. "You remember it?"

Wyatt nodded, looking down at the coffee table as he sat, the feel of the quilt on his back compounding the aching in his chest. "Yes, ma'am."

"Please call me Sara, Wyatt. And can I get you something? Coffee?"

"No, ma- no, thank you." He smiled.

"Wyatt," she said, looking into his eyes happily. "My, I can't even believe you're here. Tell me what brings you to Oklahoma."

Wyatt hesitated, not sure of how to explain it.

"I- I just got out of the Marines," he said, the words sounding strange to him. "And I'm headed back- well, I don't really know where yet."

She raised her eyebrows. "Well, that's so nice. Congratulations. I just can't thank you enough for coming by here. I'm so glad I was home. I'm headed to church later to bring some things in for a bake sale, but I'd love it if you stayed the night. Or as long as you need to, really."

Wyatt smiled. "Thank you," he said quietly. "I honestly didn't have much of a plan when I came here. I just wanted to come by and see you and–" he trailed off.

She nodded. "It's real thoughtful, Wyatt," she said, her eyes tearing the slightest bit. "My husband would have loved to meet you. He passed last fall."

"I heard. I'm so sorry," he said, not knowing what else to say.

She smiled at him, sensing his discomfort. "Thank you, Wyatt. He just- well, the doctor said it was probably an aneurysm or something of that nature, but I'll tell you, I think he died of a broken heart. I really do."

Wyatt was quiet, looking over at her. She was so strong, her chin held parallel to the ground and tears in her eyes, he could feel her strength emanating from her like a beacon. She had nothing left in this world yet she sat in front of him firmly rooted to the earth. Suddenly, he felt very weak.

"I'm sorry, Wyatt. I know it's hard for people to be around me. I swear sometimes people look at me like I'm contagious or something. Like grief and loss are catching." She smiled sadly.

"I understand that," he said honestly.

She smiled, nodding at him. "I'm sure you do. You've not had an easy road, have you?"

She looked at him just like Rose had all of those years ago. Just like the Turkish woman in the small shop. As if they knew his heart and all of his secrets.

"Only compared to some, I guess," he said, avoiding her gaze.

Sara sighed, taking a drink of her coffee. "Well, he just loved you, Wyatt. Gus just thought you hung the moon and stars." She beamed up at him. "He wrote about you in every letter he sent home. I'll show them to you if you want."

Wyatt could feel his throat catch as he nodded to her, and part of him felt guilty. He loved Gus, no doubt. He was closer to him than most other Marines, all except for Patrick. He hadn't realized how Gus must have felt about him.

"I would like that," Wyatt said quietly.

Sara smiled at him gently. “Is there something you want to say? I know you didn’t come here just to say hello.”

Wyatt nodded, looking down at the rug under him. He’d had all of that time, all of these years to think about what he should say to her. He’d rehearsed it dozens of times in his head, and yet the words escaped him.

“I came here to tell you that- he- Gus–” Wyatt fought back tears, widening his eyes and sighing heavily. “Just before he died. I was with him. And I- I wanted to say that I’m sorry that I couldn’t get him help quicker. To save him.” A tear rolled down his cheek but he didn’t try to wipe it away, instead looking directly into Sara’s eyes as he spoke to her brave face.

“He was only thinking of you and your husband when he died. He loved you both so much,” Wyatt said, his words catching in his throat. “He wanted you to know that he did what he was supposed to. That he was brave.” Wyatt stopped, looking down at the ground before collecting himself and looking back at her. “He was probably the nicest person I’ve ever met. Just the sweetest guy,” he said, smiling softly. “But he was a warrior, too. And he wanted you to be proud.”

Sara stood and moved beside Wyatt on the couch, reaching out to grab his hand.

“Oh Wyatt. You’re such an angel,” she said, stroking his hand, her eyes spilling over with silent tears. “It wasn’t your fault. Don’t you ever feel like that. He loved you and I’m glad you were with him.”

Wyatt couldn't look back at the woman. Her fearlessness and grace overwhelmed him into silence.

"Don't you know yet, Wyatt? Don't you know that God had a plan for him?" she asked, squeezing his hand, making him look back into her face. "God has a plan for you, too," she said, whispering before pulling him into an embrace.

It was strange to be in the shop without Rose. For as much as Charlotte ran the place, she realized that once Rose was gone, she needed her for almost everything. Even if it was just for her to be there, her energy surrounding Charlotte and reminding her that she was loved. She even missed having to coax her out of the lounge and get to work. But she knew her aunt and she could tell that she'd hit a wall, something about her just didn't seem right. Charlotte didn't know if it was because of the city itself, the lack of suitable men, or the booming nature of the business, but Rose didn't seem happy there, that much was clear.

The workshop was crowded that weekend and Charlotte was thankful that she'd had the presence of mind to fly Willow in for the weekend to help. She simply couldn't handle all there was to do on top of teaching Rose's class. That was what was really bothering Charlotte: the fact that she had to be Rose for a day. That she would have the burden of dozens of people looking to her for spiritual answers. She knew Rose's material better than anyone else, she could recite it all backwards and forward, but there was a difference between doing that in her head and actually delivering other information aloud, to a captive and silent audience.

"Where's Dr. Italian Sausage today?" Willow said, hanging off the counter as Charlotte looked through the papers in front of her.

"Not here," she said, not looking up from her work.

Tony had shown great interest in the shop and all things spiritual when he was trying to win Charlotte over. Even after they'd begun dating regularly, he'd made a big show of meditating and showing up to workshop weekends ready to participate. But that had tapered off recently and Charlotte couldn't say that she minded. She liked the idea of her work being something separate from him. It seemed more natural.

Willow sighed, twirling her long red hair. "Man, he's dreamy. You really held out for a good one, didn't you? Just your luck."

Charlotte raised her head and furrowed her brow at Willow. "What do you mean, 'just my luck'?" she asked, annoyed.

Willow shrugged. "I don't know," she said, standing up and looking at the students walking into the gallery for Charlotte's class. "Things just always work out for you."

Charlotte's mouth dropped open to argue, but then she remembered that Willow didn't really know anything about her. She only knew the Charlotte who showed up to Flagstaff with the world laid at her feet, endless possibilities in front of her. That was not who Charlotte felt like on the inside, though. Far from it.

But she wouldn't say that, not to Willow. She was her friend, but there was no way to make her understand what she didn't really want to know and what she probably wouldn't believe anyway.

"Yeah, sure. Everything's a piece of cake," Charlotte said, walking toward the gallery.

Charlotte's long sundress drug the ground over her flat sandals, her hair braided to the side of her face. She could feel her hands sweating and she approached the front of the room as the students began to settle and fall quiet.

I am loved. She said to herself over and over, grounding the idea into the earth. *I am loved and I can do this. Help me, Rose.*

"Good afternoon, everyone," Charlotte began, smiling out at the students. "I want to start by thanking you for coming to the workshop today. If this is your first time here, we want to welcome you and let you know to please ask any and all questions you might have today during class." Charlotte cleared her throat, trying her best to fake confidence. "I also want to apologize that Rose won't be here today. You'll be stuck with me instead, so there won't be a gallery reading at the end of class. But Rose has promised to do that double time next month," she said, smiling out into the audience.

Charlotte recounted the lessons of the day, speaking gently and clearly to the students, pausing to patiently answer questions. For as nervous as she was, it wasn't half as intimidating as she thought it would be. She found that she was confident in her answers, explaining everything in simple terms just like Rose had continuously done for her over the years. Spirituality, per Rose, was best kept simple. The answers were not as earth-shattering or as frightening as most people thought they were.

Toward the end of class a woman in the back of the room raised her hand shyly. She was middle-aged, plain-looking, and dressed for the yoga class earlier in the morning. Charlotte smiled encouragingly at her, nodding in acknowledgement as the woman stood.

"Um, hi," she said, smiling gently. "I was wondering if you could maybe talk about regression a little bit. Rose said that I- that maybe that would help me. I just was wondering what it- well, I was wondering what it is really," she said before sitting back down.

Charlotte gathered herself, reminding her breathing to stay calm. Regressions were not her favorite topic. After that day, so long ago, on Rose's couch in Patagonia, she'd never had another one. That day had been enough for her to know that she didn't want to see what all of her other lives held. What they meant for her now. It was much simpler to stay rooted in the life she had now, which was complicated enough for her.

"Regressions are a form of hypnosis where you revisit previous lifetimes. Where you learn about those lives in order to realize why you have challenges you have today. It can be a form of therapy for some people," Charlotte said, almost mechanically. "For some people, it can help them break free of cycles or phobias in their life."

Charlotte looked at the woman who stared back at her intently, her brow furrowed as she processed her words. The woman opened her mouth to speak but closed it right after, thinking better of asking a follow-up question.

"Does that make sense?" Charlotte said earnestly, walking down the aisle toward the woman so she would feel more comfortable. "Did I explain it enough?"

"Yes, I- thank you," the woman said quietly, looking down at the floor before looking back to Charlotte. "I was just wondering if it could- if it could explain why some people can't be in our lives. Why we have to lose them," she said quietly, despite her embarrassment.

Charlotte felt a chill run through her. She thought of him. Of his face. The way all of those lives between them had gone. That letter he left unanswered. She felt the hollowed-out place in her heart where he remained missing. She smiled back at the woman, fighting the tears forming in her eyes.

"It can. But sometimes, no matter what, we will never understand it," Charlotte said, her heart aching for him, yet again.

Wyatt ended up staying four nights with Gus's mom. He thought at first he would maybe stay a night then push out in the morning, uncomfortable being a burden in her home, but she'd made him feel so welcome, cooking for him, sitting in the front room with a cup of coffee, gently asking him about his life and his plans for the future. To his surprise, he talked to her. He told her about his uncertainties, about how he didn't really know what to do or who he was without the Marine Corps. And to his relief, she didn't offer any grand solutions, but instead nodded her head, furrowing her brow sympathetically.

"You will find your way," she told him with certainty one morning. "I'm going to pray about it."

He said nothing the way he did each time Garrett or anyone else talked to him about God. But it made him feel better for some reason, knowing that someone of Sara's strength and fortitude was on his side. She showed him pictures of Gus, left him sitting at the kitchen one afternoon to read Gus's letters from Iraq, all of them mentioning Wyatt, the cowboy from Arizona who was always so kind to him. Always so helpful. His friend, he said over and over again. Wyatt could hardly get through the stack without sobbing, but luckily Sara knew that. And she also knew he wouldn't want to look like that in front of her, so she excused herself, running to town as he sat on the small kitchen chair next to the farm table, holding in his hands the letters Gus had written from Iraq.

He let the tears fall off of his face and onto his lap below him, not bothering to wipe them away. Instead, he just felt it. And it was the first time he could remember immersing himself in a feeling that way, instead of pushing it away from him. It wasn't closure, not like people talked about, there could never be closure for Gus, for what Wyatt saw happen to him. But there was something therapeutic about being there in that place with his mother. About knowing that she was brave enough to keep going. To wake up each morning and believe the best of the world. To have that faith.

And so he found himself staying several nights with her, feeling much the same about her as he felt for Mama Karla, Patrick's mother. They both gave off a warmth like a fire, so different from his own mother, cold and beautiful, that he was always shocked at how good he felt after simply being in their presence. He left with an embrace on her front lawn and the promise that he would be back again, that he would stay in touch and let her know where he ended up.

"Don't you forget!" she said, holding him at arm's length and looking up into his face. "Don't you forget, you have a purpose."

He thought of that, driving away on that cold Oklahoma day. And he tried to believe it. He tried to think that maybe his work there wasn't done. That there could be something else for him, but he had no idea what that could be. Who was he if he wasn't a Marine? He was no one before that, really, just a kid. Just a boy who'd hardly left southern Arizona. A far cry from the hardened man he'd become.

Leaving Oklahoma was a lot like leaving Florida in that he had no idea where exactly he was going, only that he was headed west. He didn't want to say to himself, or anyone else, that he wasn't in charge of where he was going, that his heart actually made the decision for him, bringing him back to Arizona without choice. He stopped only once in New Mexico, waking early the next morning to continue driving, arriving in northern Arizona just as the sun crested over the mountains.

Wyatt pulled his truck over to the side of the road and rolled down his window, letting the cold air fill the cab. The grassy fields in front of him were yellow with the season, still untouched by the snow that he knew would come soon. He could smell the pine trees in the air, the scent reminiscent of so many camping and hunting trips of his youth. It was here, just outside of the tiny town of Greer, Arizona, where he'd come with his father the summers and falls of his youth, scouting the mountains for elk and catching trout out of the stream that meandered through the hills. This place was part of why he loved Arizona so much. He was a desert kid, there was no mistaking that, but this place was part of him, too, and he felt it.

Wyatt inhaled deeply, pulling his jacket tight around his shoulders. He watched as the sun peeked its way through the pine trees canvasing the tops of the mountains in front of him. Of all of the places he'd been over the last eight years, he'd never felt like that. Never felt the peace in his heart that he felt in that moment.

Home. His heart said to him, relieved.

Wyatt told himself that he was just passing through his home state. That maybe he would keep going, cross the northern part of the state entirely and head to the west coast, maybe stop in Las Vegas on the way and see what kind of trouble he could find. After a couple of nights at a small inn in Greer, relaxing and sitting on the cold empty deck to watch the sun rise and set each day, that's not what he did. Instead, he got in his truck and headed south. Winding his way down through the Salt River Canyon with its stretches of steep rock, down through the valley of Phoenix, which was even busier and bigger than he remembered, he found himself in Tucson, sitting in front of his childhood home.

He'd not been there since that day, the last time he'd seen or heard from his stubborn father. He knew then it would be the last time that place would ever be his home, although it wasn't even that at the time. Even then he knew that things would never be as they once were, and they never were again. He'd heard from his father only twice over the years, receiving cold, brief letters from him on deployments. And he never responded. Hardened into the Marine he was, he knew his father would never understand.

His house had changed a lot. It looked smaller and not as well kept as when his particular father had trimmed the hedges and raked the rocks in the front drive. There were no potted plants on the front walk, but discarded children's bikes instead, remnants of the other lives that lived there in his house. He didn't know what he would feel being back there again, but he didn't imagine that it would feel as empty as it did. His youth there was so separate from who he was now, it seemed like a different life altogether.

The air was cold that morning, unseasonably so for Tucson. Wyatt kept his window down as he got back on the freeway and headed south again, the mountains of Tucson flashing by him through his passenger side. Patagonia was the last place he wanted to go, or so he told himself, but who else deserved a visit more than Garrett did? Garrett, the man who had been there steadily throughout the years, his sturdy way always supporting Wyatt in everything he did even if he did so quietly. The man was family to him, just as Patrick was. But he steeled himself against being in that place again, that southern Arizona haven he loved so much and that place that had meant so much to him that summer.

The grass had already turned down south, the yellow hues taking over the summer green that was there before it. Whenever he thought of it, he pictured it green, the way it was after the monsoons. He never thought of it like this. In his mind, it was always summer in Patagonia. But the rest of the place remained unchanged. The same small ranch houses peppering the horizon. The same pastures with horses running free in them.

When he stopped at the crossroads in Sonoita to fill up with gas, he couldn't help but smile. He stood pumping fuel and looked across the street to the small row of businesses on the other side. The Ranch House was still there, intact and as old as ever. The dilapidated building hadn't changed at all and the owners hadn't bothered to update a thing about it. That wood deck looked even older than it was back then. Back when he'd gathered his nerve to kiss her there in the open for the first time, where everyone could see. He marveled at the fact that something could seem like it happened so long ago, but at the same time feel like it was yesterday.

The drive to Garrett's was faster than he remembered. Back then he'd always driven slowly from Sonoita to Patagonia, mostly because she was usually sitting next to him, her warm body pressed up against the side of his and her head on his shoulder. He'd always take his time getting back when she was there. But he shouldn't think of that. Wyatt shook his head, fiercely trying to stop thinking of her. He'd promised himself if he came here he wouldn't do that. Couldn't allow himself to go back to that place that was so far away, a time that was so far gone sometimes he wasn't sure if it had happened at all.

The road to the ranch was winding and overgrown, the dead brush of the impending winter spilling into the roadway. Not at all like it once was when Wyatt was there. He remembered trimming that very driveway, keeping it impeccable the way Garrett liked it. The main house and barn were worse for the wear, too, he noticed as he pulled up. The white paint was chipping from the trim with several patches missing from the roof. The bunkhouse was too far away from him to see and for that he was thankful. If he could go the entire visit without seeing it, he would, he told himself.

Wyatt parked his truck and got out, closing his door hard after him. At that moment Garrett stepped out onto the porch, brows furrowed together at the unexpected visitor. He scrutinized the truck and the large young man standing beside it and said nothing at first. Wyatt looked up at him, grinning widely.

"Mr. Garrett," he said, smiling.

"Well, I'll be damned," Garrett said staring for a moment. "Wyatt!" he said, headed down the steps to greet him.

He looked just like he always did, pearl snapped shirt tucked into worn Levis, but his hair was a little grayer and he'd let a small stubbly beard grow on his full cheeks. Friendly rancher's eyes sparkled above his slightly red nose. Wyatt walked toward him and widened his arms to embrace the old man without hesitation, patting him on the back as he did.

"I'll be damned!" he said again, "Prodigal son returns!"

Garrett pulled away from him and looked into his face, keeping hold of his large biceps. "Look at you, kid! Full grown man, my god!"

Wyatt smiled at him and felt his heart swelling inside of him. Garrett couldn't know what he'd meant to him over the years and he certainly couldn't tell the old cowboy something like that. Cowboys were much like Marines that way. Most things were better left unsaid.

"Come on in here, damn it. Tell me what the hell you're doin' here!" Garrett said, leading him into the house.

The big house remained unchanged, Garrett's bachelor decorations and sparse style consistent throughout the years. Just like the outside, the place was starting to show its age but it was still nice, still with the same comforting feeling he'd felt all of those years ago when he needed it most. Garrett settled him at the kitchen table, thrusting a Corona into his hands even though it was still the afternoon. He proceeded to pepper him with questions about where he'd been, about Patrick who Garrett had met years ago at basic training graduation, and about how it felt to be out of the Marine Corps.

Wyatt was somewhat surprised since Garrett was never one who liked to talk much. The old man was stoic, just a quiet rancher who said more with his actions than he ever said aloud, but he simply couldn't help himself having Wyatt right there in his kitchen. There he'd been all of those years in Patagonia on his quiet ranch while the young man had been out, storming the world. It was intoxicating to listen to, exhilarating to hear about Turkey, Afghanistan, and Iraq, even though Garrett knew Wyatt watered down those stories for his benefit. He kept asking follow-up questions, making Wyatt talk more than he had in a very long time, placing more and more Mexican beer in front of him as he spoke until Wyatt finally held up his hands.

"Whoa, Mr. Garrett, I've gotta drive." He laughed, pushing the fifth beer away from him.

"Drive? Where to? Bullshit," he said, feeling a buzz. "You stay here with me. I'll make up the guest room. I'll make tacos for dinner. Must've been a long time since you've had decent Mexican food, right?"

Wyatt grinned, taking another sip of the beer in front of him. "It has, yeah."

"Well, I bet, boy. Might have seen the whole damn world but you can't beat our Mexican food," Garrett said, taking a long pull himself. He nodded his head out the window to the yard, glowing in the glowing horizon. "Or our sunsets."

Wyatt looked out to the barn with the sun setting behind the mesquite trees in the distance. He felt his heart tighten, and that same voice inside of himself that told him again where he was.

Home.

"Gotta go feed before the sun sets. Come on, I'll let you clean shit for old time's sake," Garrett said, standing and slapping Wyatt on the shoulder as he walked to the door.

Wyatt walked in step with Garrett as the old man told him all about the rains that year. Bad summer, hardly any monsoons at all, he told him, although it seemed that every year Garrett said that very thing in his letters to Wyatt. There was just never enough. And Wyatt could see it, the grass and vegetation crisp with drought, tumbleweeds thick in the brush so much so that the fire danger alone gave him pause.

Once they entered the barn Wyatt tried not to make a fuss about what he saw. The place was not as it used to be and there were only four horses in the stalls, one of them Sunny who had aged significantly, hobbling in like an old man for his hay and grains that Garrett threw to him. Wyatt joined in, helping to feed and pouring the grains for each horse like he used to do. The sun was almost completely down, the winter days growing shorter and shorter. The men got quiet as they fell into the chores like they used to do together.

They walked out into the grapefruit sunset glowing in the yard, walking toward the fence line to look out at the horses still eating in their stalls. Garrett sighed, looking over at Wyatt.

"Different, huh?" he said, bringing it out in the open.

Wyatt nodded, pushing his cold hands into the pockets in his jacket. He stood with his feet wide, boots already dusty from being back on the ranch.

"Little bit," he said, then laughed. "I don't know, though. It's been a long time."

Garrett looked up at him and smiled. "Yes, it has." He sighed, looking back out into the empty pasture. "You were here during the hay day, really. One of the best summers I've ever had here," Garrett said, spitting out in front of him.

"How many cows you running now?" Wyatt asked, making conversation.

Garrett shook his head. "Nothing to speak of, Wyatt. Only a few dozen."

Wyatt checked his reaction, slowly nodding his head and looking away instead of dropping his jaw like he wanted to. When Wyatt worked the ranch all of those summers back Garrett ran upwards of 500 head. A couple dozen was nothing in comparison.

"The boys still working 'em?" Wyatt said, thinking of Luis, Santiago, and Raul.

Garrett shifted his feet and shook his head. "Luis finally retired. Well, shoot, didn't really retire, but saved enough to just do masonry work down in Sonora." Garrett smiled. "I miss my old amigo. He comes back and visits from time to time, though. Raul doesn't do ranchin' work anymore, he's into making, well, let's say, faster money. But Santiago is still here in town. Works for Clay Scott's ranch now. He's got a pretty wife, couple of babies. Turned out a hell of a lot better than I thought he would, I'll tell ya that."

Wyatt nodded and tried not to scowl. For all the time that had gone by, he found he still didn't like Santiago. The sound of his name made him stand straighter and puff his chest out.

Garrett laughed. "'Member that time you knocked the shit outta him?" he said, wheezing a coughing laugh. "Best damn thing to happen to that kid, I'll tell ya that."

Wyatt grinned, his ice blue eyes sparkling.

"I'm still sorry about that," he said, then smiling wider. "Kind of."

Garrett laughed harder, patting Wyatt on the arm.

"Boy, I'm happy to have you here, son," he said earnestly. "Your timing is perfect," the old man said, his eyes watering the tiniest bit. "Sellin' this place next month," he said, looking back at the big house.

Wyatt's jaw dropped that time, he couldn't help it. "Selling it?" he said, shocked. "Why?"

Garrett shrugged. "No proper way to say it, son. Lost my ass in this recession. The business ain't what it used to be. I just can't keep up. I'm too goddamn old to start it all over again," he said, smiling over at him sadly.

Wyatt opened his mouth to speak, then closed it again, not having the words for Garrett. He knew the ranch had been in his family his whole life, that he'd lived here with his wife, raised his kids there. He knew how much of a part of him it was and how much it hurt him to have to sell it. But Wyatt felt his heart ache for something else, too. This place would no longer be there for him. No longer would Garrett be his anchor to this southern Arizona oasis he loved so much, the place he thought of every time he closed his eyes in war, needing desperately to go somewhere else.

Garrett reached out and patted Wyatt's shoulder again, leaving his hand there for a moment as he thought. "I know what it means to you, too, son," he said, shaking his head. "I'm sorry. I really tried to hold on. I really did. I just couldn't anymore."

"I'm really sorry, Mr. Garrett. I just- I can't believe it," Wyatt said sadly.

"Eh, listen, could be worse. I ain't dyin'." He grinned. "Not today, anyway. Now come on," he said starting toward the house. "Let me make you a good white man Mexican dinner."

Wyatt stayed put, looking down at the dirt in front of him, his heart suddenly pounding in his chest. This. This was why he was here. This was why her voice and that voice inside of him told him to come back to that place.

No coincidences. He heard her say into the desert night.

And he knew immediately what he had to do. Why his heart brought him back there. He looked up at Garrett who had stopped, waiting for him to walk to the house. He felt his feet connected to the ground, to that place he loved so much.

Here. Here is where he was supposed to be.

"Mr. Garrett," he said, his deep voice steady and strong. "How much are you asking for the ranch?"

After that weekend Rose missed the workshop, her little jaunts became more and more common. She'd be sitting in the lounge on a Wednesday, sprawled out on the couch reading a book only to sit up and tell Charlotte she had to get the hell out of there again. She'd go through her normal process of begging Charlotte to go with her, somewhere, anywhere but there in the shop or in Savannah. And sometimes Charlotte complied, packing an overnight bag and giving her apologies to the always disappointed Tony, and they'd be off to some neighboring town, city, or off to the beach where even in the chill of winter Rose insisted on sitting for hours watching the waves roll in before she closed her eyes for meditation.

But Charlotte couldn't always go with her, often telling her no since she had to stay and run the shop. She sarcastically told Rose that one of them had to work, even though by that point, that wasn't necessarily true. Rose and Charlotte had a gift for hiring capable and hardworking people who could easily run things without them. The fact that Rose insisted on reading each employee before their first day probably had something to do with it, but regardless, the shop basically ran itself. Only Charlotte couldn't let go, couldn't relinquish control for very long. So she stayed and would hug her aunt goodbye on those weekends, knowing better than to ask where she was going since Rose would generally give some throwaway answer anyway.

"Brad Pitt's in Charleston. Thought I'd head over and give him a spin." She winked.

As much as she fought it, Charlotte was unsettled that her aunt wanted to leave so much. She fought the fact that it reminded her of her mother, Rose's sister. The two women were so different, she told herself anytime she thought that. Rose was not Lily. She loved Charlotte, had been there for her ever since the night she showed up on her doorstep like a dirty stray. She'd loved her relentlessly, taught her, helped her, and done more for her than any other person could ever do. No one knew Charlotte like Rose did. Which was why, even as a grown woman, formidable as she may have seemed to others, she felt quite lost without her aunt.

It was a Monday in late January and Rose had been gone the entire last weekend to another unknown destination. Charlotte showed up for work early that morning, knowing full well that Tony would come by the shop sometime before noon and beg her away for lunch, maybe more. As much as she enjoyed the attention, sometimes she missed the days when no one would come looking for her, when no one would pull her from meditations or piles of paperwork to demand time of her.

But Tony didn't seem to realize he was an inconvenience of any kind. His good looks and charm always assured him that others were graced by his presence, regardless of how he asserted himself into situations. And he was right. Charlotte had a hard time denying him most anything when he walked into a room. His booming presence and sparkling smile always washed away her annoyance. She worked straight through the morning until Tony arrived just before noon, knocking softly on the door as he opened it, a smile stretching across his face as his eyes met hers.

"I'm here for my reading," he said, his eyes dancing with mischief.

Charlotte smiled, raising from her desk to greet him. Her black slacks hugged her curvy hips and her white blouse stayed buttoned chastely above her breasts. She knew better than to wear a skirt on Mondays since that was when he visited. That almost always meant trouble.

"Hello, doctor," she said, crossing the room to greet him.

Tony placed his soft hand on the side of one cheek and pulled her to him for a lingering kiss, pushing his luck a bit before she pulled back laughing.

"No way. I have so much to do and Rose still isn't back. I can grab a quick lunch, though?" she said, striking a deal.

Tony frowned, his eyes moving down over her body. He rubbed his hand down the side of her breast to the curve of her hips.

"Fine," he sighed. "I guess I'll take it."

Charlotte laughed. "You get a run in this morning?" she asked, walking back to her desk and shutting down her computer.

"Quick one. Just five miles. Gonna need some massage therapy later, though," he said, grinning over at her.

Charlotte smirked, keeping her eyes on the computer. "Ok. I'll see if I can get you booked with one of the therapists here, then."

"I meant you. Don't be stingy with me."

The phone started ringing and Charlotte picked it up, shooting him a glance and grinning over her desk at him.

"Charlotte Holt," she said shortly.

"Well that won't do. I need to speak to Charlotte Bronte," Rose's voice said on the other end.

Charlotte's face softened and she laughed.

"You got her. Where the hell are you? Did you really find Brad Pitt this time?"

Tony settled himself down in one of the chairs opposite Charlotte and laid back, comfortably waiting for her.

"Oh no, dear. Things would never work out between us. He couldn't handle me for long. Plus, he's rather pretty, isn't he? Maybe not, well, I don't know, dirty enough for me," Rose said, a smile in her voice.

Charlotte laughed, sitting back down in her office chair. "Where the hell are you? I've been waiting for you to get home. We have a business to run, lady, and you have readings tomorrow!" Charlotte said, mock scolding.

"I'm home," Rose said simply.

Charlotte nodded, absentmindedly organizing items on her desk. A small figurine of St. Michael looked back at her.

"Ok then, come meet us for lunch. Tony just got here to pick me up. We could go for some pasta? Did you already eat?" Charlotte said, rattling off options.

The line was quiet for a moment as Charlotte waited for an answer.

"Aunt Rose?" she said again.

"Charlotte," Rose started, the seriousness in her voice a shift from how she was speaking before that. "I'm not in Savannah," she said, letting the line fall quiet again for a moment. "I'm home, babe."

Charlotte felt the blood pumping through her veins and she looked up at Tony sitting unchanged across from her. Her heart pounded as she processed the words. But all she could see, all she could feel, was the Arizona desert.

Snow fell that winter in Sonoita. It happened only some years, a winter storm blowing into southern Arizona and taking hold, freezing out the town several mornings, pipes bursting and cars crashing, all of it unaccustomed to such conditions. The snow rarely stayed on the ground past noon, the people of Sonoita and Patagonia all coming outside to watch it fall over the grassy fields, canvasing the skyline beautifully. The contrast of their desert home and the white sheet of snow was like something out of a dream.

Wyatt woke one morning to a chill in the air that he knew meant snow. He'd lived enough places to know that there was a smell that came along with impending snowfall, a feeling in the air that told you it was coming. He'd only seen it a couple of times growing up in Tucson, and once when it fell on Christmas day. He was eight then and he remembered his parents watching him from the back porch, coffee in hand and wonder in their eyes as he played in the thin sheet of snow over their lawn. For years after, he and his friends would talk about that Christmas, the one where snow fell over Tucson, sticking to the needles of the cholla cactus. Snow was a gift in Arizona, never a burden.

Wyatt was dressed and out the door before the sun was up that morning, driving his truck out to the far pasture that needed work. The fence line was almost completely gone after years of neglect. Snow or not, he'd have to have it ready for the new shipment of cattle. He'd risked it all buying the ranch and if he failed, it wouldn't be for lack of trying. It wouldn't be for lack of work. But to his credit, no one put pressure on him the way he did to himself, self-imposed deadlines and goals always ringing in his head. He was determined to turn the ranch around and determined to make it successful.

The inside of his truck fogged as he drove, so he cracked the window, allowing the frigid air to blow in the cab, sneaking its way between his cowboy hat and the collar of his thick jacket. Wyatt sipped his coffee, looking out the window at the dark sky surrounding him, thinking of the tasks ahead of him. He'd been back several months now and every day seemed to reaffirm why he was there. The work was harder than it was when he was 18. Maybe because he was older now, or maybe because it all fell to him. The success and failure of the ranch rested purely on his shoulders. But the fact remained that there he felt better than he'd felt in years, his soul breathing a sigh of relief to be back in his Arizona home.

Wyatt parked his truck in the pasture just as daylight broke behind the thick clouds over the mountains. His boots kicked at the dry grass under his feet as he walked toward the fence with his tools. He looked up at the sky as the first snowflakes fell on his bearded face. He stopped then, placing his tools down, and he looked around at the fields stretching out around him. All of it was his now. No one else's responsibility but his own. He looked back up into the sky as the snow began to fall silently to the ground below his feet. He'd been all over the world, his international travels only reminding him of one simple fact: he belonged there, with his feet firmly planted on the Arizona earth.

Charlotte drove, the silence of the car unsettling her immensely, but she couldn't bring herself to turn on the radio. She'd felt off ever since that phone call from Rose weeks before that. Her aunt picked up and headed back to Arizona, seemingly out of nowhere. It didn't make sense, but the more she thought about it, the more she understood it. She knew Rose like no one else in the world, and she knew that her aunt hadn't been happy for some time.

Charlotte had tried everything she could to pull her out of it. She cut her hours at the shop, agreed to trips with her, days off, all the things she loved. But Rose's spirit simply wasn't what it once was. Not like she was when Charlotte showed up on her doorstep back then in Patagonia. Rose was like no one else then. Unshakeable from who she was in the place she'd created for herself, the place she belonged.

Inwardly, Charlotte blamed herself. All of these years, all she wanted was to repay Rose for what she'd done for her. She'd turned the Flagstaff and Savannah shops into booming businesses, pursuing every avenue she could to create more revenue. But it seemed that the more money they made, the busier they became, the more Rose pulled away and the more she longed for something else. What that was, Charlotte didn't know, but she knew it was her fault somehow. That her priorities weren't what they should have been. She was blinded by the success that continuously made them more money. The better they did, the more she knew she was repaying Rose and the more she knew that she was not her mother.

Charlotte inhaled a shaky breath as she drove, her hands tightly gripping the steering wheel. She'd lived all over the country growing up with her mother, blowing into a town only to pack up and hit the road months or a year later, onto the next place. Even since she met Rose the moves continued, just less frequent. The gypsy inside of her would tell her to pack her bag again and move onto the next place. All her life that's how she'd trained herself to think, trained herself to feel.

Charlotte looked out the window at the sun setting over the horizon in the distance. Her breath caught as she saw it, tears forming in her eyes without warning. Yes, she'd lived everywhere and belonged nowhere. Her life was a series of places flashing by her. She couldn't understand why it was, then, as her car crested over the hill that overlooked Patagonia, her heart felt home.

SOMEWHERE IN TIME – Book Three
coming soon
www.katiejdouglas.com

Acknowledgments

I have so many people to thank for my second novel coming to fruition. First, to my mama, my biggest fan. This book is for her because she loves it so much. She's supported me throughout everything I've ever done in my life and she is my best friend. Thank you, Boma, for always believing in me.

To my editor, Megan Hennessey, who knows these characters as well as I do. Megs, thank you for your encouragement. Thank you for knowing my heart. Thank you for your friendship.

To every beta reader and friend who read this book before everyone else, Kate, Vicki, Angel, Tina, Mandy, Shan, Kittrin, Waverly, Melanie, and my sister Jo. Thank you for giving me the confidence I needed to move forward. Thank you for giving your heart to my books the same way I do.

To my husband and three incredible babies who are the most important part of my life. Thank you for making my life beautiful.

To my whole family, all of my friends, and every person who has supported me on this journey, my gratitude knows no bounds. Thank you.

To the Marines who have given their service to our country and so selflessly let me interview them for this book. Gunnery Sergeant Matthew Croy and Corporal Sean Osborn, I hope I came close to doing the Marine Corps justice. Semper Fidelis, you crazy devil dogs.

Thank you to the indie author community for your endless support. Melanie Smith, BJ Kurtz, Waverly Alexander, and so many more. Thank you for jumping me in your indie gang.

Nayes makeup (hair and makeup), Ashley Elicio Photography (cover pictures), Rachel Christmas (cover design), Debora Lewis with Arena publishing (formatting). All of you are responsible for this incredible cover and the professional look of the whole book. Thank you for your hard work.

Thank you to every person who reads my books. Those of you I know and those of you I don't. Thank you for putting yourself in this place with me. It's one of the most incredible things I've ever experienced and I'm so grateful.